Runaways

Runaways

The Long Journey Home

BRENDA C. POULOS

Copyright © 2015 Brenda C. Poulos
All rights reserved.
Printed in the United States of America
Published by Author Academy Elite
P.O. Box 43, Powell, OH 43035

www.AuthorAcademyElite.com

ISBN: 1943526060
ISBN-13: 9781943526062

To my husband, John.

Thank you for your encouragement and support.
Without it, this book would not have become a reality.

Acknowledgements

Heartfelt appreciation to Beta readers, Sandy Applegate and Dolores Guadian. Your comments were invaluable.

Thank you to Crystal Acosta, Karen Hsu, Nancy Johnson, and Dee Kincade for sharing your expertise and wise counsel.

You have searched me, Lord,
and you know me.

You know when I sit and when I rise;
you perceive my thoughts from afar.

You discern my going out and my lying down;
you are familiar with all my ways.

Before a word is on my tongue
you, Lord, know it completely.

You hem me in behind and before,
and you lay your hand upon me.

Such knowledge is too wonderful for me,
too lofty for me to attain.

Where can I go from your Spirit?
Where can I flee from your presence?

If I go up to the heavens, you are there;
if I make my bed in the depths, you are there.

If I rise on the wings of the dawn,
if I settle on the far side of the sea,

Even there your hand will guide me,
your right hand will hold me fast.

Prologue

*E*than half ran down the steep embankment. The coon was toying with him, scurrying in and out of the hollow log. He stopped, raised his rifle, finger on the trigger. *I can out wait you. You don't know who you're messing with!*

A few minutes later, with no sign of the coon, Ethan stomped to the edge of the orchard with exaggerated footsteps, attempting to lure the pest out from its hiding place. It was then that he heard Ginnie's familiar laughter, answered seconds later by a male's somewhat deeper tones. His head spun. He covered his ears with his hands.

The hair lifted on the back of his neck as a shiver ran down his spine. Gasping for breath, he crept forward. He clutched his gun to his chest, flattening himself against the rough bark of a tree.

Before he was conscious of what he was doing, Ethan emerged from his hiding place and strode with purpose toward the large apple tree under which he and Ginnie had been married only four years earlier. He choked back hot blinding tears as he approached Sam Havens from behind. Sam Havens with his hands on his wife's soft white shoulders. Sam Havens with his lips caressing Ginnie's long, silky hair.

Sam turned when he heard the click, eyes wide, and hands thrust forward in protest. "No!"

Ethan pulled the trigger, sneering as a wisp of smoke permeated the air.

He could only shake his head at Ginnie. He tried to form the words, but his throat was dry and his tongue thick.

She dropped to the ground; first to turn Sam's body over and check for a pulse, and then to crawl toward her husband, begging for mercy. "Don't, please—"

"Rot in hell, both of you!" The corner of his lip curled upward as he took careful aim. He watched her squirm, but finally pulled the trigger when she got close enough for him to smell her lilac perfume and the stench of her betrayal.

Two shots had ended it all.

The sound of the rifle and the odor of burnt flesh were all that he clearly remembered later that night as he sat on the front porch, rocking back and forth. His mind was unable to conceive that he'd shot them both dead under the same tree onto which he had carved out his declaration of love.

When he heard the toddler's cries behind him, he kicked the door shut with the heel of his boot. *What a fool I've been. Why, that boy doesn't look a thing like me.*

Chapter 1

Barefoot, Jake tripped over the worn threshold of the kitchen and onto the front porch. He pivoted on one foot and hurried to catch the old screen door before it slammed shut. He flinched and held his breath, his hands shaking as he pulled out two splinters from his big toe.

While resting his foot on the rotting porch rail, he peered through a hole in the screen door into the only home he'd ever known. The old wooden table stood in the middle of the room. Beyond that was Jake's sleeping corner, his pallet still wet with blood from last night's beating. Across the room was the faded green pullout sofa where Father slept. Next to the window sat an icebox that no longer kept things cold.

Father's boots, thrown into a corner, tempted Jake. Their feet were almost the same size. He grabbed the door handle.

He crept across the floor toward the shoes. The smell from them was overwhelming. He hesitated. His feet weren't used to wearing shoes. It might slow him down. He set the shoes back onto the floor and headed toward the door. He froze mid step when he noticed the full moon through the screen.

Escaping would have been so much easier on a dark night. He stepped outside and shivered as light sprinkles of rain and cold wind peppered against his face.

Jake winced as he pulled his trousers away from his calves. Last night's beating was the most severe he had ever endured. *He'll never touch me, again!* He wiped a stray tear with the back of his hand.

He had only been playing with Hound, but Father came running when he heard him growl. Jake had tried to explain, but Father strapped him all the harder. Blood from his bare legs spattered on the already stained and dirty floor.

Now, looking back through the screen door, his eyes fell on Father's thick black coat slung over the back of the sofa. A warm jacket would sure feel good. It lured him back inside.

He opened the door once more and tiptoed forward running his fingers along the edge of one sleeve. *It sure is cold out tonight.*

As he stood there in the moonlight, wrestling with the thought of taking the coat, he was startled by Hound when he stood up and stretched. The dog trotted up to him but Jake shook his head and put his finger to his lips. Hound went back to his pallet, circled it a few times and settled back down to resume his sleep.

Jake stood over his father, watching as his chest raised and lowered. His eyes turned to the rifle leaning against the corner. *Maybe I'll just end his life the way he did Mama's.*

Precious seconds ticked away.

The bright winter sun coaxed Ethan from a deep sleep. The almost bare springs of the old sofa poked him in his side as he rolled over. He groaned as he pulled the thin, ragged quilt over his broad shoulders. He stretched out his arm, fingers beckoning Hound for his early morning scratch behind his ears.

He shook himself awake and jumped to his feet. Something was wrong. His eyes darted to the corner. No Hound.

He gave the boy's pallet a hard kick. He was gone, too. Ethan stomped toward the bathroom door and pounded his fist on the frame. Silence.

Hopping into his pants, he scuttled into the kitchen. He threw on his shirt and used the sleeve to clear a spot from the dirty windowpane. He squinted as he looked through it, searching for any sign of the pair. He grabbed his coat and rushed to the unlatched door, tripping over a smelly bag of garbage in his path. He cursed under his breath as he ran outside.

He jumped over the wire fence, and then hit a large patch of ice at the corner of the cabin. He slid the rest of the way to the kennel at the far end of the yard. He whistled for Ghost.

The wolf appeared in an instant, his teeth bared and growling. Ethan snapped the muzzle over the pure white snout. "Sorry, boy, but we need the element of surprise on our side. Hound's older than you, but we both know he can run faster."

Intense heat began to course its way through his body. He could care less about the boy leaving, except for the fact that he served as a suitable whipping boy at times when Ethan's anger built and he found no other outlet. He was a painful daily reminder to him of Ginnie and Sam's insidious alliance. Perhaps without him around, Ethan could learn to forget and find peace for his tormented soul.

All he wanted was his dog. He'd do anything to get him back. He'd killed before. He would kill again—without so much as a blink of an eye.

Jake wiped the rain off his face with the palm of his hand. It was coming down harder now, making his trek through the unknown terrain more difficult. His ears picked up the sound of Hound loping up behind him.

Jake closed his dark brown eyes and rubbed the middle of his forehead with his thumb. Dropping to the ground, he searched the dog's face. "I'm glad to have your company but I'm afraid your being with me might make me easier to find." He put his arms around Hound's neck and wallowed in the soft, warm fur. *I wonder if he feels to blame? How can I explain madness to a dog?*

Hound whimpered and stretched out his long tongue to lick Jake's face.

After another moment's hesitation, Jake sighed and shook his head. "Ah, okay." He stood then, motioning for Hound to join him.

They picked their way down the muddy path to the river. Ice pellets hitting the water sparkled in the light of the full moon.

By now Father would have noticed they were gone. He'd probably already loaded his rifle. Jake was sure he'd pursue them—and he wouldn't give up easily.

The storm had strewn fallen branches across the path. More than once Jake slipped on leaves slick with rain. His bare feet grew numb. He looked down to see his bloody footprints on the path. He gritted his teeth and pressed on.

As he traveled, Father's curses roared over and over again in his head. Hot tears ran down his cheeks. He knew Father hated what Sam and Mama did, but he couldn't understand why he had stopped loving *him.*

Father had showered love on him as a small boy. A picture replayed in his mind of his parents snuggling, tickling and laughing with him until they all fell asleep on the big four poster bed—the one Father later burned without so much as an explanation.

Hound stayed by Jake's side as they traveled throughout the night. More than once, he kept the boy from falling asleep and sliding into the icy water below.

The sun would be up, soon.

Hound's stomach rumbled—or was it his own? "I'm afraid we're both going to miss our daily meal." He patted Hound's head. "When there's not enough scraps to go around we share, don't we? But Ghost? Never. He'd take my hand off without a second thought."

Jake collapsed next to Hound underneath the thick brush lining the river. He closed his eyes. How did Hound get out without Father hearing? He might never know how he'd done it, but he was grateful—ever so grateful—that he had. His first smile since Mama's death spread across his face.

He'd never been away from Father. He'd never even been out of the yard since Mama died. How long it had been? He had tried to climb the rusty chain-link several times before but was always caught by Father and forced to watch as the dogs ate his own portion of the scraps.

He was taller now and easily jumped over the fence. He had waited a lifetime for this day.

<hr/>

Ethan trudged down the steep embankment toward the river. He thought about the day Ginnie brought their baby into the world. He'd yelled for Ruth to come when the labor pains began. She'd come all right, but confided she didn't know what to do for Ginnie. Still, it had been of some comfort to him just having another person there. His experience with animals somehow hadn't translated when it meant helping his own wife.

He would have taken the pain on himself, if it had been possible, for he loved her that much. Her yellow hair, wet with perspiration, clung in little ringlets around her face. She'd never looked more beautiful.

The baby's first cry was the most wonderful sound he'd ever heard. If there was a God, he had certainly been smiling down on them that day.

Those tiny fingers and toes had been made possible by the love he and Ginnie shared. That was the purest happiness he'd ever known, only to be followed three years later by the most unbearable pain. *And as for you, Sam—good riddance.*

Ethan shook his head, clearing his thoughts. Why was he thinking about Ginnie, anyway? His fingers tensed their grip on the gun.

His lips curled as he thought about his prey. The tracks in the mud showed them heading for the river. The boy didn't realize that the water would rise if it stormed, again. Not a safe place for a boy and a dog. Without food and no weapon, he was totally unprepared for life outside the yard.

"Yes, Ghost, he'll be dead in a day—two for sure." He imagined seeing Jake's corpse in a grotesque position with carnivorous animals feeding on his lily-white flesh. He let out a deep, gratifying sigh and picked up the pace.

All of a sudden, Ghost ran ahead. He'd only do so if he'd spotted his target. Ethan hurried to catch up to him lest he harm Hound. It was a good thing he'd thought to muzzle him.

Ghost had a jealous streak. Without provocation, he'd tear Hound limb from limb. Only a signal from Ethan could keep that from happening.

He'd raised Hound from a pup, bonding with him during the time Ginnie became distant. She had withdrawn into herself as she mourned the loss of the baby girl she'd miscarried at five months. Hound was a lot of company to him in that dark and lonely time. He'd served as his best friend and he'd always treated him as such. He fed him his scraps first. His pallet was right next to Ethan's sofa bed.

Stepping over a log, he planted his foot in a pile of dead leaves. All at once a sharp pain pulled him to the ground. He let out a guttural scream. An old rusty trap imprisoned his right foot. He clenched his teeth as sweat beaded on his face.

With shaking hands, he strained against the jaws of the trap. He didn't stop until his fingers were numb. He rested, sucking in several breaths of air. When he could feel his fingers again, he stretched them several times, took in a deep breath, and seized the trap once more. *One. Two. Three.* With his hands on each side of his boot, he pried the jaws apart at last and ripped out his foot.

With another loud yell still echoing through the trees, he released the metal and let it fall to the ground. He winced at the pain and wiped the stinging sweat from his forehead with the palm of his hand. When it subsided, he inspected his injured foot. The flesh of his ankle was torn open clear down to the bone. He bit his lip, and then closed his eyelids and rested his foot on top of his other boot.

There was no blood at first, but in no time at all his foot was covered with it. Shaking, he took off his jacket and then his shirt. He put his coat back on and used the shirt to wrap his shredded ankle and foot before blacking out.

Jake fell asleep sometime between Mama's smile and the warmth of Hound's body against him. Mama looked so beautiful. Mama. He could hear her laughter. Mama. He longed to reach her outstretched arms.

Hound's bark broke into the boy's dream. He wanted so much to stay with Mama for a little while longer. The peace that surrounded her was a balm to his wounds, both physical and emotional. He was just on the verge of touching her yellow hair when the dog barked again, and he could enjoy her presence no longer.

Jake rubbed his eyes and stretched his lanky body. He held his hands to his eyes to shield them from swirling leaves. Dark clouds had formed a halo around the sun. It would soon be snowing. He spun around when a twig snapped nearby.

Ghost and Hound stood in the clearing behind him, facing each other. Both remained motionless except for the sporadic flinching of their huge shoulder muscles.

Jake knew Hound could defeat Ghost, but his immediate worry was the rifle. Father only took Ghost off the chain for hunting—and he never hunted without the rifle.

This time, though, Father wasn't hunting coon or weasel or squirrel. This time he was hunting for Jake.

Father was a killer. Jake had heard *the story* every Saturday night: how Father caught Mama and Sam under the apple tree; how he shot them both without hesitation.

He'd kill him, too. That was as certain as the sun coming up in the morning and going down at night. There was a bullet in that rifle with his name on it.

Jake stopped short. He dared not go closer to the pair. The hammering of his heart was so loud it almost drowned out their vicious growls. He watched in awe as Hound guarded him, his master.

Ghost was muzzled, but the dog had been working at the leather and had torn one side loose, leaving it hanging. His sharp teeth glistened as he bared them.

Jake's eyes darted in all directions. Father must be nearby.

Up on his elbows, Ethan pulled himself through the falling snow in the direction of the dogs' growls. Could he get there in time to save Hound? From the beginning, his intention was for the dog to be the boy's companion, protecting him as he grew to manhood. But, that all changed on that fateful day in the orchard seven years ago. No child of Sam's was worthy of Hound.

Ethan whistled, then ordered, "Ghost, come!"

Moments later, Jake crumpled to the ground, sighing as the wolf suddenly backed off and raced down the slippery path from which he'd come. Jake's mouth hung open. He couldn't believe it. Why did Ghost retreat?

He signaled for Hound to join him. "We've got to get out of here." Together, the two of them scrambled through the low brush. They didn't stop until Jake stumbled onto the entrance to the apple orchard. He lifted the wire latch and pushed back the wooden gate.

An enormous tree cast a shadow on the narrow dirt path. He froze. Could this be *the* apple tree? His heart raced as he took several steps forward and stopped when he saw the crude carved heart. He couldn't read, but was certain of what it said, "Ethan and Ginnie - Love Lasts - Forever." His fingers trembled as he touched the words.

His mother, some five years younger than Ethan, had flung her arms around his neck when she saw his love for her displayed so permanently.

So it was only fitting they'd married under the sweet-smelling blossoms the following spring.

The beautiful Ginnie gave birth to Jake exactly nine months later.

———

Ethan awoke on the kitchen floor late that afternoon, a fiery sunset igniting the sky outside the dirty window. He searched his memory, trying to recall the events of the day. He was in the woods…the trap snapped onto his foot…the dogs fought…Ghost returned to his side. He rubbed his chin. How had he gotten back home?

He rested under the old quilt, too exhausted to put Ghost in his pen. The wolf was never permitted to sleep on the pallet. That special place was reserved for Hound. But Ghost did Ethan a good deed, so he would allow him to lie by his side—just this once.

Ethan fell into yet another fitful sleep, waking once more in the middle of the night. He watched as Ghost's shadowy form stretched and then ambled over to the kitchen to rummage in the gray bucket by the sink.

Even though the scraps had been there since the day before, the rumble in Ghost's stomach enticed him to eat. When he finished, he circled around to Ethan, who was struggling to sit up on the side of the worn sofa. He settled down by his master's side and watched as he inspected his leg. His ears pricked when he sucked air into his mouth through clenched teeth.

Ethan reached behind him to click on the switch to the overhead light. He shuddered when he discovered his leg had swollen to twice its normal size. He dragged himself over to the bucket in the corner of the kitchen, cupped his hands, and dipped them into the cold rainwater supplied by the still unrepaired hole in the roof.

He held his breath as he washed the wound, berating himself for not replenishing the antiseptic from Ginnie's first aid kit. Still, there might be a bottle of moonshine underneath the porch...

Finding himself unable to stand on the injured leg, he belly-crawled in the direction of the porch. One by one the minutes slipped by, his progress slowed by fits of pain and precious time lost to blackouts.

Sometime around sunrise he reached his destination. He rolled onto his side and stretched his arm under the steps as far as he could, raking it back and forth in the dirt but failing to come up with anything except a few rocks and a lid from an old tin can. Too many trips there on lonely evenings may have cost him his life. He should have rationed the liquor out for special occasions, like celebrating an exceptionally good hunting trip, or times when he punished the boy—and then needed to forget...

Trudging through deepening snow banks, Jake and Hound made slow progress the following day. Shivering from the cold, they somehow managed to keep going until dusk. "I'm afraid we took too much time in the orchard. Father's sure to catch up with us soon." In the meantime, he considered what would happen if he were to be confronted by a stranger. Would he be able to defend himself? Should he make up a story of some kind? Give himself a new name?

Except for Father, the last person he'd seen was Ruth. She was Mama's best friend, but she'd left the day following the murders. She was Sam's wife, but she didn't even stay for his burial. After saying a few words to Father, she raised her hand to announce her departure into the world, the wind whipping her long red hair around her face as she headed down the dusty road.

She never looked back. She just disappeared from their lives forever, wearing Mama's blue sweater.

Jake did a double take as he looked up at the purples and pinks blanketing the sky over the mountain peaks. Maybe tomorrow they should go in that direction—opposite of the way Father headed when going into town for provisions. His teeth chattered and his head spun. "W-we would-n't w-w-ant to run—into him—now would we, H-h-ound?"

Hound barked his assent, running round and round as he often did when he spotted a rat or gopher in the backyard.

"What is it, b-b-oy?"

Hound barked again, running forward and then back toward Jake.

"You—want m-e to follow—you, b-b-oy? Okay. Let's—go."

The pair plodded through powdery snow, coming upon a rundown shack half-hidden behind the heavily laden boughs of a large pine tree. Its roof had caved in near the front door, and the porch had almost rotted away.

Jake brushed away cobwebs from the small window next to the door and peered inside. "I—don't t-t-hink anyone l-l-ives--here anymore, H-h-ound."

He lifted the crude latch and the door opened back against the inside wall. His heart raced as he crept inside.

It was almost dark, but from what he could tell, it was only one room. No table. No chairs. Nothing but an old rocker. It was shelter, though—and warmer than outdoors.

Did they dare stop for the night?

Chapter 2

———

*E*arly the next morning, Jake woke to the sound of rain peppering against the slatted walls of the shack. He swung his legs over the side of the rocker, massaged his stiff knees, and stretched his arms.

He smiled, remembering how Mama had held him throughout the night, singing her sweet lullabies and rocking him to their melodic cadence. He had snuggled close to her and drifted into a peaceful sleep, leaving behind the foreboding possibility of Father's revenge.

When Hound licked his face, he lowered himself to the floor. He ran his hand along the dog's back, up to his broad head and then stopped to scratch him behind his ears. Their stomachs growled in unison.

As the morning sun replaced the crescent moon, the shack came to life. Spiders resumed work in their webs. A rat scurried out one of the holes in the wooden floor.

Father could be around any bend. They should move on.

He pushed to his knees and pivoted toward the door. He blinked. A jacket hung next to it. A pair of boots sat off to the side. Was he dreaming? He pinched his arm.

He took a deep breath, yearning to touch the smooth surface of the boots. He scrambled forward. He put out his hand, but then withdrew it. Would the owner soon return, realizing he had forgotten them?

He jumped to his feet and raced to the window. Sunlight poked through the heavy boughs, but he was unable to see past the porch. If he couldn't see out, then no one could see in…

He turned back. It wouldn't hurt to just try them on…

He knelt on the floor and closed his eyes, imaging what such softness—such warmth would feel like. The temptation was overpowering. He spit on his hand and wiped the dirt from the bottoms of his frostbitten feet. He held his breath as he slipped them inside one boot and then the other.

"Look, Hound! They fit me perfectly." He twirled around and around. Then the dog joined in, following Jake as he marched from one wall to the other like the soldier on Father's box of breakfast cereal. Hot tears rolled down his cheeks as he laughed and stomped across the creaking floor.

He froze, marveling at the coat. He had never had one—never even dared to hope for one of his own—but it was right there in front of him, just the same.

He stretched out his hands to feel the smoothness of the hide. Taking a deep breath, he slipped his arms into the sleeves, relaxing into the softness of the lamb's wool lining. He drew it closed with the supple leather sash.

He frowned. It might be wrong to keep them, but he had to take the chance.

Any punishment would be worth this one, perfect moment.

Although he and Hound went another full day with no food, the rain provided an abundance of water. Jake turned his head to the dark skies and opened his mouth, allowing the cool liquid to fill it. Hound lapped up water as it accumulated in the boy's cupped hands. Sometimes he drank from Jake's boot prints left behind in the wet earth.

At sunset, three days after his escape, a blaze of retreating light hit the thick bushes directly in front of Jake, revealing boughs weighed down with deep purple berries. He rushed forward and picked several of them, the sharp stickers piercing his fingers. He hesitated for a moment, mesmerized by the blood they drew, but then continued to pull the fruit from the stems. He devoured them by the handful. A little pain was a small price to pay for such delicious berries.

Jake offered some to Hound. "Come on, boy, they're really good."

Hound sniffed the berries and then backed away.

"Suit yourself."

A few minutes later Jake heard Hound's growling stomach and laughed as he gobbled the fruit up, stickers and all, from his hands.

Pitch dark now, they took shelter underneath a large tree so thick with leaves that the smooth ground underneath remained dry. Jake spent the next few minutes pulling the stickers from his fingers, Hound helping him by licking off droplets of blood. Afterward they drifted off to sleep, an intertwining of wet fur and legs. Wet dog had never smelled so good.

Mama's presence filled the hours with companionship and love the likes of which Jake could only experience in the dream world he visited on nights like this. However, in the middle of the night Jake was roused from his sleep by an odd ache in his belly. As he rolled over and away from the still-sleeping hound, he vomited out a large quantity of the berries. Perhaps the feast hadn't been worth it after all.

Jake leaned into the warmth of Hound. He looked toward the sky filled with thousands of stars, reveling in their beauty, and delighting in their dance across the vast space. The interlude was short-lived, however, as wave after wave of nausea washed over him for the next several hours.

Hound, also, did not escape unscathed. He awoke with a start, shortly after Jake, regurgitating huge amounts of purple liquid underneath a nearby bush.

The rain stopped sometime during the night, so midmorning, Jake prodded Hound to join him as he resumed his journey into the unknown. "We need to make up for lost time while the sun's shining and the sky's clear."

He shielded his eyes with his hand, looking up at the ominous sky. "Let's hope it doesn't snow, again. That would slow us down and our footprints would lead Father to us for sure."

⁂

Unable to find the elusive moonshine, Ethan collapsed in the yard. He lacked the strength to crawl for shelter underneath the few boards on the porch still intact. If he lived through this, he would do some repairs next spring.

Except for Ghost, he was alone in the backwoods. At first, the cabin seemed to be an ideal place to hide, but later on, he doubted the decision. The lack of medical help was a big problem when Ginnie was giving birth. He had relied on Ruth—though he found her to be essentially worthless—and what he could remember seeing in movies—also worthless.

He spent the remainder of the day and night drifting in and out of consciousness. As the falling snow blanketed his body, fever conjured terrifying memories of his childhood.

The buckle of Father's leather belt struck hard against his back. Mother sobbed in the corner, clasping her hands in her lap, the edge of her apron stuffed into her mouth.

Near sunrise, the demons retreated and Ethan's thoughts began to clear. He raised an eyebrow. He'd get the knife he used to skin the game he'd caught in Uncle Ethan's old traps. He'd need to sterilize it somehow. He might have to use it to... No, he wouldn't think about that. At least, not now.

He used his bloody elbows to propel himself from the front of the house to the side, and then to follow the sewage trench to the back, a distance of roughly two hundred feet. Some time ago, he stuck the knife in the bark of the mighty oak for safekeeping. As he looked up at it now, he let loose a string of vile curses, realizing it was lodged much higher than he remembered. How in the world was he going to get up there?

He leaned against the tree and pounded his head against the bark, over and over again, creating a bloody spot on his scalp. The last time he'd used that knife was to teach the kid a lesson. *He didn't think I'd use it, but I showed him.* He'd tied his hands, and then sharpened the knife on the strap...nice and slow...right in front of the boy's eyes. He could still hear him beg. "Don't, Father, please——"

Ethan hit his palm against his forehead. He had to think. He needed to get the ladder from the shed. That was first and foremost.

He summoned the energy to drag himself toward the small building at the back of the yard, covering the distance faster than he anticipated. His spirits soared as he pulled himself up beside the only sturdy door on the property. He took in a deep breath and reached upward for the handle. When his hand hit the hard metal of the padlock, he crumpled to the ground in a defeated heap.

Oh, no! The key is in the cabin. There's no way I—

Flat on his back, he shook his fist at the sky. He closed his eyes, taking in deep breaths to calm his erratic heartbeats. What kind of a man executes plan "A" without a backup?

After several minutes of contemplation, and with renewed determination, he crawled the short distance to the water trough. He kicked it over, water running off in the direction of the shed. Then he came in behind it, lay down on his belly and used his arms to push it, little by little, over to the tree where he turned it on its side.

Finally, he made his way over to the ever-growing pile of junk at the back of the cabin to retrieve a rickety wooden crate. He hoisted it onto the trough, creating another level.

He focused his eyes on the knife once more. It was now or never.

With new resolve, he placed the palms of his hands onto the trough and heaved himself up with all his might, cursing as his injured leg scraped against the dry wood. Panting and sweating profusely, he pulled himself to his knees. His eyes riveted on the crate. If he lost his balance...

He took in a deep breath and grabbed onto the tree, using it to steady him as he rose in one swift movement and placed his left foot on the crate. His body erect, he snatched the knife from the bark. *Hail Mary!*

It was then that his knees buckled. Losing his grip, he sagged against the tree. The crate crashed to the ground, leaving his feet thrashing in midair and causing his entire body to pivot. His shoulder grazed the side of the trough as he landed on the ground below.

He regained consciousness some time later, with a smile on his face and the knife still clutched in his shaking hand. He was thankful for the soft mud. Without it, he could have broken his back.

The sun was low in the sky. Had he been unconscious that long? He no longer wore a watch, using only the sun to gage the time. No alarm clock roused him awake in the morning. No timepiece governed his workday.

He peeled off his outer shirt when he could no longer take the heat of his own body. He flinched as he checked his leg, an angry red line now inching upward toward the groin.

He dragged himself over to the rusty bucket. Rainwater. It certainly wasn't sanitary, but it would have to do. He drank, first, then rinsed the caked-on mud from his wound. His leg was tender to the touch. He writhed as he washed it. He'd seen his share of animals with infected wounds like this.

Knife in hand, he inched his way down the side of the cabin and back around to the front yard. He looked toward the kitchen window. He needed to retrieve the matches from underneath the sink.

He pulled himself up the porch steps, one at a time, cursing God aloud with each painful movement. He forged ahead, wincing as splinter after splinter accumulated on the palms of his hands.

His stomach growled. He hallucinated about lobster and steak, but in his lucid moments he knew he'd be lucky just to catch one of his laying hens. He licked his lips as he eyed a small one strutting about the yard.

Thankful that the screen door was still ajar, he was able to pull it the rest of the way open with his fingertips. He slid inside the cabin and rested on his side. He lay motionless on the floor, breathing hard.

He began to laugh uncontrollably, as he made up a series of lewd "knock-knock" jokes. The interlude ended with a sobering thought: *If I don't move from here pretty soon, I may die from hunger right in front of the refrigerator.*

He observed the cupboards, scratched and lacking paint. He drew in a deep breath and let out a determined *whoop*, pushing himself up to a sitting position. He scooted over to open the door under the cracked and yellowed sink. His hand shook as he removed a can that had once held coffee.

He closed his eyes, crossed his heart, and tugged on the plastic lid. When a single match fell into his waiting hand, he reacted by throwing the can with such force that it shattered the only window in the house that wasn't boarded. Fragments of glass fell onto the counter and into the sink.

He could blame the kid for the broken window if he were here. He paused a moment, compiling a list of the boy's shortcomings worthy of discipline. At the top of the list, and actually not the boy's own fault, was the simple fact that he was the offspring of an adulterous union. And for that, someone had to pay.

He perspired as he spent a fitful night thrashing to and fro, flushed with fever that would not abate even in the freezing weather, convulsing and yelling out for his wife.

When the fever waned, his thoughts became more rational. He reflected on his life with Ginnie. He still couldn't believe he was able to convince her to leave home. After all, she'd only just met him that very night at the CorNer Bar. He laughed when he thought about his two o'clock phone call to her and the sight of her stealing down the ladder in her nightgown—running barefoot down the street in the stillness of the early morning hours and into his waiting arms.

Her eyes twinkled when he suggested they lose themselves in the mountains above Otter Creek. They masqueraded as brother and sister, driving across the country without so much as one person questioning their story. Ginnie later confessed that she had been enchanted by him—older and ever so handsome.

She had no idea she was starting a new life with a convicted felon.

Hunger dominated Jake's every thought on the fourth day of the journey. He followed Hound across the flat landscape rimmed with beautiful snowcapped mountains, puzzled at budding plants poking through the frozen ground, reaching upward.

Long shadows crisscrossed the landscape as clouds rolled in to cover the midday sun. Hound's ears pricked. He ran ahead, then stopped and looked back at Jake.

"What is it, boy?"

After a moment's hesitation, the dog turned and trotted off.

Jake's knees buckled at the familiar sight of the old wire fence and the cabin beyond. His mind swirled with confusing thoughts and conflicting emotions.

Could they have come full circle?

Chapter 3

*W*aking to the sound of his own cursing, Ethan wiped perspiration from his brow with his forearm, Ghost entered through the flap. The wolf was getting used to his newfound freedom, roaming in the woods and returning whenever he wanted.

He deposited what was left of his kill into the scrap bucket, circled round three times, and lay down. Muddy and shivering from the cold, he had been out all night hunting for rabbit. Judging from his contented posture on the pallet, he must have killed a fat one.

Ethan's stomach growled. There was still some meat on the carcass... He gasped as a familiar snout pushed open the flap. *Hound!*

The dog stopped short, watching Ghost as he slept on *his* pallet. His eyes darted toward the scrap bucket. His big tongue dropped a puddle of saliva on the floor. He inched forward, one eye on the bucket, and one eye on Ghost.

Ethan caught the dog's attention and shook his head. He knew he was hungry, but he'd rather see him starve than be killed by Ghost.

Sensing the intruder, the wolf jumped up on all fours. He spun around to guard the bucket.

His fierce growl froze Ethan to the spot. He could only watch as the two dogs stared each other down, hunched over and snarling with the scrap bucket between them.

Ghost, protecting his new territory, took the initiative. He leaped over the bucket and landed on top of Hound, digging his teeth into the smaller dog's broad neck. Blood rose to the surface and then dripped onto the floor.

Ethan's heart pounded against his chest. One more bite could prove fatal.

Hound circled around, coming at Ghost with everything he had. The muscles in his strong legs rippled as he slammed against his adversary. Ghost fell against the sharp iron strap securing a box of kindling next to the old wood stove. When it slit his throat, blood spurted out of the wound. Ethan averted his eyes, then placed his hands over his ears to drown out the piercing yelps and the sound of gnashing teeth.

As an eerie calm settled over the room, Ethan raised his head to the horrific sight.

Ghost was dead. The huge wolf lay motionless near the pallet.

Hound had triumphed but continued to lose blood. He might not make it, either.

He motioned for the dog to come to his side, but instead Hound limped toward the flap. He paused then and turned around.

"Ah, coming back to your master are you, Hound?" He put out his hand.

The dog limped past him and lowered his head into the bucket, claiming for himself the delicious bounty from Ghost's late night hunting trip—the victor's spoils.

Ethan's shoulders drooped as he watched the dog push through the flap. This was an animal's ultimate betrayal—an unforgivable act of treason.

Jake looked toward the sky and beat his chest with his hands. He had gone through all of this—and for what? Hands that couldn't feel anything and an ache in his belly.

Sometime later, he regained his composure and wiped his tear-filled eyes. He crept closer to the fence that had once imprisoned him. It was then he noticed the broken window and the marks in the damp earth indicating that something had been dragged from the front of the cabin to the back. Or was it the other way around?

His hope was renewed when Hound staggered around the corner of the cabin and picked his way toward him. The dog dropped the carcass in front of his master and then backed away. He hunkered down, propped his head on top of his paws, and watched Jake sink his teeth into the meager offering.

"Thanks, boy." After eating a few bites, Jake paused. Blood trickled from a wound low on Hound's neck. "Who did you meet up with, boy? Was it Ghost?" If it was, he might be out there right now, watching... His throat tightened. He remained motionless as his eyes searched the terrain for signs of impending danger.

He dropped to his knees beside his dog and packed the gaping neck wound with snow. Then he shrugged out of his coat and placed it over Hound's body. "This will keep you warm."

Tears stung his eyes as over and over again, he begged an unknown god for his friend's life. *Please let my dog live. He's all I have. I'd rather die than lose Hound.*

He stayed by the dog's side the rest of the day, offering him chips of frozen rainwater from nearby puddles and encouraging him to clean the remaining meat off the bone. "Hey, Hound, do you remember when we found that gopher in the back yard? Remember how we sneaked up on him and trapped him in the bucket? And how he hit against the sides of it so hard trying to escape that he knocked himself out? And what about the time that Mama baked me a birthday cake? She even let you have a piece, didn't you, boy?"

Jake stroked the dog's head, humming softly until Hound's big eyes fluttered shut. That birthday had been a long time ago—when he was three.

He curled up by Hound, as clouds feathered across the dark blue sky. He ran his tongue across his lips, recalling the taste of the sweet icing and the lemon cake. He could almost feel Mama's soft cheek against his as she bent down to help him blow out the candles.

In the late afternoon, Hound raised his head and licked his hand.

"That a boy!" Jake was careful not to squeeze too hard as he hugged him. Tears trickled down his cheeks, but he didn't bother to wipe them away. He remembered Mama's words, *"Never be ashamed of crying tears of joy. They are too few and far between, Son."*

With Hound now resting comfortably, he decided to venture off. "I'll be back soon, Hound. You rest and I'll find us something more to eat."

He followed the sound of cascading water to a small brook where trees with low branches covered in moss shaded the water. He skipped across a string of smooth stones to a place where two fallen logs formed a circulating pool. When a small fish swam near his feet, he bent forward and caught it by the tail. It wriggled loose, though, and found safety underneath one of the logs.

He continued to pursue the small fry, but it was too quick for his stiff fingers. He gave up when he lost his balance, and slid into the frigid water with a *kerplop.* He rose, sputtering and soaking wet.

It was near dusk. Hunger, cold, and his curiosity about Ghost lured him to the cabin. His pulse quickened as he neared the fence. Teeth chattering, he took small, silent steps toward the window, a thin layer of snow crunching under his feet. The wolf, fur drenched with blood, lay motionless beside the pallet.

His eyes roamed over the rest of the room. A rat scurried into the corner where Father's swollen leg stuck out from behind the sofa. Was he dead? His bottom lip quivered. Was he safe at last?

———

Jake's shadow fell across Ethan's body. Through half-opened eyes, he watched the boy disappear into the small pantry. He strained to listen as he rummaged through its contents, returning with the only food remaining in the cabin: a jar of green beans Ruth had canned the summer before her departure. She had promised to teach Ginnie how to can the following summer but, of course, that never happened.

Placing the dusty jar on the table, the boy tried, without success, to open it with his swollen fingers. After searching for something to pry the lid off, and failing to come up with anything suitable, he threw the jar into the sink. He picked the beans from among the shards of glass, gorging himself on the vegetables before collapsing on his pallet.

Ethan's fingers pressed against his temples and he covered his ears. Devilish thoughts threatened to overtake him. The boy's running had started a chain of events for which he was ultimately responsible: Ethan's injury and Ghost's death. Blackness erupted from the depths of his soul, unleashing an uncontrollable surge of energy and propelling him toward the pallet. Once there, his hand shot out and grabbed Jake by the ankle.

The boy's shrill scream pierced the air as he shook his leg free from his father's vise-like grip and sprang to his feet. But his legs were weak and numb, causing him to lose his footing and crash into the wall behind him.

"So, just what do you think you're doing back here?" Ethan bellowed, as he grabbed the rifle and pointed it at Jake.

"Hound is hurt. I-I had to find out what happened," Jake stammered.

"Ghost died protecting me. That's what happened."

"Looks like you're hurt, too."

"Got caught in one of the traps."

"Now you know what it feels like, I guess." Jake's eyes shot daggers at Ethan as he instinctively touched the grotesque scar across his right forearm.

"You've deserved every punishment you ever got!" Ethan spat.

"Mama—"

"Just shut your mouth. I am so tired of hearing 'my mama' this and 'my mama' that. Your mama, for your information, was a sneak, a liar and a harlot."

"She was not! She was beautiful and kind and good and—" Jake paused. "She was everything you're NOT."

"You're just a kid. You have no idea what you're talking about." Ethan shoved the barrel hard into Jake's chest.

"Aaugh!" Jake's face turned ghastly pale. He panted, struggling to regain his breath.

"That's right. Don't forget: He who holds the gun has the upper hand."

"I'm bigger now, or haven't you noticed? I could whup you…"

"You think so, huh?"

"Yes, I do!"

"Then let's go, boy. Bring it on." Ethan ordered.

Jake wobbled to his feet. "I hate you! I wish I'd never been born. I wish I never had a father like you."

Ethan threw his head back and howled, "So that's how you feel? Well, have I got some news for you."

Jake bent over at his waist. He clenched his fists and sucked in a breath of air. "Oh?"

Ethan locked his eyes on the boy, watching him shift from one foot to the other. He weighed his options and berated himself for letting even that much slip out.

"No—on second thought—you don't deserve any good news. You ran off, stole *my* dog, and even ate my last bit of food. I think I'll keep what I know to myself." His nostrils flared as he cracked his neck from side to side.

"I know all I need to, anyhow."

"Which is?"

"I know you're evil. I know you have a black soul—a dark, cold, hard, black heart."

Ethan sneered. "And you're so perfect, is that it?"

"I've tried to be good…tried to do just what you wanted…tried to stay out of your way. But there's no pleasing you. You just look for any excuse you can find to—"

Ethan pounded his fist against the floor, "Why, you little—" He lunged at Jake's feet and used the butt of his rifle to knock them out from under him. He rolled on top of the boy, slid the barrel over his windpipe and began to apply pressure.

Jake squirmed back and forth on the floor, rotating his body as he pushed against the gun with all his might.

Ethan jerked his head in the direction of a noise outside the screen. *Has Hound come back to protect the boy?* He instinctively rolled to the side, crouching on his left foot. As he pushed up, in an effort to stand, he slipped on the pallet and lost his balance, landing hard on the old slatted floorboards. They gave way with a loud *crack*, Ethan's body lodging within their clutches.

Jake pulled in shallow breaths between fits of raspy coughing. He slowly brought himself up to a sitting position, panting as he leaned his head back against the smooth stone fireplace.

Ethan wriggled to free himself, but he remained sandwiched between the boards. His eyes flew to the knife on the floor, just out of his reach, then trained on the rifle lying between the two of them. They were his only weapons…or were they?

Ethan's lip curled, his eyes communicating his evil intent. In a split second, his fingers snatched the match out of his shirt pocket, struck it on the rough floor, and tossed it into the air. Its downward spiral, reminded him of the sparkling costume of a trapeze artist, twisting the rope while descending toward her muscular white steed.

His demonic laugh was soon drowned out by roaring flames.

Chapter 4

*F*ire traveled up the walls of the cabin and raced across the ceiling, devouring everything in its path. The sofa bed was the first to go, followed by the old table. A trail of flames zigzagged from one side of the room to the other, a game of checkers played by unseen hands.

All at once, the floor gave way. Ethan fell onto the dirt below. Jake landed nearby. Unsupported, fiery boards cascaded down from above. Ethan strained to free himself from one landing on top of his legs. He recognized it as the armrest from the "punishing chair." His diabolical laugh was met with dancing flames that seared into his face and marched up his back.

All of a sudden, arms of fire reached out toward the boy. They dragged his limp body out from under the burning timber and carried him away. His groans were the last sounds Ethan heard as he drifted into unconsciousness.

Ethan stretched, then sat up. He sneered at Jake's lifeless body covered with a light dusting of snow. Crawling over to him, he placed his fingers around his throat. He hesitated. He preferred a slow death for the boy.

He cocked his head toward the cabin, the last of the flames now dying down. The match...the fire... How had they escaped the cabin alive? Had the fiery arms been a hallucination or did something, or someone else, save them? If so, why? So they could apologize to each other? The boy for even being born and him for laying his heart open to a temptress with yellow hair?

Leaving Jake behind, Ethan dragged his body through a minefield of rocks, tree trunks, and even a small ice-covered pond on his half-mile journey to Sam's cabin. Sweating profusely and muttering to himself *(the "fever talking," as his grandmother would have said)* he pushed past his own limits to reach the only shelter within a twenty-mile radius.

At dusk, the cabin came into view. Sitting on a bluff, it would be an uphill battle for him to get there. Come to think of it, that was the phrase the newspaper had used to describe his trial. He turned over on his back to rest, laughing at his own twisted humor. It was too bad he was the only one there to appreciate it.

He started to "army crawl" again, trying to ignore the pain in his elbows as the tender scabs tore loose and began to bleed into small patches of snow. The gnawing in his gut had long passed, but he was running on fumes with little energy left. *Keep moving. Keep moving.*

He kept his eyes to the ground, straining every muscle to maintain the pace. He had to make it by nightfall. If he dared let himself rest... The thought formed a knot in his gut.

An abrupt movement caught his eye, followed by loud growls. His head jerked up. A bear cub was heading straight for him. *This can't be! Not after it all it took to get here.*

His arms shook as he pulled them out from under him and covered his head. He slowed his breathing and kept still, waiting. Was its mother close by?

The cub sniffed up and down Ethan's body, taking his time as he licked blood from his fingers and elbows. The hair lifted on the nape of his neck as the animal rocked him back and forth with his already-powerful paws. He braced himself for the inevitable; half-wishing the bear would quit playing around and just get it over with.

In an instant, descending shrieks filled the air as a large buzzard swooped down on the bear, its sharp talons pulling at the soft fur on his back. He lifted the cub off Ethan and carried him several feet away.

Without hesitation, Ethan scrambled under the protective branches of a small tree and wedged himself between two rocks. He covered his ears once again, muffling the bear's vociferous outcry as the vicious bird overpowered him. He remained there, heart beating wildly in his chest, as the victor claimed his spoils. It was already dark when he left his hiding place and pressed forward.

Sometime later, he allowed himself a few moments of rest. With only a crescent moon above the forest canopy, he was barely able to distinguish the outline of Sam's cabin. The view from there was spectacular. No doubt about it. However, it sat just high enough to be visible from the road. Not the best place to hide, but then again, no one would be looking for him.

It took the remainder of the night for him to make it up the steep incline, snaking his way around exposed and twisted roots, taking detours around large rocks. He was near the steps when fatigue overtook him. He curled up in the fetal position, hunched his shoulders against a pre-dawn downpour, and succumbed to the heaviness of his eyelids.

An hour later, wet and shivering, he pulled himself up the steps.

It had been years since he was inside Sam's cabin. After the incident in the orchard, he swore he'd never go in there, again. But these were desperate times. He needed food and shelter. He gave the door a kick with his good leg. The brittle wood broke easily, creaking as it opened back against the frame.

Now, in the early morning light, he made his way into the living room and rested his head against the wall. He looked back through the kitchen window in the direction of his own cabin, tendrils of smoke still rising into the sky.

He forced his frostbitten fingers to tear away the remnants of his pants, exposing his wound. He squeezed his eyes shut. Even the hind leg of Sylas Scroggin's Labrador, mauled by an angry Doberman, had looked healthy in comparison.

He needed to view this objectively. After all, he was an experienced vet. He'd performed dozens of amputations.

He found a suitable replacement knife in the kitchen. Then, gritting his teeth, he crawled to Sam's closet, stole the tie from Ruth's bathrobe and a stretched-out sock from inside one of Sam's boots. He snatched Sam's driver's license from the shelf above them. It just might come in handy one day.

Coming out of the closet and into the kitchen, he chuckled when he found a full bottle of moonshine sitting on their Formica-topped table. It had been there all those years, like a bottle of champagne left by management in the Presidential Suite of the Waldorf Astoria Hotel. Once more, he gave in to a fit of irrepressible laughter.

He pulled himself up onto the bathroom toilet. After binding his leg with the tie, he chugged down most of the liquor. When the warmth of it reached his gut, he poured the rest of it on his leg and the knife. He clenched his teeth until the burning subsided, took in a deep breath, and picked up the knife. He made his incision just above the knee. Turning the knife, he used a sawing motion to cut around the entire leg, exposing the kneecap.

His screams bounced back to him, unheeded, unnoticed. Black spots before his eyes prompted him to take another breath. He dared not pass out now. He shook with pain as he pulled his lower leg toward his body, repeatedly twisting it back and forth until it gave way. "Son of a b——" He fell sideways onto the floor, panting.

Lightheaded and drenched with sweat, he tightened his makeshift tourniquet and slipped the sock over the stump. After he finished wrapping the site with remnants of Ruth's robe, blackness enveloped him.

Feverish dreams haunted him throughout the night. Ginnie's fingers caressing the heart he had carved into the apple tree. Ginnie bathing their baby boy. Ginnie laughing with Sam.

Two little girls screamed and ran toward him. They were trying to tell him something. But what? He couldn't hear the words, though he leaned closer and closer...

———— ⌘ ————

Jake awoke to feel intense cold pressing down on his thin body. He tried to stand on wobbly legs, but fell face down onto the snow-soaked earth.

His eyes darted all around the clearing, falling on the charred remains of the cabin. The air, still filled with smoke, burned his lungs and stung his eyes.

Was Hound still alive? He crawled to the place he had left him, but the dog was gone. The coat remained on the ground, Hound's pawprints leading off into the trees.

Jake sat down on the coat and put his face in his hands. Tears found their way down his cheeks and onto his chest.

Leaves of nearby bushes shook. A lump formed in his throat. Was it just a gust of wind? Or could it be Father's ghost? He squeezed his eyelids shut and held his breath, waiting...

The leaves stirred once again. He opened one eye, then exhaled.

Hound trotted through the foliage, carrying a squirrel in his mouth.

For the next few days, demons of Ethan's past played the night of the hit-and-run over and over in his head. He drank too much at the game—and afterward. That was the truth. He didn't see those little girls run out from between the parked cars. That, also, was the truth.

But Elvira Eastman saw his car and copied down "BESTVET" from the license plate. She watched from her kitchen window as the girls' parents ran out of the house and clutched their small bodies in shaking arms.

Ethan had scoffed at the witness sitting on the stand with her hand on the Bible. All smug and pious, like none of them knew she was having an affair with her golf caddie. Rumor had it that she'd even tried to have her husband killed once to collect the insurance money. They said she just batted her false eyelashes at Owen and swore she couldn't ever think of doing such a thing. He took her back after not so much as a night apart. Weakling.

His trial lasted a month, but the jury deliberated for only three hours. He was branded a convicted felon that day. Later that night, he escaped from the antiquated jail. His heart raced as he slipped past an easily distracted guard with a penchant for cinnamon rolls. Another weakling.

Once out the side door, he stole down the dark alley without a sound, his breath rising in the cold air to form wispy haystacks under the streetlights as he passed by. At the end of the street, a police cruiser pulled over to the curb, its siren squealing.

There in the moonlight he froze, his escape lacking in precise execution. After a few minutes spent recalculating, he ran halfway down the block and broke into his own clinic. He holed up there for a few hours, then headed for the CorNer Bar.

An hour later, he met Ginnie for the first time. She had delicate features, fair skin, and hair the color of spun gold. Her crystal blue eyes drew him in. He was intoxicated by her perfume, her laugh, her smile.

He told her stories about his many travels—all lies of course. As he talked, a plan to hide out at Uncle Ethan's cabin had already begun to take shape.

When the lucid moments broke through the fever, he explored Ruth's pantry where he found a bountiful supply of canned carrots, green beans, turnips, and a variety of fruits. He ate a cold meal of something labeled "soup." It lacked flavor, but it was filling.

He rummaged through an old cardboard box in the bathroom and found a bottle of pain pills and antibiotic ointment. In the medicine cabinet, he discovered a prescription heart medication with Sam's name on it. *Well, old buddy, you should thank me for saving you the trouble of experiencing a heart attack by putting a bullet right through it!*

—⊶∞⊷—

That night, the fever returned.

Christopher Harding picked his son's small body up and threw him, limp and feverish, over his shoulder. He stumbled toward the carriage house at the far corner of the estate. He slid the massive door open without a sound, propped Joshua against a large workbench, and returned to the door to slide the bolt in place.

Father placed his hands under Joshua's arms, pulling him up to meet his dark eyes face-to-face. The alcohol on his breath stank. He snarled at his son, and then threw him headlong against the side of the Rolls.

Please, Father, no!

He gave Joshua's ribs a sharp kick with the toe of his polished boots. When his son cried out in pain, he delivered a second blow.

Joshua raised himself onto his elbow. He pulled himself across the smooth floor, inching toward the side door.

Father wobbled in his direction. He grabbed Joshua by the shoulders and flung him toward the window, shattering the glass.

A week later, and somehow spared from death, Ethan sawed off two sturdy branches from the pine tree shading the kitchen window. Balancing himself against the porch rail, he fit the cross pieces and smoothed them with the use of Sam's whittling knife.

After wrapping the armrests with kitchen towels, he eased them under his armpits and stood erect. He wobbled, at first, but over the next few hours he continued to practice walking up and down the overgrown garden path. With each lap, he grew more proficient. *It's amazing how much can be accomplished when one has a goal in mind...*

Chapter 5

Winter turned to spring. Trees budded, beautiful monarch butterflies began to visit the region, and brooks overflowed with clear, cold water.

One day, Jake encountered a bear cub holding a honeycomb high above his head, allowing the sweet liquid to fall onto his waiting tongue. When he abandoned the comb to chase a curious porcupine, Jake rushed to pick it up and finish it off.

Father had brought home honeycombs, now and then. He enjoyed the sticky sweetness, taunting Jake by moaning and licking his lips. Now Jake knew why he liked it so much.

Jake soon acquired a taste for the once-forbidden honey. It grew to be the main staple of his diet, along with juicy green apples, blueberries, black raspberries, gooseberries, and cherries.

When spring gave way to summer, he spent each day in the vast meadows adorning the base of the lower mountains. There, he discovered curious-looking insects, interesting terrain, and animals he never knew existed. He and Hound romped in lush green grasses, basked in the warmth of the sun, and delighted in the fragrance of wild flowers.

On an especially hot and humid day, Jake went for a swim in a clear brook. As he pulled himself out of the water, a gunshot rang through the air, shaking the leaves on a nearby bush. Jake scrambled behind a dense grouping of trees. Was that Father's rifle? Hadn't he died in the fire?

Sure enough, Father's muscular form stood in the clearing. He reached his hand deep into the bush, pulled a large rodent out from among the leaves and threw it into an already-bulging bag. He had often told Jake hunting stories of animals that took too long to die, requiring that he wring their necks or plunge a knife into their hearts. Yes, Father enjoyed killing.

Father put his bag on the ground and rested himself on a large boulder. He reloaded his rifle and took a drink of water from his canteen, wiping the excess off his chin with his sleeve.

It was then Jake detected the absence of Father's right leg. A knot formed in his stomach.

He'd need to be careful Father didn't see him. If he wanted him dead bad enough to burn the cabin down, Jake was certain he would try to kill him again.

His legs ached as he crouched, waiting for Father to go on about his hunting. He turned to look at Hound, also hunkered down, one of his huge paws resting on Jake's back.

Minutes later, Father stood, leaning against his crudely made crutches. He wore a satisfied smirk and laughed aloud as he weighed the bag in his hand.

If he were on the other end of that gun, it wouldn't be so funny. Jake breathed a sigh when, at last, Father hobbled off carrying the bag, his rifle strapped to his back.

⸺◦∞◦⸺

Jake tossed and turned all night, dreaming about being killed by Father's rifle and stuffed into his bag. In the darkness of the sack, the animals revived, scratching and biting his hands and feet.

A rustling in the vegetation nearby woke him with a start. The beam of a flashlight shined into his eyes and Father's tall form towered over him.

He cowered. An ax!

He scrambled to his feet and ran for safety just as the ax came down. He followed the tree line, crawling on his belly to keep the low branches out of his face. He grabbed onto abundant scrub brush to keep from falling into a deep ravine.

Once he escaped down the mountain and reached more familiar territory below, he paused. He bent over with his hands on his knees, breaths coming in ragged spurts. It was pitch black and silent, except for the hooting of a distant owl. *Where are you, Hound?*

He strained to listen for sounds of Father's pursuit. Sweat beaded across his forehead. Smothered in the darkness of the moonless night, he inched farther and farther back until he connected with the rough bark of a tree and slid to the ground. It was as good a place as any to hide until daylight.

He sought comfort in the memory of Mama's blue eyes, dimples, and slow smile—a smile that had a way of building, little by little, until it erupted into contagious laughter. He could hear the sound of her breathing and feel the fierceness of her hug as she caught him by the shoulders and squeezed with all her might. As he drifted off to sleep, he heard her voice as she repeated the familiar nighttime prayer: "Now I lay me down to sleep, I pray the Lord my soul to keep; If I should die before I wake, I pray the Lord my soul to take."

Had the Lord really taken Mama's soul? If he had, where did he take it?

———

Near daybreak, the sound of chopping echoed through the woods. As his muddled thoughts cleared, Jake's eyes widened. *The apple tree. He's cutting it down!*

He jumped to his feet, charging at full speed. Low tree branches scraped his arms and face. He tripped, grabbing at exposed roots to pull himself upward and propel his body forward.

The sound became more ominous the closer he got. Was he too late to save it?

When the orchard appeared in full view, his worst fears materialized. Father stood in front of the tree, ax in hand, attacking his demons with an unholy vengeance.

A large vein pulsed in his neck as he ran headlong toward Father, "Noooooooo!" He shoved him to the ground with one mighty push, sending his crutches flying through the air and the ax to the ground with a heavy *thud*.

Father fought to right himself and then balance on one foot. Jake lowered his head and rammed him a second time. Father leapt to the side, causing him to run headlong into the trunk of a nearby tree and a familiar blackness to wash over him.

———

Ethan pulled himself up and collected his crutches. Giving the boy nothing more than a backward glance, he resumed his attack on the base of the tree. Again and again, he raised the ax and swung at the trunk, the force of his tortured determination causing bits of wood to scatter over the forest floor. "I'll rid myself of you for once and all. I'll wipe every memory of you from this earth!"

As he raised the ax to administer yet another blow, a movement to his right caught his attention. He looked toward the place where the boy lay to see a most unexpected adversary. His heart skipped a beat. "Hound, it's good to see you. Come here, big fella." He put down the ax and wiped his sweaty palms on his shirt. He leaned forward, holding out his hands toward the dog.

Hound remained by the boy, guarding his unconscious body.

"Now, Hound, you know I wouldn't hurt you."

Hound growled and lowered his head.

"The boy got in the way—" He hopped forward on one foot.

Hound answered with several loud barks.

"Okay. Okay. I won't hurt the boy. I promise."

He moved slower. He reached out, again, continuing to talk in soft whispers. "I'm living in Sam's cabin, now. You'd like it. It's a lot warmer than the old place. I even sleep in Sam's bed. Imagine that." He belly laughed at the very thought of himself stretched out in Sam's bedroom.

At the sound of laughter, Hound lunged at him, forcing Ethan to hobble back. The dog snarled, lunged again, and pushed him back even farther.

Ethan's lip drew up at the corner as he reached into his pocket and pulled out a piece of jerky. He held the bait in front of Hound. "Look, boy, what I have for you. Come on. It's yours. Just come and get it from my hand."

The dog hesitated, then whimpered.

"Ah, doesn't this smell good? Haven't had anything this delicious in a long time, now have you?"

Hound licked his lips, saliva flowing down, dropping onto the ground between them. He took one cautious step forward. Then another.

Everyone has a price. Once Hound returned home, he'd show him who was boss. He was a traitor—and traitors must be punished. The boy had somehow turned Hound's heart against him. He'd get what he deserved, too.

Hound was just a few feet away from the jerky, supple and promising, when Jake groaned. Returning to his side, Hound stood his ground. Head tall and erect, he glared at Ethan with cold eyes.

⎯⎯⎯∞⎯⎯⎯

Jake pulled himself to his feet. The fingertips he ran over the top of his head returned sticky with blood.

"How dare you take my dog away from me. You're both nothing more than fugitives now. And I won't rest until you come to justice," sneered Father.

His eyes searched Father's face, slowly taking in every wrinkle, every stray hair, every detail making him appear more human. *What does the devil look like? Could Father could be him?* Only the devil would try to kill his own son.

"I didn't take him. Hound made his choice. He followed *me*," Jake replied.

"That's a lie! You dirty piece of trash! You've turned him against me."

"I thought about sending him back to you, but—"

"Why didn't you?"

"Because I love him, too." Jake reached down to stroke Hound's broad head.

"Oh, how touching. A boy and his dog." Father cleared his throat and then spat in the dirt. "You two make me sick."

Hound sprang to his feet, his chest thrust out, growling.

Father continued his tirade. "I tell you what, if you want to leave, I won't try to stop you. But you must send Hound back with me. That's the price of your freedom."

"But I need him. He's my only friend."

"In that case, if you'll excuse me, I have a tree to demolish."

Father hobbled toward the tree and swung his ax. The leaves shook on impact, but the trunk held firm. He stumbled back toward Jake and perched atop a large boulder. He scratched his head, glaring at the tree.

"Father, what if something—or someone—is protecting it? Like God or maybe his angel?"

"So, you're a man of the world now, are you? Believe in the supernatural, boy?" With the heel of his boot, Father crushed one of the juicy apples that littered the ground.

"Maybe. Someone left a coat and boots for me last winter."

"So, now you'd have me believe that angels are bringing you gifts?

"Could be." Jake smiled and raised his eyebrows.

"Well, I'll clue you in. You're nobody special that angels would bother with the likes of you. Ideas like that are pure fantasy."

"The tree's still standing, isn't it?"

Familiar anger burned in Father's eyes. "Not for long!" He grabbed his crutches and managed to get to his feet. He faced Jake, his back to the tree. "I just needed my second wind. Now, I'll finish the job."

A strong wind blew through the leaves of the apple tree. As it sang its eerie song, the tree began to sway. *It's coming down!*

"You look like you've seen a ghost." Father sneered.

"It's just that—that—" Jake held up a trembling hand and pointed his index finger upward, leaping sideways as the massive tree fell.

Its loud *boom* echoed through the orchard. Leaves and splintered branches rained down, scattering debris across the entire area and pinning Father underneath.

"Ahhhhhhhhh!"

Following a moment of stunned silence, Jake crumpled to the ground. He clutched Hound's head to his chest. "Are you all right, boy?"

Hound wriggled from his grip, barking as he backed away. When Jake failed to move, the dog turned back to stare at him. He barked louder the second time.

"Okay, boy, I understand. I'm coming." As he turned, the toe of his boot caught on a twisted root, his right knee landing on the upturned ground.

Hound continued to bark, urging him to his feet.

He climbed onto a large flat rock overlooking Father's motionless body. He shook his head. The trunk of the tree lay across his back. *Was Father dead?*

He bit the inside of his cheek as he pushed his hair out of his face. His eyes drifted toward the eastern sky, watching clouds as they formed over the mountaintops.

He jumped off the rock. He kneeled next to Father and placed a quivering hand on his neck.

Father groaned. He lay on his stomach, his torso bent beneath the weight of the tree. His head rested sideways, partially covered with dirt. Arms flailing, his plea was no more than an exaggerated whisper. "H—help."

Jake stepped back. His eyes darted from Father, to the trunk of the apple tree where the Father had carved his declaration of love into the bark more than a decade earlier.

Now he knew the truth: Love must not *really* last forever.

He dropped to his knees beside Father. "I'm here."

Father cleared his throat and swallowed several times. He reached up and caught Jake's wrist. "Get me out!"

Jake jerked free. He considered his options. For once, *he* had power over Father.

"Did you hear me, boy?"

Jake retrieved the rifle from the ground. In one swift movement, he cocked the hammer and pointed the barrel at Father. His breathing ran labored and short. Myriad thoughts plagued him—sights and sounds of the past, hopes for the future, memories of a life long ago, visions of Mama—all grappling for a foothold in his consciousness, all vying to dictate his actions. If it were the other way around, Father wouldn't hesitate for a moment.

"Go ahead. Do it." Father narrowed his eyes—black and hollow—the eyes of a madman.

Jake stared at the one who had abused him for so many years, now helpless and face down in the dirt. Images of the fire, and the strong arms lifting him flooded his memory.

Someone loved him. Someone cared.

His trembling hands fumbled to unload the bullets, dropping them one by one—three in all—onto the earth near his feet. He used the butt of the rifle to plow through the loose dirt and push branches aside. But even after an hour of digging, Father was still imprisoned under the enormous tree.

Father bombarded him with orders. "Faster, boy, faster!"

Sweat poured down Jake's neck and back as he clawed at the dirt. He tried to ignore his father's demands and keep his mind on the rescue at hand, squelching the desire to walk away and never look back.

No one would blame him.

———<>———

Ethan mumbled in his sleep most of the night. He shivered as a light rain, promised by the afternoon's dark clouds, fell in the early morning hours.

As soon as it was light, he woke the boy. "I've got a plan and we can't waste any time." The boy was afraid of him. He'd do what he said.

Jake wiped the sleep from his eyes, and sat up. He crawled over to the tree. "What is it?"

"We're going to use Hound to pull me out. You'll need to get a rope from Sam's cabin. It's about a mile from where we are now. If you walk due west, along the creek, you should be able to get it out of his shed and be back here by noon."

"What if I leave and don't come back?"

"Check out the bathroom when you get there. After you see it, there'll be no doubt in your mind that I'm capable of anything. I'll get out of here on my own and I'll hunt you down. Be assured, I'll show you no mercy."

The rain stopped and the day turned bright and sunny. They had only gone about a quarter mile when Jake squatted down to get a close look at a caterpillar. He prodded it with a stick, turning it over and over again, watching it wriggle to right itself.

Sometime later, a small rabbit caught his eye and the chase was on. In and out of bushes, around and under fallen tree trunks, he and Hound pursued the scrawny brown animal. Jake lost sight of it when he sat down on a tree stump to catch his breath.

His eyes roamed around the small clearing. Nothing looked familiar. He poked his tongue from one cheek to the other as he paused to listen for the flowing of water in the creek. He walked a few feet in each direction from the stump until he finally heard it in the distance. He let out a long breath and licked his bottom lip. "This way, boy."

Hound panted, his long red tongue hanging down as he followed Jake, retracing their steps toward the creek. He trotted toward the water, lapping it up for a full minute before Jake coaxed him onward.

They followed the creek as it twisted and turned. Sure enough, it led them precisely to their destination. Jake shaded his eyes with his hands. So, this is where Sam and Ruth had lived. The cabin, with an expansive glassed-in porch that wrapped around the sides, was overgrown with weeds. Intricate patterns of cobwebs covered the windows.

A swing, painted with small red and purple flowers, hung from a large tree near the stone walkway. It creaked when Jake gave it a gentle push. At one time, colorful flowers must have grown in the row of dusty blue pots lining the steps.

Jake pushed the door open and led Hound into a small mudroom adjacent to the kitchen. He pinched his nose with his fingers. It smelled like spoiled scraps inside.

A crusty dog dish sat by the door leading to the living room. That's right. Ghost had been Sam's dog. Ruth had traded him to Father.

The price? One blue sweater.

The counter was littered with an array of unwashed dishes. Six wooden chairs sat around a large table covered with a blue-and-white checkered tablecloth. A canning jar sat at one end of the table.

Jake whistled as he looked for silverware in several drawers. Finding none, he used the edge of an apron from a nearby hook to wipe off one of the dirty spoons he found in the sink. He pried the lid from the jar with its handle, poured some of the thick gravy into Ghost's bowl, and gulped down the rest of it himself.

Hound licked Jake's face with gratitude and whimpered for more.

"Sorry, Hound. That's it for now. We have a job to do."

All set to retrieve the rope from the shed, Jake started for the bathroom. As he inched his way down the dark hallway, the smell intensified. He whacked the bathroom door with the side of his fist. It was unlatched and swung open, hitting the wall with a *bang*.

Jake's heartbeat throbbed in his ears. *I just know it's his leg. I just know it. What else could it be?* He shut his eyes, unable to bring himself to look. He grabbed the doorknob and closed the door. He darted toward the kitchen, tripping on a braided area rug by the fireplace.

As he pushed himself to his feet, a row of pictures on the wall caught his eye. This must be what other families are like—happy, smiling, hugging. *Our family might have been like this if Mama hadn't died.*

On the end of the row, by the door, he studied a picture of Sam, blowing out candles on a cake. Several people were gathered around him, blowing horns and cheering. He examined each face, his eyes at last falling on a beautiful young woman with yellow hair. He fought for each breath, his heart pounding in his ears. He felt lightheaded as he marveled wide-eyed at the image before him.

In a flash, he jerked the frame off the wall. His nervous fingers turned it over and fumbled to remove the photograph. He let the frame fall to the floor, hugging the picture to his chest and then holding it out at arm's length to study every detail. *Mama!*

He slumped into a wicker rocking chair and put his head between his knees. He closed his eyes, squeezing out the last of his tears.

When he lifted his head, the joy that he first felt at seeing the picture had twisted into something unexplainable—a fire that started in his belly, growing hotter as it traveled upward. His smile turned to a frown as he clenched his fists, knuckles white.

Minutes later, leaving the shed, Jake gritted his teeth and snapped the doubled-over rope in his hands.

Chapter 6

They should be at Sam's by now. Another couple of hours and they'd be back to the orchard, pulling him to safety.

Ethan would still need the boy's help, though. He wasn't in any shape to overpower him. No, he'd need to evoke his sympathy...make him believe that this accident had caused him to rethink his life...how shallow and selfish it had been. He'd tell him he was aware of his worth as a companion...a son.

Of course, that would require quite an acting job on his part. He'd need to do better at it than he had done when the police questioned him after the hit and run.

That whole evening was a blur. The questioning: "Where were you at 7:15 tonight? What was the name of your last patient of the day? Can anyone corroborate your story? Did you report your car as stolen?" And on and on.

He had done those parents a huge favor in the long run. Those little girls were destined to give them a lot of grief as teenagers. He'd spared them a lot of sleepless nights, the expense of braces, dance lessons, and new cars for their sixteenth birthdays.

Yes. He'd declare his intentions to change...be a good person... promise to teach him things, like how to hunt, maybe even how to read. He'd let him go into town with him. Maybe he'd buy the boy some clothes, shoes, a rifle of his own...

Hot breath on his neck brought Ethan back to the reality of the present. *Back so soon?*

He turned his head, gulping as he saw the greenish-yellow eyes of a pure black wolf focused on his arms, caked with dried blood. He moved his hand, little by little, toward the rifle, laying slightly to his left. *One. Two. Three.* As his fingers closed in on the rifle, his eyes caught sight of the bullets lying on the ground just a few feet away. *Stupid boy!*

Saliva flowed from the wolf's huge mouth. He pricked his ears at shrill howling in the distance.

That's right. Go on with your pack...

He eyed Ethan once more before he growled and loped away.

Ethan's head dropped onto a cluster of leaves, his chest heaving and his mind already considering possible scenarios involving the wolf's inevitable return.

Not far from the orchard, Jake slowed his pace. Curiosity drew him to the creek where the water flowed wild and free. He paused to examine a bright turquoise stone lying on the mossy bank. He turned it over and over in his hands, then threw it into the water, and watched as it sank to the bottom.

He had a decision to make.

If he helped Father, he would be just like that stone. Stuck. Lying at the bottom of the creek forever... waiting for someone to find it.

But that someone might never come…might never see it there…so blue and so beautiful…shining among the other stones.

It was very possible that no boy would ever rescue that stone from the bottom of the creek…might never put it safely in his pocket, carry it home and place it in his treasure box.

It was a special one, all right. But even the most extraordinary stone couldn't help itself… couldn't get back out of the water on its own.

But Jake had run away. He was no longer imprisoned in the yard. He was free from a life of constant abuse… endless nights of punishment. *If he went back to help Father…*

He stroked Hound's smooth coat as he studied Mama's picture. *What should I do? Help Father, or change course?*

He stepped into the water. Maybe, just maybe, *he* would one day have a treasure box…

The splashing of his feet surprised a black water moccasin lurking in the shallow water. Trapped between the creek bed and the intruder, the snake shot forward, biting him on his left leg.

"Ayyyyyeee!" Jake grabbed his leg and fell onto the bank. Two angry puncture marks mottled the flesh high on his calf. He choked back his tears. "Help! Help!"

Hound shot into the water, grabbed the snake's body with his teeth and whipped it back and forth against the rocks. Then he bit into its side, killing it in an instant.

Jake clasped a handful of Hound's fur in his hands and nuzzled him. "You're the best." Once again, he examined the wound made by the sharp fangs. Then he snatched the rope, pushed through the pain, and trudged on in the direction of the orchard.

Minutes later, his belly clenched into a hard knot. His head throbbed as he bent over and heaved up a vile-tasting liquid. A burning pain traveled up his already red and swollen leg.

He staggered forward, as dizziness overtook him, then tripped over his own feet. He brought his knees up to his chest and rocked back and forth. His teeth chattered. "I—can't—feel—my—leg!"

Charlie Claiborne checked his air speed as he prepared to land the Cessna at the airpark approximately five miles away. His new bride clutched the bottom cushion of her seat. At least she'd calmed herself enough to enjoy the view out the window. Anna had acted like this, too, the first time he took her flying.

"Take it easy now, Charlie. I feel like my stomach is in my throat." Claire panted.

"Now, honey bunch, don't you fret. I've logged many an hour in this baby. I can turn this thing on a dime and land it on the head of a pin."

"A nice, easy landing on the runway will be just fine."

"Comin' right up." He still missed his first wife, of course, but she'd be glad he'd found happiness with Claire. They had talked about this more than once. She'd made him promise to enjoy the years ahead with someone kind and loving. Someone who'd make him number one in her life—just as Anna had.

"Wait! Charlie, there's something just to my right. Can you get a little closer?"

A swirling blue mist covered a small area by the creek. It glowed from underneath with a pulsating light.

Charlie banked to the right, nosed the plane downward, and leveled off. "What in the—Claire, have you ever seen anythin' like this?"

"Not in all my born days."

When the mist parted, allowing him a glimpse at the ground below, Charlie did a double take. "It looks like a woman lyin' there. No, no, it's a child." Even after all his years as a rescue pilot, he was still never prepared to see a youngster...

Claire covered her mouth with her trembling hand. "She's not moving. Maybe she's hurt or—I can't stand to think what might have happened."

"The airpark is just about a mile away. We'll land, jump in my SUV and be back here in about five minutes."

Claire continued to scan the area until the entire scene was swallowed up by the forest below. She tensed when Charlie began the descent, skimmed over the airport sign, and brought the plane down on the tarmac.

He taxied to the hangar, transferred two small suitcases to their vehicle, and headed for the narrow road that would take them near the creek. Its twists and turns brought them within a hundred feet of the swirling mist, which disappeared as soon as they arrived. Charlie stopped the car and they both jumped out.

A large brown hound loped up, greeting them with a series of loud barks. He guided them the short distance to the body and then lay down beside the child.

"Claire, I think it's a girl." Charlie stood over the lifeless form, muddy and wet on the soft earth. He watched the child's chest rise and fall, agonizing over each shallow breath. "A kid has no business bein' alone in such an isolated area."

Claire rolled the youngster over and choked back a sob. "A long ponytail, but it's a boy. And, I think he's coming to!"

As darkness descended, Ethan flinched at each unfamiliar sound. Cold and hungry, he dreaded the moment when sleep would overtake him. When he finally let himself doze, it was Sam's voice that broke into his repose.

"Looks like you're in quite a predicament, old boy." Sam jumped on top of the tree trunk and looked down on Ethan with amusement.

A lump rose in his throat. "Listen, Sam—"

"Shame to waste all of these fine apples, don't you think?" Sam reached over, plucked one, and took a bite. "Delicious. You really should try one."

Ethan stretched out his arm, fingers walking themselves along the rough bark, but unable to reach even one. The more he tried, the longer his arm stretched—longer and longer until it was back at his cabin, which had somehow continued to burn.

"Help me! Somebody help me...help me...help me..." His voice echoed throughout the entire forest, the earth and into the universe beyond.

Jake awoke in an unfamiliar bed. He looked around the room. A repeating pattern of roses and vines covered the walls. A pink blanket was folded at the foot of the bed, and there was a pink chair in the corner with a matching rug under it. Mama would have called this room "beautiful."

He sat upright on the side of the bed, struggling to remember the events of the last few days. *I got the rope. Hound and I got as far as the pond. The black snake bit me. I got sick—wait, wait—I saw Mama's picture.*

Jumbled thoughts of Father, trapped under the tree, swam in his head. The smooth wood floor creaked as he stepped down and limped toward the open bedroom door.

Embers glowed in the fireplace at the end of the living room. He gravitated toward its warmth, stretching out his hands. He winced as he rested his calf on the plush rug in front of it, blowing gently on the ashes and coaxing the fire back to life.

How did I get here? Jake's pulse quickened as a picture reformed in his mind. *Bluish white...pink cheeks...shining...yes, lots of light...*

The sound of faint footsteps outside the door prompted him to crouch in the corner of the room. He held his breath as they moved closer. He raked his tongue across his lips and closed his eyes. He let out pent up air when he heard the sound of toenails clicking on the wooden floor. "Hound!"

When the door opened, he held out his arms and the dog came to him, licking his face, ears, and neck. He laughed. "What would I ever do without you?"

"I'm Claire Claiborne."

Jake gasped and withdrew back into the darkness of the corner.

"I didn't mean to startle you." A lady glided through the door and into the living room.

Jake's tongue felt thick and unwilling to cooperate. His entire body shook as he sat in stunned silence.

She moved nearer. "I'm sorry, uh—what's your name, son?"

Jake's gulp was loud. He took in a deep breath. "Um. Jake."

"Nice to meet you, Jake."

He couldn't stop staring at her—couldn't resist her intense gaze. "Are you the one who saved me?"

"I had a little help."

The lady's kind voice and lovely face matched perfectly. She sat down in the padded rocking chair, some distance away from him. She had light gray hair, pink lips, and crystal blue eyes that twinkled as she spoke.

She looks like the... His heart skipped a beat. "I like your shoes."

She chuckled, her pink toenails protruding from furry white slippers. "Well, thank you. Slippers are both warm *and* comfortable."

Jake moved away from the fireplace. "It's plenty warm in here."

"Even though it's summer, it's still chilly in the evenings. I like to keep the screen door open to let the fresh air inside, but if the fire is too warm for you, we can let it die down."

"Is this your house?" He studied her face. He liked her smile, but he should be careful. Grownups might look nice, but their real selves hid behind their eyes.

"This cabin belonged to my husband's father before he passed away. My husband and I live in the southern part of the state. We just flew here a couple of days ago. In fact, it was when we got near the airstrip and descended that we saw you lying on the ground a few miles from here."

"You can fly?" Jake could hardly keep from laughing as he imagined the plump, gray-haired woman flying through the air wearing her fluffy slippers.

"No, silly. We flew in Charlie's plane."

Jake's brow furrowed. "I see them fly overhead sometimes, but I sure didn't know that people could ride inside."

Claire gave him a quizzical look.

"Until last winter, I'd never been out of my yard. There's a lot of stuff I don't know. But, it's not because I'm dumb or stupid." He took in a gulp of air, letting it out in short measured breaths.

She filled the growing silence with a question of her own. "So, what's your dog's name? We tried every name we could think of, but never found one he'd respond to."

Jake reached down to scratch him behind the ears. "His name is Hound."

"I can't imagine why we didn't think of the obvious," she laughed.

"Where's your husband? Is he nice?" He folded his arms to his chest, suddenly conscious of his scars.

"As a matter of fact, he's very nice." She glanced at the clock. "Tell you what, let's get you some clothes to wear and then we can continue this interrogation over supper. Charlie's great-nephew is about your size. I rummaged around in the hall closet and found a pair of his pants and a t-shirt."

Jake picked up the clothes from the coffee table, hobbled back into the bedroom and closed the door. He fumbled with the drawstring on the pants, unable to tie it securely. He doubled over with laughter when he saw himself in the mirror, wearing the multi-colored and tie-dyed t-shirt. He peered around the corner as Claire emerged from the pantry with a basket of vegetables in her arms.

"Well, come on out and let me take a look."

With a sheepish grin, he ventured into the kitchen.

"You look very nice. And they're just your size."

"Um, I was wondering about this shirt..." He looked down at the myriad swirling colors.

Claire chuckled, "It probably isn't what you are used to, is it? But, I assure you, these clothes are very typical of what the boys wear nowadays."

Jake joined in the laughter. "If you say so."

"I suppose you're hungry. Here, have a carrot to munch on while I cook." She handed Jake a long one. "You've been a pretty sick young man. Another day or two of rest and you should be good as new."

He shuffled to the counter, licking his lips. "Can I watch?"

"After we put some more medicine on your leg." Claire took the cap off of a tube of ointment.

"It doesn't really hurt that much, so I—"

"Come on, lift that pant leg up and let's take a good look." Claire raised her eyebrows and sent a curious smile in his direction.

He hesitated, but then pulled it up. He flinched as Claire smoothed the salve onto the pink edges. "See, it's almost healed."

"Almost." Claire's eyes met his. "We may need to get a second opinion when Charlie comes back tonight."

"So, is it time to eat, yet?" He popped the last of the carrot into his mouth and headed toward the kitchen.

"Do you like stew?"

"I'm not sure." He wouldn't tell her what Father fed him. Maybe if he were very polite, she'd let him eat with her at the table.

Claire opened several cans and emptied the contents into a big pot. She took a knife from the block and cut tomatoes, potatoes, and celery into small pieces. Once everything was simmering on the stove, it wasn't long until a wonderful aroma filled the air.

His mouth watered. Their cabin used to smell like this when Mama cooked for them. But that was such a long time ago...

Claire put food on the table for her and Jake, and a plate on the floor for Hound. The two guests buried their heads in their dishes and didn't come up for air until they were empty and licked clean.

"This is the best food we've ever had."

"Well, I'm glad you liked it." Claire grinned and poured Jake another glass of milk.

"How long have I been here?"

"Two days."

Jake's eyes widened. He jumped up from the chair. "Two days?" Could Father still be alive? Was he out from under the tree, like he said, and coming after him?

"Are you okay? You're as pale as a ghost."

Jake bit his lip. "I just thought of something I was supposed to do."

"Whatever it was, I'm sure it can wait until you feel better. Let's sit and talk awhile in the living room." She sauntered toward the recliner and Jake took a place on the floor beside Hound. "I'm thinking we need to get in touch with your parents. They must be sick with worry. Want to tell me why you ran away?"

"I never said I ran away."

"Does that mean you didn't?"

"No. It's Father I've run away from. Mama died when I was just a little kid."

"I'm sorry to hear that." She reached forward and touched Jake's hand before he pulled back. "Well, every family has its problems, but when you love each other, you can work things out. Running away doesn't really solve things. Being that it's just the two of you, don't you think that makes it even more important for you to maintain a good relationship?"

"You don't understand what it's like living with him—how he…" He closed his eyes. A single tear followed the silhouette of his nose, dropping onto his lips and coming to rest on his chin.

"It's okay, you can tell me. Sometimes just talking things over with a friend can help us realize what we need to do."

His eyes searched Claire's for a reason to trust. "Maybe I could just start with the good stuff first." He'd save the part about Father for another time.

"Of course. You can tell me whatever you feel comfortable sharing. It's between you, me, and the fencepost." Claire's soft face and kind eyes calmed his initial fears.

"Mama was beautiful. We built snowmen in the winter and planted seeds in the spring. Oh, and she read to me from a special book each night." He lowered his head to study his hands.

"She sounds lovely. And, what about your father?" Her raised eyebrows expected an answer.

"Father used to be nice, but he changed after Mama died. Look, I have a picture of her." Jake hobbled into the bedroom to retrieve the photo. He held his breath as Claire studied the image.

"Yes. She was very beautiful, Jake. And you know what? You look a lot like her."

"I do?" He smiled from ear to ear.

They talked late into the night. Claire shared funny stories of her students and their antics, the tragic death of her first husband, and her recent marriage to "Big Charlie." Before she sent him off to bed, she gave him a warm hug that reminded him of Mama.

Chapter 7

Charlie headed home from Bucky Hansen's ranch on the dark winding road. His stomach growled. Claire understood he needed to help Bucky out, since the vet was out of town. Bucky had no experience in delivering calves but his call for help, just as they were tending to the boy's snakebite, couldn't have come at a worse time.

As he rummaged around in the console of the SUV for his stash of snacks, he neared a fork in the road. He made the sharp turn to the right. Claire would have guessed by now he wasn't going to arrive home in time for supper. This shortcut would knock about thirty minutes off his drive time. He might make it there in time for pie.

A mile down the single dirt lane, he tensed when the low hanging trees brushed up the front windshield and over the top of the SUV, slapping along the sides of the doors as he drove by. It sure was dark in this part of the woods. The vegetation was so thick he couldn't see the moon or stars overhead. *Looks like the county's been neglectin' its highway maintenance.*

He massaged a muscle spasm in the calf of his right leg, but it persisted. He applied the brakes, let the car roll to a stop, and eased his plump body out of his seat. He'd just have to walk it out.

He was only twenty feet or so from the SUV when he heard it—faint—but distinct.

"Help! Help!"

Charlie hobbled back to the SUV, turned off the motor, and listened. When he heard the cry again, he restarted the engine. He turned the wheels, pointing the headlights in that direction. He grabbed his flashlight from the glove box and flicked it on. When the cry became a shout, Charlie followed it. He ducked to avoid low branches and, at times, stumbled over the uneven ground. He'd played in these woods as a boy. There were lots of foxholes and such, even back then.

"I'm over here!" the voice yelled.

Charlie shined his flashlight around, almost tripping over the man before he saw him. He cringed at the sight of the injuries to his face and exposed arm. Leaves and branches covered the rest of his body. He looked like a soldier, camouflaged in the safety of a foxhole. "Are you all right? Of course, you're not. Pardon my ignorance."

The man tried to speak, his voice hoarse. "You're a sight for sore eyes. I'm Ethan." He blinked back the moisture gathering in his eyes.

"Charlie Claiborne." He squatted down, shaking his bald head as he observed Ethan, pinned to the ground by the massive tree. "How'd this happen?"

Ethan's voice quivered. With the weight of the tree on his back, he pulled in short breaths and sputtered. "Three days ago, I...chopped this tree...down. I misjudged which...way...it would...fall. My hound dog...ran off. I'm...guessing...he went for help...but he's never...come back."

"Looks like we may need a crane to get you out of here." Charlie grabbed the mobile phone attached to his belt and hurried over to the clearing. He walked in ever-widening circles until he got a signal, then dialed 9-1-1.

After the call was made, he returned to Ethan's side. Seeing his motionless body, he dropped to the ground and put his fingers against his neck. He was relieved to feel the rhythmic throb of his jugular. "Whew! I thought I'd lost you for a minute, buddy."

When the Appalachian Rescue Team arrived, they confirmed Charlie's suspicions and radioed for an all-terrain crane to help with the extraction. While they waited, the men told a variety of stories—from strange rescues, to the antics of family pets, to clandestine encounters.

Three hours later, the crane's jaws lifted the trunk off of Ethan's torso, dropping the tree off to the side with a heavy *boom!* They waited for the "all clear." When they got it, the men positioned a sling under his body. On the count of three, they lifted him up and positioned him on the waiting gurney.

Ethan looked up at Charlie. "I would have…died…out here…if it wasn't…for you. Be sure…to let me…know if you…hear anything… about my…dog."

"I'll stop at the hospital and check on you in a day or two. Maybe I'll have some news about your hound by then. Keep lookin' up."

Ethan's eyebrows squished together and he gave his head a slight shake.

As soon as the sling was removed, the EMT put the cuff on his arm, took his blood pressure, and performed a preliminary assessment.

All at once, Ethan's eyes rolled back and his body went limp.

The EMTs scurried to load him into the waiting ambulance.

"What's the matter?" Charlie moved forward to get a better look.

"Must've had some internal bleeding. The weight of the tree trunk probably kept it at a minimum, but now that it's removed, we've got a real problem." The driver slammed the doors closed and hopped behind the wheel. The ambulance left, spraying leaves and dirt into the air and nearly fishtailing as it hit the open road.

———— ∞ ————

Jake stayed at the "summer house," as the Claiborne's referred to it, for the next several days. He enjoyed hearing Claire's stories, especially the account of how she and Big Charlie had met at the grief support group.

"Charlie's wife, Anna, and my husband, Mike, both died from cancer last year," Claire said, her voice soft and low. "The group is where Charlie and I met and fell in love. We got married the weekend before we found you. Charlie thought this would be a good place for a honeymoon, but I'd be happy to live here forever."

"Me, too." Jake rolled with Hound on the soft area rug. "Ouch! Be careful, Hound. My leg still hurts a little."

"The woods are so restful and the fresh breeze feels so good, don't you think?" Claire smiled, her dimples showing.

"I guess so. But the winters are cold."

Big Charlie said he found a man trapped under a tree in the orchard two days after they'd found Jake. He was taken to a hospital in town. Jake didn't tell them that he was his father. He'd keep that a secret.

Each day brought new things for Jake to experience. Among them was learning to read. Claire, being a retired elementary school teacher, used her *Woman's Day* magazines, the back of the *Frosted Flakes* box, and even the assembly directions for Big Charlie's new gas grill as her unconventional textbooks.

"Put screw (A) and nut (B) together and insert into (C). Tighten with the Allen wrench (included) and turn…" Jake flopped onto his back, laughing. Would the grill turn out to look anything like the picture on the box?

Claire turned her attention from watching the rain out the screen door to observing the pair as they worked to assemble the grill on the living room floor. "You're very smart, Jake. You're learning fast. A year from now, you may well be reading at grade level."

He handed Big Charlie a wrench. "What grade is that?"

"Well, you come about to my shoulders when you're standing, so I'd say maybe fifth grade."

"I'm not sure I want to go to school. Maybe I'll just stay home." Other kids might think he was dumb. So would the teacher. *Do they punish kids for being stupid?*

"I'm afraid it doesn't work that way. It's the law that children go to school." Claire relaxed into the smooth leather of the sofa..

"I think I'm learning just fine from watching television. For instance, did you know the world is divided up into continents and those are divided up into countries, and those are divided up into, um—"

"States." Charlie rolled his eyes.

"Right. And, those are divided into, well, smaller and smaller stuff." Jake's smile was animated and engaging. "And, did you know that the world is so big that all the continents don't have the same seasons at the same time?" He rushed on, almost out of breath. "Did you know that—?"

"Jake, I'm glad you're interested in learnin' about the world, but it's almost time for Gilligan's Island, so get your bath and put your pajamas on. Then, you can join me. You're gonna love this show. We'll finish the grill tomorrow." Big Charlie stepped over a sleeping Hound on his way to his favorite recliner.

"Geez, why do I have to take a bath every night? I'm not even dirty!" Jake held his hands out, twisted his arms back and forth, and displayed his elbows. "See?"

"House Rules." Big Charlie wiggled his fingers, waiting for the remote control.

"Who makes the House Rules?" Jake whined, a pout on his face.

"Claire made the one about daily bath requirements." Big Charlie laughed. "I had this same conversation with my own dad more than once."

Jake sat down on the coffee table across from Claire. "Did you make the rule about no eating with our hands, too?"

"How'd you know?"

———

Ethan received emergency surgery to stop the internal bleeding. His pelvis was broken, requiring traction. He lay flat on his back for days on end, waiting for the doctor to make his rounds, complaining about the hospital food, and barking orders at the nurses.

He tried to act relieved when Charlie told him about finding the boy and his dog. He said he'd appreciate it if he and his wife could keep them for a while, but what he really wanted was Hound confined in a place where he could retrieve him once he was discharged from the hospital. It might not have been a good idea for them to keep Jake, though. Charlie acted a little strange when he visited. Had the boy been talking?

Chrissy, the nurse assigned to him, entered the room, her voice breaking into his thoughts. "So, how are we feeling today?"

"I guess I'm about a six on the pain scale." He gritted his teeth and panted as he tried to adjust his position in the bed.

"Your pain medication should have you feeling better in no time."

His eyes narrowed. "You're about thirty-five minutes late with that, you know. Have your supervisor drop by and see me later. Maybe what you need is a few days off without pay, or a demotion to bedpan duty."

"There are other patients in this hospital, too, and I do my best to get around to each one of you. Sorry you had to wait." Chrissy stuck the needle into his I.V. The warmth of the drug coursed through his veins within minutes. He dropped his head back down on the crisp, clean pillow. He should be able to sleep another afternoon away. *Ah, that's it. Slow and easy.*

It wasn't long until Cleo Watts, tall and serene, disrupted his foggy world. "My, you are pretty banged up, aren't you Joshua?"

"What are *you* doing here?" Beads of sweat formed on his forehead.

"You deserve every bit of the pain you're feeling right now. None of it could compare to what my girls felt in that instant when you ran them down. You escaped from the punishment the courts dictated, but you're going to suffer for what you did in the life beyond. There will be no rest for your eternal soul."

"I didn't run them down. It was an accident. I didn't mean to hurt your girls." There was nothing he could do to calm his racing heart. "I told the truth, but the jury got it wrong. I lost my practice and my reputation."

Cleo brought her face near his. Her breath was as cold as ice. "Maybe. But you'd been drinking. You ran. You left my girls to die like dogs in the street. You're an evil person. My girls are in heaven, but you'll never set foot inside its gates. You'll live in everlasting torment. Cast into utter darkness."

Charlie looked up from his newspaper as Claire entered the kitchen. She was worried about the boy. She looked like the weight of the world was on her shoulders.

"He's finally back to sleep. You know, dear, he has nightmares every night. It's so sad, really, his calling out for his mama." Claire placed her hand on Charlie's pudgy one.

Charlie covered her hand with his. "Yes, and in those same dreams, he's tryin' to get away from his father."

"And you're absolutely certain the guy you rescued—this Ethan—is Jake's father?"

"Both found only a quarter mile apart. Both have a dog named Hound. He as much as admitted to being his father when I saw him yesterday." Charlie played with Claire's fingers on the table between them.

Claire leaned in toward him. "How did he react when you told him about Jake's snakebite?"

Charlie shook his head. "He just said, 'Oh'. Can you believe it? His son is found half dead from a snakebite and all he has to say is, 'Oh'? Hound is all he seems to care about."

"What do you make of their situation?" Claire's eyes searched his.

"I'm thinkin' there's been some kind of abuse goin' on." Charlie planted a soft kiss on Claire's cheek. "The boy is covered in scars."

"I found a bag of chips and several cookies in his dresser drawer, this morning."

"What in the world?" Charlie stepped toward the open window, watching wispy clouds dance across the face of the moon. "I wondered about him being so skinny. You think Ethan punished him by withholdin' food?"

"I'm afraid so." Claire joined him, slipping her arm through his.

"It's little wonder he's reluctant to talk about his father."

Claire nodded. "And you said Ethan clams up when you ask him anything about Jake."

He swallowed the last of his coffee. "What do ya say we force Ethan's hand?"

Claire lowered her voice. "What do you mean?"

"I mean, let's take Jake on a little outin'. I saw where the circus opens in town, tomorrow night. Let's surprise him with an evenin' at the circus and an overnight stay in a kid/pet-friendly hotel. You know, one of those with a swimmin' pool and a slide. Before that, though, we'll go visit Ethan. We'll urge Jake to go in to see him, too, along with us—so he feels safe. We'll watch how they interact. Maybe ask some pointed questions. This may be the only way to see what is really goin' on between those two."

"That's a good idea. At the very least, we should get Ethan's written permission for Jake to continue staying with us." Claire squeezed dish soap into the sink and started running the hot water.

Charlie pulled out the phone book and ran his fingers through the Yellow Pages, copying a phone number on the corner of his napkin. "I'm gonna give The Bureau for Children and Families a call in the mornin'. I really think we're too old to take care of a young boy for an indefinite period of time. After all, this *is* our honeymoon. Maybe they can locate a relative who'll be willin' to look after him."

"Jake says he has no relatives and I hate to see him placed in foster care with people he doesn't know. He's just now getting comfortable with us. I don't want him to have to start over again with strangers." Tears formed in Claire's crystal blue eyes.

"Now, honey bunch—" Charlie put his arms around her shoulders.

She turned and put her forehead to his. "I don't expect you to understand. You had a child, but I never had a chance at motherhood. I admit I'm too old for all of this on a permanent basis, but I'm not ready to give him up just yet. Could you give me just a few more weeks, Charlie?"

"I'll see what the Bureau says in the mornin'. If it's permissible with them, it'll be okay with me—honeymoon, or not."

Chapter 8

*J*ake stretched as he woke from a sound sleep. He breathed in. "Ah, bacon's frying…"

A knock on the bedroom door was followed by Claire's voice. "Are you awake, Jake? Mind if I come in?"

"I'm awake. And I smell bacon!" Jake pushed up onto one elbow, closed his eyes, and took in another exaggerated breath.

Claire breezed into the room and opened the blinds, letting in the bright morning sun. "It's going to be a lovely day." She sat on the edge of the bed. "You've been with us two weeks today, so we thought we'd celebrate by going into town. We have a surprise for you."

"What kind of a surprise?" Jake threw off the rose-colored sheet and sat up. "Are we going ice skating?"

A smile danced across her face. "A hundred alligators couldn't make me tell. Now, get dressed. Charlie's already at the table."

Jake dressed as fast as he could and then let Hound outside. At the table, their smiles and small talk fueled his curiosity. He never was surprised by anyone before—at least not in a good way. His momentary frown turned into a broad smile. Maybe they planned to take him to a movie, or the zoo. "Can Hound go with us?"

Charlie snatched the last piece of bacon. "Of course. You wouldn't want to go anywhere without him, would you?"

Once in the SUV, his stomach full of scrambled eggs and bacon, Jake's eyes stayed glued to the windows. He asked question after question about the things they passed on the way to town, but still it seemed like the drive would never end. "Are we there, yet?"

"I remember posin' that same question to my own parents more than once. And I'm gonna tell you just what they told me." Big Charlie's eyes met Jake's in the rear view mirror.

"What's that, Charlie?" He stroked Hound's smooth coat as he lay beside him on the seat.

"Just a few more minutes. Be patient." Big Charlie chuckled, and then winked at Claire.

Jake groaned and turned back to the window. He tapped his fingers on his leg. "That means wait, wait, wait."

As they got closer, the landscape changed from trees, lakes, and hills to buildings, fences, and roads. Big Charlie slowed the vehicle as they reached the city limits.

"Look at all the people. Just like in your magazines, Claire." Jake rolled down the window and stuck his head out. The wind blew his long hair in all directions.

Big Charlie pulled the "Hornet," the name he had given his bright yellow SUV, into a parking space. He opened the door, groaning as his feet hit the pavement. "Oh, my achin' back."

Jake let Hound out to stretch his legs on the plush green grass. It wasn't long until the dog returned, retrieved a Frisbee from the open rear door, and brought it to him.

"I know you want to play, Hound, but we can't right now. You're going to stay in the car for a while and take a nap. We have someplace special to go. We'll come back for you. I promise." He motioned Hound back inside the hatchback.

Walking down the crowded sidewalk, Jake's heart beat faster. He clung to Claire, flinching each time someone came too close.

Rounding the corner, he sounded out the sign on the huge building in front of them. "Hos-pi-tal." He stopped short, letting his trembling arms drop to his sides. His knees locked. "What are we doing here? I'm not sick."

"Of course not, dear. There's someone here we'd like to talk to," Claire explained. "We thought you might like to have a little visit with him, too."

It could only be one person..."No, I don't want to! Let's go back to the car."

"Now, Jake, we've talked to the guy. He says he's your father—"

"He's lying!" Jake interrupted. He turned to run in the opposite direction.

Big Charlie caught him by the wrist and bent down. "Listen, this is the guy I told you about—the one that was trapped under the tree. Now, what are the chances that you'd both have a dog named Hound?"

There would be no sense to keep lying. They knew the truth. "I don't want to see him. You can't make me!" Jake tried to wriggle loose from his grip.

Big Charlie led him to a nearby bench. "Listen, Jake, I told him all about the snake bite and he doesn't blame you for not comin' back for him. He knows you wouldn't have been able to get him out of there by yourself anyway. Remember when we saw the story on the news and how the reporter said it took a crane to get the tree off the man?"

Jake nodded. *Please don't hate me, God, but I wish Big Charlie had never saved Father.* His legs wobbled as he stood up. He took a deep breath and forced a smile. He'd make them think he was going to do this, but then…

"We'll have to ride the elevator to the second floor," Big Charlie explained, his bald head gleaming in the sunlight.

Jake squinted. "What's an elevator?"

"It's like a room with sliding doors that's able to take small groups of people up to the higher floors in buildings without their having to climb stairs," Claire answered. "But don't be afraid. They're quite safe, and anyway, we'll be riding with you." She grabbed his hand and led him down the sidewalk toward the towering brick building.

"There are sure a lot of strange things in the world. Strange good and strange bad." Jake followed Claire and Big Charlie across the expansive lobby. He did a double take when two boys wearing black clothes, nail polish, and make up breezed past them. "Then there's just plain strange."

They halted in front of the elevator. Jake jumped back when it arrived at the ground floor and the doors opened. "Sorry."

"It's okay. We know all these things are new to you. Let's give this a try, shall we?" Claire asked.

Jake took a deep breath before allowing the couple to lead him inside. When the doors closed, and the elevator started to move upward, his stomach flip-flopped.

Claire squeezed his hand, "Take a deep breath. We'll be there in a few seconds."

As the elevator reached their floor, a big smile erupted on his face. "That was fun! Can we do it again?"

"Sure," said Big Charlie, "when we're ready to go back down. But, right now, we're gonna turn to our right and go into the first room. Your dad will be so pleased to see you."

Jake licked his lips. He looked behind him toward the elevator. "He doesn't know I'm coming?"

"No. This is a surprise for him, too." Claire's smile looked too big for her face.

Jake slumped into a chair in the small waiting area and looked up at Big Charlie's kind eyes, rimmed by large metal glasses. Father wouldn't want to see him any more than he wanted to see Father. Maybe he could do them both a favor. "Couldn't we just leave and come back a different day? How about next week? Or, maybe *I* could just sit here and wait while *you* visit him."

Big Charlie bent down and looked Jake straight in the eye. "Talk to me, Jake. Help me understand why you're behavin' this way."

Jake jumped up. "I-I—want to—but—" Silent tears rolled down his cheeks.

Big Charlie pulled him into a playful hug. "Hey, we're really not tryin' to upset ya, son. I feel terrible about this, but if there's any chance of you and your father workin' out your problems, this may be it."

Jake shook free from his embrace. "You don't understand what he's like. Couldn't you just talk to him first, and I'll come in when I get my nerve up?"

Big Charlie squished his eyebrows together, forming one shaggy band across his forehead. "I wish you'd tell us what you need to get your nerve up for, but if that will make you more comfortable, I guess we can do it your way."

Jake sighed and fell back into the chair. "Thanks, Charlie." *That was a close call. Whose side are they on, anyway?*

Big Charlie knocked on the door to room 212 and held it open for Claire.

Father greeted the couple. "Good to see you, Charlie."

The door closed behind them with a *click*.

Father had lied to the Claiborne's. If Father thought he had told them anything, he would get the beating of his life—or worse. Maybe he shouldn't trust Claire and Big Charlie. Maybe life was just one big game of adults versus kids. The elevator doors were closing! He sprang to his feet too late. There had to be another way out.

⸻ ❧ ⸻

Charlie led Claire over to the bed. "Ethan, this is my wife, Claire."

Ethan's squinty eyes stared at her, his long beard and hair making a formidable impression. "Pleased to meet you, ma'am. You must be the one responsible for sending me this nice flower arrangement." He pointed toward the mixed bouquet in a sparkling cut glass vase.

Claire blushed. "Well, I thought they might cheer you up. I know your accident must have been a terrible experience."

"Not one I'd like to repeat, I can tell you that," he agreed.

Charlie lumbered toward a peach-colored vinyl chair in the corner. "How are you doin' physically? Are you scheduled to get out of here anytime, soon?"

Ethan's voice boomed. "I have no idea. I haven't seen the doctor in two days. I think the way they run this hospital is disgusting. I'm trapped here with food that isn't fit for human consumption and nurses that don't know what they're doing. Heads are going to roll around here, I can promise you that!"

Claire cleared her throat and inched toward the door. "I think I'll just wait outside and give you men a chance to visit. Take your time."

"Okay. See if Jake is ready to come in." Charlie looked toward Ethan. "Your boy is sittin' right outside the door, but I must admit we're puzzled by the fact that he was hesitant to come in to see you. Is there more to this story than you've told us?" He stole a leftover French fry from the food tray on the bedside table.

Ethan's face reddened. "Oh, you know how it is with kids and their parents, Charlie. Nothing we can't work out, though."

Claire looked back at Charlie and rolled her eyes as she swung the door open. Her hand was still on the doorknob when she made an about face. Her smile was rigid and her eyes brimmed with tears. "I need to see you right away, dear. We have a-a predicament. I'm afraid we're going to have to cut our visit short."

"What are you talkin' about, Claire? What's the matter?" Charlie asked, leaning forward.

Claire gave Charlie a "knowing look" and rushed over to him, pulling him to his feet with one quick jerk. "There's an emergency that I have just—um—learned about. We must go, *now*, Charlie!"

With a shrug of his shoulders, Charlie allowed himself to be hustled out of the room, "I'll see you, soon, Ethan. Keep lookin' up."

"But—"

As the door closed, Claire blurted out, "He's gone!"

Charlie's eyes swept around the small waiting area, empty except for an older woman engrossed in a soap opera on the overhead television. "We pushed too hard."

As they rushed to the elevator, the Claiborne's stopped mid-step at the sound of glass breaking against the door of room 212.

Chapter 9

With his heart hammering in his chest, Jake made his way down the block, and crossed to the other side of the street. Turning the corner, he caught a glimpse of the Claiborne's as they ran toward the SUV. He slipped into an alley behind the Beehive Cafe, flattening himself against the rough brick wall. He put his hands over his ears to drown out the sound of Claire screaming his name.

He was sorry to have left like that, but someday Claire would get tired of him anyway, and decide to send him back to Father. And, he could never let that happen.

As he stood in the alley, next to a smelly garbage Dumpster, the entire hospital scenario replayed in his mind. He had bolted the moment the door to Father's room had closed, found the door labeled "Stairs" and descended the concrete steps two and three at a time. Reaching the landing, he placed his hands on the rail. He pushed himself up high and over, but his ankle twisted when his foot hit the edge of a step, causing him to lose his balance. He cried out as his shoulder—and then his cheek— hit the wall.

Stumbling out the door at the bottom of the stairs, he avoided a security guard by hiding behind a group of uniformed cleaning people. Once outside, he ran for the SUV. He pulled open the back door, motioned for Hound, and snatched his backpack. It was filled with snacks, a hooded sweatshirt, and even a few dollars—his "chore" money.

Hound ran by his side, dragging his new red leash behind him.

Charlie, under Claire's direction, drove up one street and down another, searching for Jake and Hound. He felt a special connection to the boy. He'd been through a lot. He wanted to make it possible for him to lead a healthy, safe life from now on—a life free of violence and fear of abuse.

"The streets are so crowded, Charlie. How will we ever find them?" Claire sniffled, wiping the back of her hand across her eyes.

"Oh, we will. They didn't have that much of a head start on us. Anyway, Jake isn't familiar with this town."

Claire's lips quivered. "If he heads back into the woods, it'll be next to impossible for us to catch up to him."

He reached over to pat her shoulder. "Don't forget. He has Hound."

"Yes, those two are quite a pair. They're very protective of each other. And, from what that boy's *not* saying, he's probably got good reason to be secretive." As Charlie drove, Claire scanned the sidewalks, parking lots, and landscaped yards.

"I think he's suffered abuse worse than what we could ever imagine." Charlie pulled over to let an impatient driver go around. "Everyone in this town is in a big hurry."

Claire caught Charlie's arm in a vise grip. "Look! I think that's Hound lying in the grass by the lake. Turn left."

Charlie headed toward the entrance to the city park. As he pulled into the parking lot, he saw the dog. "That's a German shepherd, Claire. How could you think that it looks anythin' like Hound?"

She shook her head. "I guess you're right. But, there's a patrol car. Let's see if we can get some help."

"I guess it's worth a try." He eased the car to a stop.

Claire threw the door open and headed toward the cruiser.

Charlie lumbered behind, panting as he caught up to her. "Hello. Officer Michaels, is it?" Charlie asked, reading the nametag on his uniform.

"Been on the force fourteen years." The policeman put both thumbs in the waistband of his pants and rocked back on his heels. "What can I do for you folks?" He tipped his hat back from his forehead and removed his sunglasses.

"We've got a missing child. He ran off about thirty minutes ago. We were hoping you could give us a hand searching for him." Claire's soulful eyes pleaded her case.

"He probably just wandered off. He'll show up in a few minutes or so. You'll see."

"No, Officer. He's definitely run off. It's a severe case of—" Charlie glared at the officer, offended at his brusqueness.

"All right. All right, let's stay calm, folks. I'll need to collect some information from you, first. Then, if I think the situation might be serious, I'll call it in to the station."

Claire let out an audible sigh. "Thank you, Officer."

"Name?"

"Jake," she answered.

"Last name?"

Claire hesitated.

"Ma'am?"

"I-I—" She shot Charlie a helpless look.

"We don't actually know, Officer," Charlie blurted out, rubbing his hand over his chin. The officer's tanned face and gleaming teeth reminded Charlie of a famous male movie star.

Officer Michaels sucked air into his cheeks and then expelled it. "So, you aren't related to the child?"

Charlie looked down at the cracked pavement. "Not really. You see, we found him in the woods a couple of weeks ago. His father had been hurt in an accident and Jake had no family to take care of him, so we allowed him to stay with us—with his father's permission, of course." *Why does the truth sound so...untrue?*

"Well, let's start with what you *do* know."

Claire flashed the officer a big smile. "Ok, he comes about to my shoulders. Very thin. He has a long brown hair and a strange birthmark that circles his entire forearm—"

"Eye color?"

"Brown," stated Charlie.

"Age?"

Claire flinched at the question. "We aren't sure."

Officer Michaels looked up from his notepad and frowned. "You didn't ask this boy his age?"

"Well, of course we did," Claire huffed. "It's just that he doesn't know. He was raised by his father in the remote woods, isolated from the world with no way of marking time or any kind of education. He just simply doesn't know."

The officer cleared his throat. "But, if you had to make a guess?"

"About nine or ten, I suppose." Claire folded and unfolded her arms.

The officer licked the end of his pencil and jotted down the information. "Let's see what we've got so far: a nine or ten-year-old boy, about four and a half feet tall with a long brown hair and brown eyes. Oh, and a birthmark on his forearm."

"That's right." Charlie gave Claire's shoulders a gentle squeeze.

The officer reached through the open window and grabbed a two-way radio from the console of the patrol car. Before he clicked it on, he turned back around to them. "Had you folks considered he might have been kidnapped? Or might be a runaway?"

Charlie's eyes widened. *He was a runaway, all right.* "His father is in the hospital down the street. You're welcome to check our story out, if you'd like."

"You *do* know how convoluted all this sounds to me, don't you?" His badge reflected the sunlight as he raised his eyebrows and shook his head.

"Well, I suppose it might, but do you think we'd have come to you for help if we thought we'd been guilty of doing somethin' wrong? We've got nothin' to hide. Just a lot of information we don't know—yet." Charlie pulled a checkered handkerchief from his back pocket and wiped his forehead.

Jake's stomach growled. Living with the Claiborne's, he'd become used to eating regular meals. He kept his eyes on Hound as he slept on the sidewalk outside Ken's Barbershop. He popped his knuckles as he waited for his turn in the chair. He wondered if he should take such a drastic measure...

"I guess you're up next, young fella." A husky man with a thick mustache and a crisp, white shirt called him to the chair, swooping a blue-and-white striped cape onto his shoulders with a flourish. "Is that your dog outside?"

Jake nodded. "His name is Hound." He held his breath and clutched the arms of the chair as the barber pumped it up higher and higher.

"I'm Ken. This is my shop." He opened a drawer and took out a clean comb. He parted Jake's brown tresses. "It must have taken a long time to grow your hair this long. It's almost to your waist."

"My mother's been wanting me to cut it. This'll surprise her." Jake took a deep breath and closed his eyes. Now why did he say that? Perhaps, just for a moment, he wanted to know what it felt like to be an average boy with a mother at home—a mother that cared about normal things, like her son's haircut.

"What style do you have in mind, son?" The barber wiped the shiny scissors on a towel.

He shrugged his shoulders. "I hadn't thought much about it. Just short is all."

"Well, it's a big decision. Shouldn't rush it. How about browsing through this magazine? When something appeals to you, just point it out and I'll do my best."

Jake thumbed through the pages, studying each picture, imagining how he'd look in each style. More confusing than helpful, he ended up handing it back.

A bright yellow poster on the far wall caught his attention. "Can you just cut it to look like that?" A makeover. Just like on T.V.

Ken chuckled. "All right, then. Let's get started."

———⚬⚬⚬———

Charlie sat the small blue overnight bag on top of the dresser. Children outside the hotel window lined up for turns on the giant water slide.

Jake would have enjoyed this. His stomach churned as he wondered where he and Hound would spend the night.

"This hasn't turned out to be very much of a honeymoon for you so far, now has it, dumplin'?"

Claire laid her head against his shoulder. "I wouldn't trade one day of it for a Mediterranean cruise."

"You are the sweetest woman I ever did meet. I can't imagine what you see in me." He laid a slobbery kiss on her rouged cheek. "What do ya say we walk down to the Big Top, get us a hot dog, and see the show?"

Claire hesitated. "I feel guilty about giving up the search before dark."

Charlie's shoulders drooped. "But, sugarplum—"

"Still, we've been at it for hours and I just don't know where else to look." Claire picked up the gray suede jacket she had worn for several winters. "I'm glad I brought this. It's cool this evening." She turned back to him, smiling. "There are some things that just feel right—like this coat and you, Charlie. Then there are others that just don't add up—like Jake and his father. Maybe we should pay Ethan another visit on the way."

Charlie raised his eyebrows as he held the door open for his bride.

As Jake exited the barbershop, Hound sprang to his feet, growling. He narrowed his eyes, turning his head to one side and then the other.

Jake put out his hand. "Hey! It's just me, silly."

Hound's ears perked when he heard Jake's voice. He sniffed his pants and shoes. Finally, he jumped up and put his paws on Jake's shoulders, licking his face.

Jake unzipped his backpack and retrieved the hooded sweatshirt. He looked up at the darkening sky and pushed the hood over his gelled and spiked hair.

The pair traveled down the back streets of Elkins, hiding behind thick hedges when people approached them or when headlights shined in their direction. As they neared a busy street on the outskirts of town, Jake noticed a crowd filing into a large red-and-white striped tent. "Come on, Hound, let's see what the excitement is all about."

They crossed the street, coming up alongside an enormous sign. "The Big Top," Jake read. He reached a hand out to pull the tent's flap back, and leaned forward to peek inside.

Someone coughed behind him and jerked on his hood. A stern voice boomed overhead. "Trying to sneak in, are you, young man?"

Jake whirled around. His jaw fell open as his eyes traveled up the thin frame of the tallest person he'd ever seen. He wore a top hat and a fancy coat. His face, covered in white makeup, reminded him of Claire at bedtime. He blinked and then stammered. "No. I-I...just wanted to see what all these people were doing. I wasn't meaning to go inside. Honest."

"You've never been to the circus before, sonny?" The man bent down, meeting him face-to-face.

"A friend of mine read me a book about the circus when I—um—stayed with her awhile back, but I've never been to one."

"Well, this one is first rate. I'm Wally, by the way. I travel with the circus."

"Really? What do you do?" Jake looked up and down Wally's towering form.

"I'm the Tall Man. And I can see by the expression on your face that you must think I'm really this tall. No, look." Wally held his pants legs up to reveal wooden stilts. "Say, why don't you come in and watch the performance?"

"Thank you, but we've got to get going."

"Ah, rest awhile and enjoy yourself. Look, I'm allowed to give away two free tickets. Here, take this one to the window over there and I'll meet you inside. I'll get you a good seat." Wally pointed toward a small building several yards away, its roof rimmed with blinking lights.

"I'd sure like to, but—"

When two police officers strolled in their direction, Jake grabbed the ticket out of Wally's hand. "Okay. Sure. Why not?"

"I'll put your dog under a bleacher. No one will notice." Wally took the leash from Jake's hand. "Come on, boy."

Jake's heart throbbed in his chest as he hurried to the counter. He'd seen a few detective shows on television. He wondered if he'd learned anything useful in helping them to travel undetected—living *on the lam,* they call it.

Once inside, Jake found a seat on the bench next to Wally, leaning over to pat Hound's back. He settled in to enjoy the show, but when the drum roll signaled the high wire act of Blythe and Billy, Hound reacted by growling and pulling against the leash. Wally fed him a corn dog to get him to settle down.

Jake drew in a deep breath when the lights went out and the spotlight shined on the small platform above his head. The aerialists, clowns, horseback riders, and lion tamers had him spellbound for the next two hours. He was surprised when the lights came up and the crowd stood, whistling and applauding at the end of the show.

Maybe he'd consider joining the circus when he got older. He should start training Hound, soon. It would probably take him a long time to learn to dance on his hind legs. But running in a circle? He was already good at that.

He blended in with the other circus people and followed Wally out the performer's exit. He declined Wally's offer to let him bunk in his trailer for the night. Instead, he led Hound down a deserted alleyway littered with garbage cans and boxes before gazing back at the circus tent one last time.

Charlie admired Claire's face. She was such a pretty thing. He questioned what she saw in an overweight, bald-headed guy like him.

"They weren't at the park, Charlie. Could someone have picked them up? Taken them in? Or, could they be *here?*" Claire mumbled, fighting against the large wad of cotton candy stuffed in her mouth. "A boy and a dog shouldn't be hard to locate, even in a crowd."

"I beg to differ, my love. This tent is full of animals. Some of them are dogs. I'd think they would blend in quite well. That is, in the event that they're here. Which, they may not be." Charlie guided her toward the exit.

"Well, what do you say we stand here awhile and watch as everyone leaves? Just in case." Claire raised her eyebrows at her husband.

He grinned. "You take the right. I'll concentrate on the left."

An assortment of people filed past them, laughing and recounting their favorite acts in the show.

When the tent was empty, Charlie shook his head. The gnawing feeling in his gut intensified. *God, please keep them safe.*

He thought back over the events of their second visit with Ethan. He was sure the man was hiding a secret. That face he made when they asked about Jake's birthdate—the way he shouted, accusing them of messing in his personal business—that wasn't typical of a man concerned about the well being of his son.

Claire lapsed into an uneasy silence as they strolled back to the hotel. "We've got to take action to find that boy and make sure Ethan never hurts him again."

"What more do you think we should do, buttercup?" He pressed his lips into a fine line and raised one bushy eyebrow, then the other.

Her jaw twitched. "Well, for starters, we need to find out Ethan's true identity."

His head snapped in her direction. "So, you don't believe his story about bein' in the witness protection program either?"

Chapter 10

A train thundering overhead woke Jake. He bolted from the protective covering of the old trestle bridge where he and Hound had spent the night. He shivered in the coldness of the early morning wind, his teeth chattering. "Hur-ry, H-h-ound! Let's f-find some place warm."

They took shelter under a large tree with long drooping branches— boughs so thick that not only was the wind blocked out, but most of the sunlight as well. Jake felt around in his backpack for something to eat, choosing a granola bar for himself and a special treat for Hound. "Look, your favorite. Chipotle Beef Jerky."

By the time they emerged, the sun had climbed overhead. The light dusting of snow that blanketed the ground during the night was already melting. The ground sloshed under Jake's feet.

Making their tracks over several open fields, they slowed when they arrived at an RV park on the west side of the road. Curious about the strange looking "homes on wheels," Jake crept up the steps to a porch with stars, planets, and clouds painted on the floorboards. He peered through the sliding glass door, red and yellow beads casting rainbows across the walls inside.

"And just what do you think you're doing, young man?"

His body stiffened. A lady in a vaguely familiar blue sweater, curly black hair caught in a shiny blue headband, stood beside him. Her hands were on her hips, tapping her foot...waiting for an answer.

He took a step sideways, his own brown eyes searching the green ones that scowled back at him. Catching a flicker of recognition on her face, he leaped off the porch, Hound in hot pursuit.

"Wait, wait! Hound? Jake?" The woman hurried after him, her long flowing skirt swishing around her ankles, her large looped earrings swinging back and forth.

Jake's legs burned as he sprinted down the driveway. He was almost out of the park when an old brown truck speeded around the corner, just missing him. He slipped on the loose gravel. "Why don't you watch where you're going?" He pushed to his feet.

The lady bent forward, hands on her knees, sucking in air. "I'm sorry. I didn't mean to scare you. I thought I recognized Hound, but then I wasn't sure. It is you, isn't it, Jake? I'm Ruth. I used to live near your family when you were just a little tyke." She cringed as she looked at his scarred and frostbitten hands.

He brushed himself off, examining the heels of his hands. His eyes narrowed. "Ruth had red hair."

"And, you... Well, your hair is different, too." Her eyes crinkled at the outer edges when she smiled.

Jake ran his hand across the shaved sides of his head. "It's a disguise."

"Mine, too." Ruth laughed, bunching up her dark curls and releasing them with a flourish. "Come on back with me and I'll put something on those for you." She motioned toward his hands.

"I'm fine. They're just skinned up a bit."

"But they could get infected. I'm a nurse now, Jake. I know about these things."

Hound seemed to like her. And, he was a pretty good judge of character. "Well..."

"Last time I saw you, you were just knee-high to a grasshopper. Now look at you. You're almost grown."

He backed away from her, his chin trembling. Why would a nice lady like her be friends with Father?

"I'm glad to see you. Please stay and talk for a bit." Ruth put her hand out to pet Hound. "How have you been, boy?" She scratched him behind his ears.

"You left me there with him. You just traipsed off like nothing happened." He spat out the words, his face warm and neck muscles tense.

"I knew he'd take good care of you. Why, that man worshipped the ground you walked on. You were his pride and joy." Ruth's dimples accented her smile.

"He sure had a strange way of showing it." He took a step backward. "He's a killer!"

Ruth rushed to Jake's side and guided his shoulders in the direction of her trailer. "Shh. Don't let people hear you say that. Let's not be asking for trouble."

"It's the truth." He wriggled out of her grip.

"Please, Jake. We can visit out on the porch if you'd like. Hound looks thirsty."

Hound shot his long pink tongue out, as if on cue. He threw in a soft whimper for good measure.

Jake stuck his hands in his pockets, using the toe of his sneakers to make a circle in the wet gravel. "Okay, but we'll stay outside."

"That's fine. I'll get us each a glass of lemonade and we can have a little chat. It's clearing up to be such a beautiful day. Warm sun. Nice breeze." Her eyes sparkled as she twirled around under the huge trees.

He followed her, dragging his feet and scuffing the once-shiny white rubber of his new sneakers. Dust filled the air. When they reached the trailer, he sat down on the blue steps amid the painted yellow stars and waited for Ruth. He'd stay here, in case he needed to make a quick getaway.

A few minutes later, Ruth joined him. She wiped his hands off with an antiseptic wipe and smoothed on a thin layer of ointment. "There. That didn't hurt, did it?"

"Not really." She had a nice smile, but that could be a trick.

She poured lemonade into two glasses filled with ice, handing one, along with a cookie, to Jake. She sat down on one end of the porch swing, kicked off her shoes, and tucked her bare feet up underneath her multicolored skirt.

Jake grabbed another cookie from the tray. He watched as Hound lapped from a bowl of fresh water. The overflow fell onto the porch, making it look like the sun and stars were crying.

Hound licked crumbs from the porch, circled around the planets and then curled up on the top step for a nap in the warm sunshine. His side rose and fell with each rhythmic breath.

Jake drained his glass of his lemonade. "What do you call this again?" He moved to sit beside her on the swing.

"Lemonade. Do you like it?"

"More...um, please." The ice cubes clinked together as he thrust his glass toward Ruth.

She poured more lemonade. Then she offered him the one remaining cookie.

Grabbing it, he relaxed to the up and back rhythm of the swing and the caress of the gentle breeze. Ruth must have been *Mama's* friend.

"So, do you like your haircut?" A deep chuckle escaped her rosy lips.

He ran his fingers through his stiff hair. "I didn't want to be found, but now I think I look like a skunk."

She raised her eyebrows. "You ran away?"

"Yeah."

She cocked her head to the side. "Care to tell me why?"

Jake looked down at his new high-topped sneakers, shaking his head. He spit on his finger and rubbed the dirt off the toes. Just because he ate her cookies and drank her lemonade didn't mean he wanted to tell her a bunch of stuff.

Ruth touched his arm. "Jake, everything has been okay, hasn't it?"

He pulled away. "Not really. Not since the day that…you know." He retreated to the far end of the porch.

"I'm so sorry. I thought—" She pinched the bridge of her nose and looked away.

"The day Mama—um…died, Father changed." Jake fought to control the torturous memories of the past churning inside him. He ignored the tears that splashed down his face and the mucus flowing from his nose. "He beat me. He even broke a ladder on me, once. When he'd drink, he'd burn me—or worse…"

His face grew hot. His balled fists hung rigid at his sides. "He made this chair— and if I didn't sit exactly straight—" He closed his eyes. He wouldn't—couldn't—tell the rest. "I had to eat scraps out of the dog's bucket and he made me sleep on the floor." He collapsed in a heap. It felt good to get even that much out.

"I'm so sorry. So, so sorry."

He melted into her arms. He sobbed as she rocked him, nestled between the rainbow and the shooting star.

<hr />

Jake stayed with Ruth the next few days, sleeping on the foldout sofa in her small living room. Little by little, he opened up to her, talking about the surety of the past and the lack of a promising future. One night, as they ate supper on a picnic table in the common area of the trailer park, he found the courage to tell her about what happened to Ghost and to ask her about her own actions.

"Ruth, you knew Father killed Sam and Mama. Why didn't you tell anyone?" He narrowed his eyes, glaring at her.

She placed her elbows on the cracked and weathered table, resting her chin on her folded hands. She bit her lip before answering. "I know it's hard for a boy to understand the way it is in the world, but some things are considered wrong to do. In this case, it was wrong for a married man, or woman, to be—uh—romantic with someone else's wife or husband. I know you loved your mother, but what she and Sam did was wrong."

Mama would never... Jake leaped to his feet and screamed at Ruth. "But Father KILLED them!"

When she grabbed his hand, her tears flowed all at once, rivers of them. "I should have—told the police—even though Ethan threatened—me not to. I was—weak and I was scared of what he—might do to me, so I just—stayed quiet. For months, I—kept looking over my—shoulder. I was afraid he might—find me. When he didn't, it just got easier—and easier to believe—it had all just been a very bad dream." Her shoulders quaked as she choked back her sobs.

"But it wasn't a dream. He's dangerous." He rubbed his eyes with the back of his hand.

"I know." She nodded and dabbed at her eyes with a tissue. "And after hearing all the things he's done, I'm more ashamed than ever that I didn't go to the authorities. I might have prevented all this."

Charlie took in a couple of breaths before knocking on the door to room 212. He held the door open for Claire. His mouth dropped open when he saw the vacant bed with crisp, clean sheets. "Well, I'll be. He's either died or gone to rehab."

"The man was pretty banged up, dear. I can't imagine what kind of doctor would release him." She wandered around the room, her eyes falling on the only thing out of place: a folded newspaper.

A stern voice from the hallway startled the couple.

"May I help you?" A nurse with mousy brown hair tapped her foot on the spotless tile floor.

Claire was the first to speak. "We visited with the man who was in this room, just the day before yesterday. Has he been moved?"

The nurse exhaled a long breath. "I wish it were that simple. As badly hurt as he was, you'd think he wouldn't be capable of it, but he actually got away from us."

"Have you called the police?" Charlie puffed out his chest.

"Yes. Do you know anything that might help us?" She lifted a single eyebrow. "We're interested in his health, you understand, but he used an I.D. of a deceased person. It took our legal department quite a while to untangle all of that. By the time they did, we were caught with a huge medical bill pending. We still have no idea of his *real* name."

"We only know him as Ethan, but we're positive that's not his real name, either. Charlie was the one that found him and led the rescue team to him. We haven't known him long, ourselves." Claire smiled in Charlie's direction.

The nurse blushed and moistened her lips. "Well, it isn't every day one meets a hero. I'm Maggie." She twirled a section of her long hair around her index finger and lowered her eyelashes.

"Charlie Claiborne." They barely had time to shake hands before Claire landed an elbow to his side. "And this is my wife, and the love of my life, Claire."

Nurse Maggie stepped back and cleared her throat. "Good to meet you both. If you think of anything significant, please contact the police or the hospital business office."

When the nurse was out of hearing distance, Claire thrust the newspaper into Charlie's hands. "Look!"

He read the small headline on page ten: "LOCAL TEAM HELPS TRAPPED MAN. HOSPITAL SEEKS TRUE IDENTITY."

Claire anchored her hand on her hip. "Not a very good picture, but the article was probably too close for comfort. I told you he's hiding something."

"Yes, sugarplum, you did. You're smarter than a house cat." He gave her a long hug. Ethan had better watch out. She was on his trail.

"Thank you, dear. Now are you ready to have a little talk with the police?"

"I think that's precisely what we need to do. I fear for the boy's life if Ethan finds him before we do." Charlie pushed the door open with a flourish.

"Hold still, Hound, you're getting me all wet!" As Jake poured more flea and tick shampoo onto the dog's coat, he twisted and jerked to get away.

Jake turned on the hose, a strong, current surging forth. "Calm down. Just look at all of this dirt roll off you. You're going to feel so much better when you're nice and clean." He held onto his mesh collar as he rinsed off the squirming canine.

"Need some help?" A freckle-faced boy with two missing front teeth marched into the small yard in front of Ruth's trailer. He put his hand over his mouth, chuckling.

"No. I've got it under control." Jake slipped on the soapy grass, but managed to hang onto Hound.

"I have a yellow Lab. I know some tricks to keep him still when I give him a bath."

Jake tilted his head and paused. "Well, okay. Wouldn't hurt to have you hold him still for me." He rubbed soap out of his own eyes.

"Sure. No problem." The boy put his arms around Hound's neck, while Jake rinsed him with water from the hose.

"I'm Eric. We just moved into number 26." Hound tried to pull away, but the boy held on tight.

"I'm Jake. I'm staying with my friend Ruth for a few days." He turned the water off and picked up a pink-and-green beach towel. He dried Hound's rump, tail, head and back. Then he locked eyes with Eric. They nodded to each other and let Hound go.

The dog took off for the picnic area, putting his head down on the rich carpet of grass, and rolling over and over.

"You crazy dog!" Jake bent over and hugged his stomach, laughing aloud.

A lady shouted from the porch of the trailer across from Ruth's. "Eric, you have a dental appointment in half an hour. Get in here and change out of those wet clothes."

Eric's shoulders slumped. "Okay." He turned toward Jake. "Maybe I'll see you around."

He waved as Eric jogged toward home. "Maybe."

"I should be back before dark. We can play then." Eric yelled from his driveway.

"Okay. Sure." *Play?* Jake's eyes widened when a police car pulled up in front of the manager's trailer.

An officer with a slight limp exited, said a few words to the manager, and tacked a poster onto the bulletin board. He left in a cloud of dust.

Jake walked in the direction of the bulletin board, recoiling when he saw a picture that looked exactly like Father at the top of the paper. A drawing resembling Jake was underneath. At least he had a ponytail in the picture. Maybe no one would recognize him. He snatched the paper, ran toward the trailer, and slid the glass door open.

"What is it?" Ruth looked over the top of her reading glasses, crossing her arms over her chest.

He stopped to catch his breath, placing the paper in front of her. "I can't read all the words. What's it say?"

Her eyes widened as she read the flyer. "Have you seen this man? Goes by the name of 'Ethan'. May be seen with this boy, 'Jake,' and a dog named 'Hound.' The boy is thought to be between nine and ten years old, four and a half feet tall, with brown eyes, and long brown hair. If you have any information as to their location, please call the local police. And it gives the number."

The hair lifted on the nape of his neck. He gripped the back of Ruth's chair until his knuckles turned white. Father was out of the hospital. He'd be coming after Jake, trying to take Hound away, and exacting his revenge...

———

Before the first light of day, Jake checked on Ruth. Her eyes were closed and appeared to still be asleep. He eased her bedroom door closed and headed for the pantry. The door squeaked as he opened it.

He retraced his steps and put his ear to the door. No noise from inside. He returned to the pantry and added to his already bulging backpack a box of raisins, two candy bars, and some beef jerky. He motioned to Hound to follow him onto the porch, pausing for a moment to look at the bright yellow moon with the spotted cow jumping over it.

He tiptoed across the loose gravel, leading Hound in the direction of the train tracks. They hadn't gone far when a locomotive roared around the bend, large and menacing, sounding its clamorous whistle. He jumped back into the shadows of the trees, sucking in his breath. He sank onto the ground, resting his forehead in his hands until his heartbeat slowed.

"These tracks go two ways, Hound, in opposite directions. Should we go right or left? Either way, it'll be someplace new."

He pulled at the delicate chain hanging around his neck until the locket fell out of his shirt. He rubbed his thumb across the gold cross on top of the silver case. He put the smooth metal to his cheek, recalling what Ruth had told him the night before: "I know it was wrong of me to steal it, but at the time I didn't have a cent to my name. I pawned it to buy food and get a place to stay. Later, I was able to buy it back. I hoped to someday be able to give it to you. Your mother wore it every day. The case is sprung, so I couldn't get it open. Whatever's inside was very special to her—and now it's yours."

He stretched out the neck of his shirt and let the chain fall back inside. He slid the backpack off his shoulders and rummaged around inside, coming up with a packaged fruit pie for himself. He popped the top off of a small can of chili for Hound.

The day following their visit to the police department, Charlie drove toward home in silent contemplation. He snuck a glance in Claire's direction. His little cupcake was brooding over Jake.

Charlie knew they'd done everything they could to find him. All that was left to do was to go home, wait, and pray. The shadows formed a crisscross pattern over the front windshield. He brought up his right hand to cover his eyes and squinted at a familiar poster attached to a pole next to the railroad crossing.

He slowed and looked both ways before he pressed his foot down on the gas pedal. The "Hornet" sprang ahead. The extra money for the turbo had been worth it. Anna didn't think they'd need this kind of power, but he—

A loud *thump* sounded from the direction of the right front fender.

"Well, I'll be!" Charlie stopped the car, his eyes meeting Claire's.

"Charlie, did you hit something?" She flung her door open and slid from her seat to the pavement below.

He killed the motor and hopped out to survey the damage. How had he let this happen?

"Oh, no!" A familiar voice broke the silence. Jake ran up to join them.

They clutched onto one another as they beheld the still form of his best friend.

Chapter 11

The morning following Ethan's escape from the hospital, he had managed to travel all of one mile down the road, near the outskirts of town. Using new aluminum crutches stolen from the man in the room next to his, and wearing scrubs he snatched from a hook on the wall of the doctors' lounge, he marked time on a bus stop bench in front of a strip mall department store.

When a male clerk unlocked the door, Ethan slid inside. Following the overhead sign to the men's section, he found a white, long-sleeved t-shirt and a pair of red-and-black flannel lounge pants, size large. He noticed a round security mirror in the upper right corner of the store, so he slipped around the corner before he shoved the clothing into the waistband of his scrubs. He tried on several ball caps on the next aisle, and then edged his way toward the exit.

The automatic door was shutting behind him when the clothing, encased in plastic wrappers, dropped out of his pants and onto the walkway. He leaned one of his crutches against the door and bent down to retrieve them, but the crutch fell onto the cement, alerting the clerk with its loud *clatter*.

The overweight teenager stuffed the remainder of a Twinkie into his mouth, rushed from his post at the register, and chased after Ethan. As he approached the door, Ethan grabbed a metal trashcan and wedged it between the door and a grab bar, rendering the door inoperative. The clerk was forced to run across the front of the store to the other side and exit through the delivery door.

Wedging the packages under his arm, Ethan stumbled around the corner and toward the alley. When he reached the second corner, he stuck out a crutch, a foot above the ground, blocking the narrow passageway.

The teenager exited into the bright afternoon sunlight on the west side of the building. When he rounded the second corner, he tripped over the crutch, landing flat on his face and toppling a stack of boxes. "Ahhh. You broke my arm, you crazy b——" He held one arm close to his body and used the other to raise a fist toward Ethan as he disappeared behind the fast food restaurant next door.

Ethan escaped between the last two buildings at the end of the strip mall and found a place to hole up behind the vet's office/lending library. He ripped open the wrapper from the t-shirt and then jerked the hangtag from the lounge pants. He chuckled to himself, thinking what a sight that must have been—a teenager chasing a poor guy on crutches.

He was pulling the t-shirt over his head when the sound of sirens filled the streets. He yanked the pants on over his cast and then hid behind a smelly Dumpster. As the sirens grew quiet, a nervous chuckle escaped his lips. He had over-reacted. Of course law enforcement wouldn't care about the loss of a cheap t-shirt and flannels.

Ruth placed the gold-rimmed coffee cup into the sink and went back outside. Jake and Hound had romped on the grass across from her trailer just a day earlier. Her eyes clouded as she lay down on the green-and-orange striped hammock. If she called the police, he'd never trust her again. *Dear God, please keep him safe.*

The midmorning sun was warm on the east side of the trailer. She was just closing her eyes when noisy footsteps on the wooden porch startled her. The burly park manager's face loomed only inches from her own.

"What is it, Merle?" She sat up, throwing off the soft turquoise afghan.

"A little trouble down by the train tracks, Missy." His voice trembled, his familiar toothy smile gone.

Ruth yawned and shook her head. "What does that have to do with me?"

"Samuel just got back from town. He saw the whole thing." He removed his ball cap, turning it over and over again in his large hands.

"Which was?" Ruth slipped on her flip-flops.

Merle cleared his throat. "Your friends that are stayin' with you... the dog got hit by—"

"Oh, no!" Ruth jumped up, grabbed her keys and was down the steps in one giant leap. She crossed the sidewalk—her large earrings tinkling—and opened the squeaky door of her '72 Camaro. She gunned the motor and took off, laying rubber when she reached the single lane running parallel to the train tracks. A few hundred feet further, the car screeched to a halt. She flung the door open and ran to join Jake, kneeling by his dog.

"Ruth!" Jake reached up to grab her hand and pull her down beside him.

Ruth stroked Hound's head. "What happened?"

"He ran over him." Jake pointed to the baldheaded man standing next to an attractive gray-haired lady.

Ruth swallowed hard. "Did the dog run out in front of you?"

"No. The sun was in my eyes and I just—" The guy hung his head, big tears splashing onto the tops of his dusty boots.

Ruth sent a feeble smile his way. "What we need to do right now is get Hound to the vet's. Do you know where it is?"

The woman standing next to him shook her head. "No. We don't live here. We were just trying to find Jake. When I opened the door at the hospital, he was—"

Ruth interrupted the lady's explanation. "You know each other?"

Jake stood up from his vigil by Hound. "These are the Claiborne's, Ruth. You know. I told you about Charlie and Claire finding me."

Ruth rubbed her lower back as she stood to face the couple. She forced a smile. "Hound's lost a lot of blood; if we all try at once, maybe we can pick him up and get him into the back of your vehicle."

Charlie nodded and hurried around to open the hatch. Claire grabbed an old army blanket and spread it out on the road. Together, all three adults slid Hound onto it, hoisted it up by the corners, and settled Hound into the back of the SUV. Jake hopped in beside him.

Charlie squatted down in front of Jake. "I wouldn't have had this happen for all the tea in China. I hope you know how sorry I am. Please forgive me."

Tears glistened in Jake's deep brown eyes. "I know it was an accident."

"Even if Hound should—um— die?" Charlie choked on the words.

"He won't. I know it." Jake's face radiated forgiveness and hope.

"Are you sure?" Charlie whispered.

"You've been nothing but good to us. I know you wouldn't hurt Hound any more than I would."

Charlie smiled. "Let's get him fixed up then."

Ruth jumped into her car, beckoning Jake to join her. "It's not far to the vet's office, Charlie. Follow Jake and me."

"No way. I'm staying back here with Hound." Jake motioned for Charlie to close the hatch.

Ruth peeled out, leading the way. She hoped they could make it there in time. Jake had been through so much, and yet somehow he had found it in his heart to forgive. She wished she could say the same for herself.

She parked her car in the "No Parking" zone in front of the veterinarian's office. As she waited for Charlie to pull up alongside, she noticed the "Closed" sign hanging in the window. They just couldn't lose Hound like this.

She was standing on the curb when Charlie pulled his car into the space next to her car. Jake jumped out when Charlie raised the hatch. "What's wrong?"

"The office is closed. The vet won't be here until Thursday."

"Can we take him to the people hospital?"

"I'm afraid not." Ruth bent forward, giving his shoulder a squeeze. "We'll think of something."

"From the looks of it, we'd better think of it quick." Charlie stroked Hound's coat, washed clean yesterday afternoon, now matted with blood.

The voice coming from the front of the building sounded like the boy's. Ethan maneuvered around the Dumpster and stumbled to the corner to confirm his suspicion. "What's going on here?"

"Father!" Jake inched back toward Claire's protective arms.

Charlie did a double take and stammered, "E-Ethan!"

"What are you doing here?" Ruth bit her lower lip.

"Ruth? I could ask you the same thing." Ethan stared at her dyed hair, guessing he could be the reason why the woman decided to make such a drastic change. She might soon regret she didn't use her senses and leave the state long ago. He turned away from her intense gaze. "And we're all gathered here to—?" He sneered.

Jake and the Claiborne's stepped aside to reveal Hound, lying inside the SUV.

Ethan hobbled forward. His face paled. He laid his ear to the dog's chest. "He's alive, but his breathing is shallow. He needs attention."

"The office is closed. What can we do?" Ruth probed Ethan's scruffy face.

"Precisely. What can *we* do?" His face contorted as he mocked her.

"Break in." Jake exclaimed, turning to face Charlie.

"What?" Charlie's eyes widened.

Jake yanked the tire iron out of the Hornet's side pocket. "There's got to be some medicine in there. You're a nurse, Ruth. You'll know what kind he needs."

"It's not that simple, Jake. Even if I knew what to do, we'd still be breaking the law." Ruth ran her fingers through her hair.

"I don't know about laws so much, but I do know I'm not going to stand here while Hound dies." Jake ran to the door on the side of the building and heaved the metal bar through the glass. "Who's going to help me?"

Ruth hesitated. She looked toward the Claiborne's, eyes pleading. "We all love Jake—and Hound—come on, we can save him." She put her hand through the jagged hole in the glass and unlocked the door.

Ethan would use the accident to his advantage. He inched his way along the sidewalk to stand in front of the group. When he cleared his throat, all heads turned in his direction. His eyes narrowed as he stepped up to the boy. "This is my deal. Take it or leave it."

Jake took a step back. "What do you mean?"

"I mean, I will help you—under certain conditions."

"Why would I want your help? You're a killer."

"I'm a veterinarian," Ethan smirked. "How's that for a little surprise?"

"You're a-a…doctor?" Ruth rolled her eyes and shook her head.

Ethan's laugh was diabolical. "Why would you find that so hard to believe?"

She glared in his direction. "I'm sure you know why."

"I can save Hound, so listen carefully— all of you."

Claire squeezed Jake's hand. She sneered Ethan. "Why, you piece of—"

He kept his eyes on Jake as he spelled out his terms. "I will use all of my surgeon's skills, however rusty they may be, to save Hound— provided one of you furnishes me a place to stay while the dog is recuperating and that when he's well enough to travel, you give the dog to me. Do you understand, boy? Hound is *my* dog and I will take him with me when I go."

"Dag nab it, now, Ethan—" Charlie squared his shoulders.

Ethan's cold eyes bore into his. "Those are the terms, Charlie. The boy can make his choice."

Jake's fingers trembled as he stroked the dog's head.

"Well, boy?" Ethan snapped.

Tears rolled down Jake's chin and onto Hound's fur. "If there's a chance he can save you, Hound, I have to take it." He lowered his head and closed his eyes. "Okay."

Ruth and the Claiborne's carried Hound into the office of W.J. Burns, D.V.M. They traveled down a long hallway and laid him on the cold, stainless steel operating table.

Ethan followed and began at once to stock a surgical tray and ready Hound for surgery. "It's going be okay, Hound. I'll have you fixed up in no time." He shouted orders at the others. "Claire, close those blinds.

Charlie, park both of those vehicles in the back alley. Ruth, I need iodine—now!"

—⊷⊶⊷—

Jake closed his eyes and rested his forehead against the glass separating him from his dog. He reached up with both hands and splayed his fingers on the cold barrier. *God, please save Hound. He's my best friend.*

"Jake, you get that broom and I'll get the dustpan." Claire motioned to the corner near the door. "Let's make ourselves useful and clean up all this broken glass."

He hesitated before he turned away from the window. "Okay. I don't think I should watch this anyhow."

"Probably not."

Once the sweeping was done, Claire settled into an overstuffed chair in the corner and Big Charlie knelt beside her.

"We're going to pray for Hound, Jake. Would you like to join us?" Claire asked.

Jake nodded and dropped to his knees beside the chair. "Do you think God cares about animals?"

"I think he cares about all of his creation." Big Charlie closed his eyes and bowed his head. "Dear God, we lift up our friend, Hound, to you. We ask that you'd see him through this operation and heal his body. Please give Ethan the skills necessary to mend what's broken. Help him do the right thing by Hound. Amen."

Jake prayed a silent prayer, too. *Are you there, God? Hound's hurt. Father will do his best because he wants Hound back. But, it wouldn't hurt if you could give him a little extra help.*

While Claire read a magazine, Jake and Big Charlie spent the next hour thumbing through a bound stack of local maps from the library shelf. Heads together, they planned a future camping trip. They searched the aerial views of the town center, surrounding land, and finally the entire region.

Big Charlie began to trace one of the maps by hand, but stopped when his fingers began to tire. "It might be easier to borrow the book."

Just about the time Jake thought he could wait no longer, Ruth walked into the waiting room, smiling. "You can see him now."

The book of maps fell to the floor as Jake ran toward the small surgical room. He approached the table and stroked Hound's matted fur. "I can feel his heartbeat. He's going to be okay." He frowned at the cast on the dog's back left leg and the large bandage around the middle of his body.

"He has a broken leg, as you can see, and a little damage inside. Nothing major." Father stood in front of the boy, blotting the sweat from his forehead with a white surgical towel. "In about eight weeks, he should be as good as new."

"Why didn't you ever tell me you were a doctor?" Jake crossed his arms on his chest.

Father dropped to a stool, letting his crutches clatter to the floor. "Uh—it just never seemed important."

"Maybe I'll be a vet when I grow up." Jake thrust his chin out. He wouldn't be like Father, though. How could someone who is supposed to help animals be so cruel to humans?

Father grunted. "You know, they'll never let you in school with a haircut like that."

"I—I didn't want to get recognized." Jake looked down at the floor. He'd changed inside, too. He was no longer the little boy Father used to kick around.

"And you didn't think that a hound following you around wouldn't be a dead giveaway?" Father raised an eyebrow.

"I guess I didn't—"

Big Charlie stuck his head around the corner. "Oh, don't be so hard on the boy. Seems to me, we need to focus on *why* he felt he needed to run away, don't you think?"

"No one needs to do any explaining to you, Charlie," Father snarled.

"Oh, no? We'll see about that, Ethan, or whatever your real name is." Big Charlie muttered, patting Jake's head.

"What do you mean by 'whatever your real name is'?" Jake looked from Big Charlie to Father and back again.

"Because, Jake, it seems like we might have ourselves *two* runaways here." Big Charlie smacked Father hard on the back as he exited the room.

Father glared him. "Like I said, Charlie, it's none of your business."

Jake opened the motel room door the following morning on the first knock. Ruth entered, a coffee carrier in her hands and a box of donuts under her arm.

"Ruth, how's Hound? Is he feeling better? Does he miss me?"

Claire tied the bow at the neck of her blouse. "You're up bright and early. I like your skirt—the way it swishes when you walk. I may have to buy me one of those."

"I have one in about every color. Seems like skirts are all I'm comfortable in." Ruth set the coffee and donuts on the desk.

Jake squeezed between the two ladies. "Well?"

Ruth laid her hands on Jake's shoulders. "Yes, he's better. I didn't hear a whimper from Hound all night long. He took a drink of water this morning and ate a couple of bites of food."

"And?" Jake bobbed up and down on both feet.

"Yes. He said to be sure to tell you that he misses you." Ruth's eyes danced in the morning light.

"I can't wait to see him."

Ruth's voice remained calm. "How about us eating a little breakfast first. My hands were too full to carry the orange juice. Would you mind getting it from the front seat of the car?"

Jake darted out the door, retrieved the juice, and was pouring himself a glass as Big Charlie exited the bathroom.

"Mornin' Ruth. You're up bright and early. Nice skirt." Big Charlie pulled his red suspenders up and over his shoulders.

"Just thought you might want a little something to eat before you get on the road." Ruth handed Big Charlie a Styrofoam cup and motioned toward the open box of donuts.

Jake swallowed a bite, then frowned. "We're staying here, right? We can't leave Hound."

Charlie popped a donut into his mouth. "We haven't quite decided what we're gonna do. It's too expensive to live in this motel room while Hound recovers. I guess we could drive to town once a week to see him though."

Jake looked toward Ruth. "Can I stay with you? Please? I'm sorry I ran off like that before. I just couldn't stand the chance I'd get picked up. You understand, don't you?" Jake licked his lips and rocked back and forth on his feet.

"I know it's difficult, Jake, but someday you're going to have to put your trust in the people that are trying to help you." Her face was solemn.

Jake blinked. "It's hard."

Ruth bit her lip. "I know. It's taken me quite a few years to be able to do that again myself. Believe me, I do understand."

"So, can I stay with you?" Jake pleaded, his hands folded in front of him. "Oh, please, oh, please, oh, please."

Ruth shook her head. "You know Ethan is staying there, Jake. That was part of his deal with you, remember?"

"But—"

"I just don't have room for all of you and, anyway, think about what it might be like for you living with your father. I have to work. I can't always be around to protect you from him—I'm not even sure that I could. He's a strong man. Nothing scares him. Even on crutches, I'd be no match for him." Ruth let out a long ragged breath.

"You can't protect me. I can't protect myself. I get it." Jake forced a smile. "Okay."

Ruth gave him a big hug. "Thanks for understanding. We'll go see Hound after breakfast and you can stay as long as you'd like. Then, if Charlie and Claire can bring you into town once a week, I'll make sure you have a nice visit with him. Just remember, though, when he's well, Ethan will be leaving. And Hound will be going with him."

Big Charlie raised his half-eaten donut into the air. "Unless, of course, we turn Ethan in."

Jake jumped to his feet. "No!"

Big Charlie's bushy eyebrows met in the middle. "What do you mean? Wouldn't that solve your problem?"

"We need him to look after Hound—for now." Jake's voice strained as he argued his case.

Big Charlie shrugged. "Good point. But, after that, we call the police. Agreed?"

Later that morning, Charlie picked up a newspaper at a local convenience store while he gassed up the Hornet. As he headed back to the summer house, he half-listened as Claire read the account of the unusual break-in at the veterinary office, the use of surgical equipment, and the missing book of maps.

"A lot of information was left out of the article. But, then again, I was there the whole time, and I still don't know the whole truth. What's Ethan's real name? And, why has he lived for so many years in the back woods? If he's a doctor, why is he choosin' to live as a recluse?"

Claire looked at him with sleepy eyes. "I want to know the answer to those questions as bad as you do, dear. And, just between us, I think Ruth knows more that she's letting on." Claire laid her head back against the headrest.

"I do, too. We need to have a little talk with her when we come back next week."

Claire's snoring didn't surprise him one bit. "Honey bunch?" He shook his head. That woman could fall asleep on a dime.

He glanced over his shoulder into the backseat. Jake was staring out the window, eyes red from crying off and on all day. Charlie hoped he didn't live to regret not turning Ethan in. He had done it for the boy. Life had sure been hard for him. He was determined to make the future better, if he could.

"Maybe we can start on that puzzle this afternoon. You know, the one with the snow-covered mountains. What do you think?" He raised his thick eyebrows.

Jake shook his head. "Nah."

"Or maybe repair that chicken coop out back. Then we can go out to the Taylor's farm and get us a couple of layin' hens. Most people like fresh eggs for breakfast. Of course, if we get chickens, you'll need to help us take care of 'em."

"Sure." Jake sagged against the seat and closed his eyes.

"Those are great ideas, but I think I've come up with the best idea of all, for what we should do on our first day back." *There's no boy on earth can resist …*

Jake's eyes flew open to meet Charlie's through the rearview mirror. "What?"

"How about us goin' fishin'? Have you ever had sushi?"

Jake scratched his head. "What's that?"

"Raw fish is about the best way to describe it."

Jake frowned. "Oh, yeah. I've had that all right."

Chapter 12

*E*than slipped up behind Ruth as she worked in the waning light at her desk in the corner of the living room. *Just look at her. She thinks she's so clever. I could snap her pretty little neck with one swift motion.* He gave her shoulders a vise-like squeeze. "You just can't stay out of my business, can you?"

Ruth's breath caught in her throat. "Not everything is about you, Ethan."

"Oh? Am I wrong, or are you searching that stack of veterinary magazines because you've taken a sudden interest in animals?" he jeered.

Ruth gulped as she looked into his menacing eyes. "You're wrong. They're *Family Circle.*"

"Really? Let's have a little look, shall we?" He reached around her and grabbed one of them. "Looks like a Bulldog on the cover to me."

Ruth flicked on the overhead light and backed away. "So what?"

"Where'd you get such old copies, anyway?"

"Remember the vet's office we broke into? Well, it's also part library. Turns out the lady that runs it just can't seem to throw anything away. She let me go through their storage room and take anything I wanted. Can you blame me for trying to find out who you *really* are?" Her lip quivered as she spoke.

"Who I am—or am not—shouldn't concern you. And, if you want the boy to remain safe and sound with the Claiborne's, I suggest you just forget all about me. I'll be out of your life just as soon as Hound can travel."

"So I should just continue to keep quiet about your killing Sam and Ginnie?" Tears welled in her eyes.

"It's your word against mine. There's no way for you to prove anything." He sneered.

She narrowed her eyes, taking a bold stance. "You're forgetting about Jake. He's a witness."

His muscular arms pushed her back down into the chair. He stood over her with a defiant snarl. "He didn't see anything. He just knows what's he's been told. A little story repeated over the years to scare a kid with an overactive imagination into obeying his father. Why, for all he knows *you* killed them both. Yeah. You were jealous. And after you killed them, you took off. The boy and I were terrified that someday you'd come back and kill us, too." His eyes glowed as he constructed his story.

"Anyone would be able to see right through that." She ran her trembling fingers over the desktop.

"Suit yourself. It's my story and I think I'll stick to it." Maybe she should be afraid. Maybe he would kill again. It might be the only way out for him.

Jake and Big Charlie picked their way down the narrow dirt path, pausing once or twice to allow for the inspection of a stone or insect along the way. When they reached the bottom, Jake gasped at the size of the lake. The mid-afternoon light danced across the surface. Fish jumped into the air, flipping their tail fins back and forth, before returning to the water.

"My father used to bring me here as a youngster. Back then we didn't own the cabin. We just put our tent up over there and camped out." Big Charlie pointed to the opposite shore. "We fished every day and ate bluegill or catfish every night. It might not sound excitin', but I can tell you I never had a better time than when I was with my dad."

"You were lucky. You had a nice one." Jake shaded his eyes as he looked up at Big Charlie. He would have preferred almost any other father in the whole wide world.

"Let's sit for a minute." Big Charlie pulled Jake over to a smooth, flat rock. "I don't want to mislead you into thinkin' things were perfect. I got punished now and then. But, most of the time, we enjoyed each other's company. Doin' stuff together—just like we're doin' right now."

Big Charlie handed Jake a fishing pole.

"Your dad loved you." Jake's eyes misted.

Big Charlie took a handkerchief from his pocket and wiped his cheeks. "I know your relationship with your father has been a big disappointment, but believe me when I say that you have a lot of people in your life now who love you and are gonna see to it that things are a whole lot better for you in the future. And did you know God has an amazin' way of takin' the bad things that happen in our lives and turnin' them around and makin' somethin' good out of 'em?"

Jake shook his head. "I don't see how God can take all the stuff Father's done to me and make it turn out any good."

"I understand, son. But I'm confident He will—and I can't wait to find out how He does it!" Big Charlie groaned as he pulled himself to his feet. "How about you? Can you trust the God who created this beautiful world—the stars, the birds, and this humongous lake full of fish for us to catch—to create a life worth livin' for you?"

Jake hesitated.

"You know what? That's a question you don't need to answer right now. Trust is sometimes somethin' a person just has to grow into. That's what Pop would say."

"Who's Pop?"

"Was. Pop was my grandfather. Sometimes he'd come with us. He's the one that taught me the fine art of fishin'. That man never left the lake without a creel full of 'em." Big Charlie's eyes stared off into the distance.

"What's a grandfather?" Jake shifted back and forth on the rock.

"Ah, I guess you wouldn't know about that. Well, it's simple. Most people have two grandfathers: your father's father and your mother's father. A grandfather can be a very special person in a kid's life when he's growin' up. They do things together. Talk and stuff." Big Charlie gave Jake's arm a playful push.

"So, I might have a grandfather—or maybe *two* grandfathers?" Jake captured a long, juicy worm from the old coffee can and followed Big Charlie's example to bait his hook.

"You might at that." Big Charlie stood behind him, held onto the rod, and helped him cast his line into the water. Then he let out a contented sigh when his own line landed in silence just a few feet away from Jake's.

It wasn't long until two sets of bubbles broke on the surface.

"It looks like we're both going to get a bite." Jake froze, anticipating a tug on his line.

Big Charlie's eyes narrowed. He nodded at Jake and put his index finger to his lips.

Charlie's pole bent at the end. He mouthed an exaggerated, but silent, count: one, two, three. Jerking the rod upward, he started to reel his fish in. It ran with the line, back and forth across the lake. He gave him his lead, reeled, let him take off, and reeled again. "He's a big one. I'm lettin' him tire himself out. Then he'll be easier to bring in." He noticed movement on Jake's line. From the looks of it, he'd soon need a little help.

Jake took several large steps toward the water and began to reel his fish in. When it neared his feet, he let his pole fall into the water and reached down to pick up the fish with his hands. As it squirmed to get away, he threw himself on top of it, grabbed it in a bear hug and wrestled it until it gave up. Jake emerged from the water, soaking wet and smiling. "I got him! I got him!"

Big Charlie stood on the shore, holding up his own fish, and laughing. "I'd say you put your whole body and soul into catchin' that one."

Two hours later, Charlie guided the Hornet into the driveway. They were later than expected, but the fish—and sharing the stories about how they caught them—would be worth it.

Claire was waiting on the porch, reading a magazine when the Hornet pulled into the driveway. When Jake skipped toward her, she pointed her finger toward the back of the house. "Peel those wet clothes off and leave them on the back porch. Then come on back out and tell me all about your afternoon."

After he returned, he and Charlie wasted no time telling her about their adventure. They stumbled over each other's words in their eagerness to relate their own version of events.

"As exciting as all that sounds, I'm hungry. I'll fry the fish, but I won't clean them. Out back with those, you two. Bring them in when you're done. I've got a salad made and I'll put a pan of cornbread in the oven." Claire closed the screen door behind her.

The skillet was hot and ready when Charlie and Jake traipsed into the kitchen with a pan full of catfish fillets. In less than a half hour, the food was on the table.

Jake took several big bites. "This is the best fish—"

"We know, we know," the Claiborne's replied in unison, "—that you've ever had."

"Claire, you should have seen Charlie bring that big catfish in," Jake said between bites.

"She shoulda seen you wrestle that big one to the ground." Charlie's eyes twinkled as he reached for the coffee cups. "Is that pie I see on the counter?"

"Your favorite." Claire smiled back at him.

"First things first." Charlie set the coffee cups on the table and reached for another piece of cornbread. It wasn't long until he pushed back from the table and rubbed his belly. "Who wants some pie? I'll cut. Jake, you get the vanilla ice cream out of the freezer." He shook his head when he turned around to see Jake, face down on the red-and-white checkered tablecloth, sound asleep.

"I'll get the ice cream. You put him to bed. You wore that poor boy out this afternoon." She made her way toward the freezer.

"He gets any heavier, I won't be able to do this." Charlie grunted as he hoisted Jake up from the chair and over his shoulder.

The pie was cut and topped with ice cream when Charlie returned to the room. "You know, I think we need to give careful consideration to what we're gonna to do about that boy. After all he's been through, the stability of a lovin' home is what he needs most. But we're in our sixties, sugarplum. The home he needs is just not gonna be with us."

Claire's face reddened. "But we agreed we don't want to see him put into the foster system."

"True. But even though I care about him and we've had some good times together, I just don't have the patience for children anymore. And, Claire, there's a good chance he's gonna need counselin' and then there's the involvement parents should have if kids are in after-school sports, and lessons of all sorts. I may be selfish, but I pictured a life with just you and me tourin' around the country in an RV havin' ourselves a good 'ol time with no one to answer to but ourselves."

Claire fell silent for a few moments before she took in a deep breath and let her eyes meet his. "Maybe Ruth would want to take care of him. They're very fond of each other. We're getting along with her pretty well now, so I'm sure we could see him whenever we'd want to."

"But she's not married. Maybe she wouldn't want to be tied down with a kid."

Claire grimaced. "I wonder what happened to her husband?"

"Divorce?" Charlie held his cup up for Claire when she grabbed the coffee pot from the stove.

"I'm not sure." She kissed the top of his head before she sat back down at the table.

"Jake told me Ruth used to live near them. She was a friend of his mother's." Charlie stood, stretched, and put his cup in the sink. "That last cup was cold. Anyway, let's get some sleep, darlin'. We can always talk tomorrow." Charlie wound his arm around Claire's waist.

"Maybe we could take a drive sometime and see where Jake used to live. Then, he could help us find Ruth's old place." Claire flicked off the overhead light.

"What for?" He guided her shoulders down the hallway.

"You can learn a lot about a person from the way they live."

Charlie smiled and shook his head. "Curiosity killed the cat, you know."

∞

Ethan placed his purchases on the conveyor belt at Food Mart. A freckle-faced cashier with braces on her teeth rang them up and a girl with bright purple hair and thick-rimmed glasses placed them in a small paper sack. Deep in animated conversation, they didn't give as much as a glance in his direction.

"The news said the instruments that were used indicate the people that broke in knew a lot about animal care. One of them, at least, must've had medical training. Probably a vet." The cashier held out her hand toward Ethan. "That will be four dollars and forty-five cents."

He handed her the five-dollar bill he'd stolen from Ruth's cookie jar earlier that morning. "Talking about the break-in down the street?"

The purple-haired girl with a nametag in the shape of a grocery sack with "TRINA" etched in tall red letters looked up at him. "Yeah. Be on the lookout for a hurt dog." She handed him the sack.

"What makes you think it was a dog? Could just as easily been a cat, a bird, or even a turtle." He spat out his comments and snatched up the sack.

"Detectives found dog hair all over the operating table. Whoever did this didn't cover their tracks very well." Trina smirked as she pushed her glasses onto the bridge of her nose.

Ethan frowned at her purple hair. "The animal could have been run over, fallen into a well, or in a hunting accident. Maybe its owner was a sadistic, evil person that just took pleasure in breaking body parts, torture, setting animals on fire…"

The girls turned to each other, faces ashen, gulping down their quickened breaths.

He left the market, his ghoulish laughter lingering in the afternoon air. *That was fun.*

———⬤———

Jake rolled down the window and stuck his head out of the Hornet. "See, I told you Father burned our cabin down. There's nothing left but that old tool shed back there. Let's just turn around and go back to your place."

"You weren't exaggerating, that's for sure." Claire's mouth hung open, observing the charred remains.

"Well, nothin' to see here. Next stop is Ruth's cabin." Big Charlie turned the SUV around and headed back toward the main highway.

Jake was jostled back and forth in the backseat of the Hornet as Big Charlie drove the vehicle over the rocky road. "Really, I don't think I can find it." He bit his fingernails, tearing one close to the quick. "I was only there once—with Hound. I guess he followed the scent—"

"Scent of what?" Claire raised her eyebrows, waiting for Jake's answer.

"Um, Father. He'd been staying there since the fire. Wait. There it is!" Jake cringed. He should have just let Big Charlie drive on by. They wouldn't have known the difference.

"Over there?" Big Charlie pointed to the cabin high on the bluff.

"Yeah." Jake's voice was almost a whisper.

As Big Charlie guided the SUV up the steep grade, Claire braced her hands against the dash. She shuddered when he parked the Hornet, at last, in the rutted and overgrown driveway.

Jake froze. His hands felt clammy. "Please. Don't make me go in there. I don't want to see it."

Claire rushed around and opened the passenger door. She put her arms around him. "It's all right, Jake. Take deep breaths. Now, that's it. You're going to be fine."

He nodded and let out a sigh.

She gave him a pat on his back. "Whatever it is, you don't have to go in there if you don't want to. Just sit here and wait for us. I think we need to see this for ourselves."

He drew his legs back inside the Hornet and closed the door. He sat, body rigid, as Claire and Big Charlie trudged through the tall weeds toward the porch where wind chimes harmonized in the gentle breeze.

Even from the porch, Charlie gagged at the smell. He opened the door and handed Claire a handkerchief to cover her nose as he batted away a torrent of flies. "What in the world?"

The couple followed the smell down the darkened hallway, past the unmade bed, toward the bathroom. The door creaked when Charlie opened it. Their shoes stuck to the vinyl floor.

A large knife, blade bent and covered with sticky mire lay in the claw-foot tub. Next to it lay something unrecognizable. Its purples, blues and yellows were covered in maggots. Towels and clothing, stiff with dried blood, were scattered on the floor.

Claire ran down the hall and out the front door, heaving next to the steps. Charlie followed behind her in short, but unbroken, strides. He slammed the door shut and prodded his wife toward the car. Once inside, he bent over the steering wheel and reminded himself to breathe.

Claire curled up in the passenger's seat, whimpering and shaking uncontrollably.

Jake reached over the seat and shook Charlie's shoulder. "It's still there, isn't it?"

Charlie nodded. He grabbed onto Jake's arm, muttered something unintelligible, and then started the motor.

Jake screamed until Charlie pulled the Hornet onto the main highway.

⸺⸺

Arriving home after working a double shift at the hospital, Ruth unlocked the trailer door. She clicked on the light over the kitchen table. Strange. Ethan and Hound weren't there. The weather was so nice this time of year, he'd probably taken the dog out for a walk.

She opened her lunch bag, reaching for the other half of her tuna sandwich left over from lunch. She nibbled on it as she thumbed through her mail, washing it down with a bottled iced tea. She walked into the bedroom, took off her uniform and grabbed her velour robe from the hook on the back of the door.

Pulling out the bench from underneath the antique dressing table, she sat down and removed the tortoise shell clip from her hair. When she picked up her brush, a folded piece of paper with her name written in capital letters fell onto the worn blue carpet. She dropped the brush back onto the dresser, retrieved the paper, and returned to the living room.

Her heart raced. En route to the sofa, she grabbed her reading glasses from the kitchen table. She crossed the room to the sofa, pushed aside the pillow that Ethan had been using for the past two months, and drew her feet up under her. She unfolded the note, scrawled on the back of the envelope to last month's electric bill:

> *Ruth,*
>
> *I know you and the Claiborne's are hatching up some scheme to steal Hound and turn me in to the authorities when they bring the boy for his good-bye visit. So, I'm moving on down the road before that happens. Hound is MY dog. Always has been. The boy's taking him was an unforgiveable act of treason*
>
> *I live my life as I see fit. There's no way I'm going back to prison.*
> *Ethan*

Chapter 13

*J*ake bounced from one foot to the other as he watched the bacon fry. "It's been a whole week since I saw Hound. I hope he still remembers me. I just can't wait. I just can't wait!"

"I know. I know!" Claire's eyes twinkled.

Big Charlie looked up from his newspaper. "Yes, I suppose we're all anxious to get on the road. But first things, first. Pour yourself a glass of orange juice and sit down here by me."

Jake stood next to Big Charlie at the primitive kitchen table and poured the juice into a small glass decorated with the likeness of Daniel Boone. "I've missed Hound so much. I don't know what I'll do next week when Father takes him away for good."

Big Charlie's admonition to "Watch what you're doin'!" came a little too late.

Jake overfilled the glass. Orange juice ran across the table and onto the floor. He rushed to the counter for the roll of paper towels and sopped up the sticky liquid next to Big Charlie's feet. "Sorry about your slippers." He remained on his knees, cringing. He was sure some kind of punishment was in order.

"Too busy thinking about Hound." Claire wiped orange juice from the legs of the table.

"My fault really. I got him goin'——"

"Charlie Claiborne," Claire interrupted, "it won't help him learn to take responsibility if you offer excuses at every turn."

"You're right, honey bunch. Okay, then. Let's move past this unfortunate incident and get on to the business at hand—eatin' breakfast." Big Charlie folded his soggy newspaper and set it aside.

Whew! I thought I was going to get a beating, for sure. Jake threw the wet paper towels into the trash. "I'll say grace today if it's okay with you."

"Well, of course it is, Jake. By all means." Claire raised her eyebrows at Big Charlie and then lowered her head.

"Dear God, thank you for healing Hound. Thanks for letting me live with Claire and Big Charlie and not getting beat for spilling the juice. Oh, and thanks for all this good food—especially the bacon. Amen."

Claire's laid her hand on Jake's arm. "That was as nice a prayer as I've ever heard."

Jake beamed as he took a handful of bacon from the platter.

Ruth fiddled with the tissue paper, crunching it between her hands as she placed it in the colorful gift bag. She knew this wouldn't make up for losing Hound, but maybe it would ease the pain. Jake would be surprised. That was for sure.

She spent the next two hours twisting and hanging crepe paper and balloons. She followed the instructions on the box of chocolate cake mix and started baking midmorning. Everyone likes chocolate…

She made the lemon icing with Ginnie's recipe—the one she had used for Sam's thirtieth birthday. She dragged her finger across the inside of the near-empty bowl, placed it in her mouth, and closed her eyes. The taste and the smells transported her back over the years to a time of happiness in their little cabin by the creek—to a party shortly before Jake's birth.

After supper, the four of them had gone outside and danced barefoot to the rhythm of Sam's banjo. Ginnie left Ethan's side more than once to curtsy in front of Sam, a coquettish smile playing on her lips.

Why hadn't she seen then what was so clear to her now? Why hadn't she questioned why Ginnie wanted to be the one to make the cake? Could it be possible that they were "together" even then? Could it be that Ethan was right about Jake being Sam's child? That would make Ruth his stepmother. The very circumstance that made Ethan hate him might just be the one that would bind her and Jake together.

She dropped onto the sofa, resting her head in her hands. Her mind whirled as she half cried, half laughed. She and Jake might have another connection—other than the one they were celebrating today.

<hr>

"How much longer?" Jake watched out the Hornet's side passenger window for familiar landmarks on their trip into town. They passed the little pond under the stand of tall pine trees, then the bridge carrying cars that would travel north toward the higher mountains, and finally Mrs. Jackson's fruit stand.

Big Charlie's smile met Claire's. They had booked a room at a hotel they hoped would be fun for him and planned on taking him to a movie. The only stickler would be today's visit with his father. If they could get him over that hurdle, it would be smooth sailing from then on out.

"Well?" Jake cranked his neck higher and smiled so wide it showed all his teeth.

"It's about fifteen minutes more, I'd say. Look on the watch I gave you and see if you can figure it out."

Jake counted by fives on Big Charlie's well-worn, but still workable, fishing watch. "That's a long time." Jake moaned, then covered his face with his hands.

Claire looked up from her magazine. "Not that long, really. Before you know it, Hound will be licking your face and wanting to play ball in Ruth's driveway."

Jake's smile was immediate. "He's the best, isn't he?"

"You've had each other through thick and thin your whole lives. It makes every bit of sense that you'd love each other so much." She reached over the seat and gave Jake's knee a pat.

"I had a dream last night that Father gave him away because he was mad at me." Jake twisted his hands in his lap.

"Well, there's no reason to think he'd do such a thing, is there? He loves that dog. After all, he saved Hound's life, didn't he?" Claire winked in his direction.

Jake turned quiet. "I guess so, but you don't know Father like I do."

"People don't just give away their pets. Why, it'd be like givin' away a member of their family. Nobody would do that." Big Charlie's smile was exaggerated.

Jake laid his head back against the headrest, relaxing to the rhythmic 'thump, thump' of the tires as the car drove over the uneven road toward town. Father's voice, loud and clear, dominated his uneasy sleep.

His little hands burned as they worked at the rope that held him to the fence post in front of the cabin. All the while, Father played auctioneer to an invisible crowd. "Come one, come all! What am I bid for a boy born out of wedlock? A whimpering weakling of a boy without a mother to care for him? A boy with no name?"

"No. Let me go!" Jake woke with a start, his body thrashing back and forth, tears trickling down and mingling with the perspiration on his cheeks.

Claire reached her arm between the bucket seats to stroke his hair, damp with sweat. "You were dreaming, Jake. Hear me? It was just a bad dream."

Ruth's heart skipped a beat when she saw the Hornet pull off the pavement and onto the gravel driveway. Who was she kidding? With Hound gone, this party would never happen. From her position in front of the mailboxes, she forced a smile and waved to get Charlie's attention. He pulled over and rolled down his window.

"Hope you don't mind. We're a wee bit early." He took a sip from his thermos.

"Not at all. It's good to see you, but where are Jake and Claire?" Ruth's brow furrowed. Both the passenger and the backseat were vacant.

"They're down the road a bit. He had a bad dream on the way here and Claire thought if they talked it through, he'd be able to calm down before he saw his father. The dream had somethin' to do with him."

"Well, park in that space between my trailer and number 22. I'll help you unload. Then you and I can talk about what's gone on here. And what, if anything, the three of us can do to keep Jake from going ballistic."

Charlie scowled, rolled up his window, and steered the SUV down the narrow driveway. He opened the back hatch and removed a large cardboard box, grunting as he carried it up the steps and into the trailer.

He pushed several brightly colored helium balloons aside. "Ruth, the place looks great. He's gonna get the surprise of his life."

"Thanks. Decorating was fun. Anything in there that needs refrigerating?"

"Not really. Just fried chicken and some cornbread. And, of course, a little gift for the birthday boy—and girl." Charlie handed her a small box with a bright pink bow.

"Charlie, you shouldn't have. That will teach me not to confide in Claire anymore." She blushed at the unexpected attention. "But it is a nice surprise. I haven't had a gift in years."

"Claire said this was a very special occasion, and anyway, she hadn't been shoppin' in a while. When a woman says that, a man knows not to argue!" He grabbed a handful of jellybeans from the bowl on the kitchen table.

"Well, sit down. I'll get you a glass of lemonade. I'll open this when Jake and Claire get here." Her green eyes directed him to the sofa. She grinned as she placed her gift next to the others.

Charlie leaned to look down the short hallway. "So, where's Hound and Ethan? Out for a morning walk?"

Ruth handed the glass to Charlie and sat down on the leather ottoman in front of him. "That's what we need to talk about. This was on my dresser when I got home from work last night." She removed the envelope from her pocket and thrust it into his hand.

Charlie drained his glass, placing it on the small end table. He pulled his reading glasses out of his shirt pocket, slipped them onto his nose, and scanned the handwritten note. "That dang-blasted son-of-a-gun!" He rested his elbows on his knees, his head in his hands.

"Exactly. I don't think any of this we planned for today is going make up for what Jake will feel when he finds out his dog is gone." Her voice quivered with emotion as her nervous fingers twirled the collection of bangle bracelets on her wrist.

"You've got that right and——" Charlie looked up as the door slid open.

"Jake!" Ruth pushed aside a cascade of balloons.

"Hey, what's all this?" His eyes danced among the streamers and rested on Ruth's simple, homemade sign. He sounded out, "Hap-py bir-th-day, Jake." He looked from one adult to the other. "It's my birthday?"

"Yes, dear, and Ruth's done all of this for you." Claire's arms opened wide to encompass the festive room.

Jake grabbed Ruth and squeezed with all his might. "How did you know? I mean, is this really my birthday? Really and truly?"

Ruth directed him over to the sofa, sat down beside him, and began her well-practiced speech. "It really is your birthday. I know it is, because I was there when you were born—I think you already know that—but it was a very special day for me for another reason. You were born on *my* birthday. And, how could I ever forget a thing like that?" *Thank you, God, for a few minutes of happiness before he notices Hound is gone.* She braced herself for the inevitable.

He hugged her a second time. "Happy birthday, Ruth! You're really sure about all this?"

"Yes, I'm sure. I made a special cake, and we have some presents for you, too. And I am pleased to announce that you are officially ten years old!"

"Ten. How about that." He danced around the room, happiness written all over his face. "Hound, I—wait, where's Hound?" He dashed the short distance into the bedroom, coming back a moment later to three solemn faces. "He took Hound?" He raced toward the door and flung it open. He scrambled down the steps and across the small front yard.

Ruth turned to Claire. "I just knew it. He gets the worst possible news on what should be the happiest of days."

Charlie hustled out the door, down the steps, and tackled him as he headed for the road. "Come on, boy. They're long gone by now. And— I'm out of—wind. So—let's—go—on back—in. What do—ya say?"

"I—say 'get off me.' You're squishing—me—to death!" Jake choked out the words.

Charlie looked at him, nose-to-nose. "Promise not to run?"

Jake hesitated. "I promise." He jerked free, glaring at Charlie.

Charlie rolled over onto the grass and remained there—flat on his back.

Claire and Ruth rushed to Charlie. Each took an arm and helped him up, voicing their concern in unison. "Are you okay?"

"Yeah. I haven't moved—that fast in—years." Charlie chuckled and shook his head.

Claire turned her attention to Jake. "Honey, let's go inside and talk this out. Please."

Jake looked up at her. "He took my dog, Claire. I don't care what anybody says. Hound's meant to be with me!"

Jake stomped toward the trailer, kicking the door facing as he entered.

Following him, Claire turned back toward Ruth with a shrug and shook her head. "There are many years of anger built up in that boy. I'll try to keep him from destroying your house." She turned to Charlie. "Keep an ear out. I may be calling you for help."

"I can come with you now if you want."

Claire hesitated. "Thanks for the offer, but I don't want him to think we're all ganging up on him, especially in that tiny bedroom."

"Whatever you say, dumplin'. Why don't you leave the door open a smidgen, though."

"I will."

Ruth remained on the porch with Charlie. "Your elbow is cut, Charlie. Let me get something from my first-aid kit for that. You've got a lot of spunk for an old man. You're lucky to have come out of this with only a minor injury."

Forty-five minutes later, Charlie was sound asleep in the swing and Ruth was pacing across the colorful universe.

The *clomp, clomp* of Claire's clogs on the kitchen tile signaled her return. Joining them on the porch, she poked Charlie in the ribs.

"Hey—what—oh. It's you, sweet pea." Charlie sat up, moved to one side of the swing, and patted the space next to him. "How's he doin'?"

Claire sat down and snuggled close. "Cried himself to sleep. So much for learning to trust." She looked up at the darkening sky. "Looks like rain."

"I hope lightning strikes Ethan."

"Charlie Claiborne, what a thing to say." Claire frowned at her husband.

"I know. I know." He bit his lip. "But, how can another human bein' be so cruel—and to his own son?"

"Well, that's the thing, Charlie." Ruth moved onto the footstool in front of the couple. "He doesn't believe Jake is his son. Oh, he did at first—and he really was a good dad—but one day he found his wife and my husband together. He went into a terrible rage. A few minutes later, they were both dead."

Charlie pounded his fist down on the arm of the swing. "He... killed them?"

Ruth nodded, her eyes flooding with tears. "He said he'd done us both a favor. He said he'd kill me, too, if I told anyone. I believed him."

"You poor dear." Claire opened the door, reached inside for the box of tissues on the kitchen counter, and offered one to Ruth.

"I'll never forgive myself for leaving. Believe me, if I had ever thought he would hurt Jake, I would have taken that child with me."

Claire's smile quivered as she pressed another tissue into Ruth's hand. "There's no telling what dreadful things he's done to that boy. But, don't blame yourself for any of it. You couldn't have known what he would do."

Charlie narrowed his eyes. "Wait a minute. If he doesn't believe Jake's his child, then who does he think his *real* father is?"

"Sam. My husband, " Ruth whispered.

Claire's shaky voice broke the intense silence. "Then you'd be his next of kin."

A smile flooded Ruth's face. "That very thought occurred to me this morning. I mean, I'm not a *blood* relative, but I might be the closest thing to one he's ever going to have."

"This could be wonderful news for you both." Charlie's face glowed with the possibility. "I don't know a lot about these things. There's probably no way to confirm a link between them. I'm assumin' Sam's buried somewhere out in the woods." His shoulders drooped.

Ruth's face lit in a slow smile. "But, we can get our answer by doing simple DNA testing of Jake and Ethan."

She turned to Claire, standing at the far end of the porch alone, her shoulders quaking.

Charlie and Claire rode home in silence. He tried to talk to his bride, but she just turned her head to look out the passenger window into the blackness of the late summer night. *Women. Got to love 'em. Got to somehow live with 'em. But, I guess I'll never understand 'em.*

"No stars out tonight. That's real unusual." Charlie pulled the Hornet under the carport. "Watch your step. I'll go around and turn on the light so you can see where you're goin'."

Claire bolted from the car, making her way across the lawn to the steps of the cabin. She was inside in a flash, leaving Charlie alone to weave through the maze of Jake's outdoor toys.

Once inside, Charlie lumbered down the hall only to face a closed bedroom door. "Claire, you could've fallen. Why didn't you wait for me to turn on the light? You're the sweetest, most stubborn woman I've ever met. I wish you wouldn't clam up. I can't even think of what could've sent you into a tizzy like that."

"Oh, a tizzy now, is it?" Claire retorted from the other side of the door.

"Now, dad gum it, I need to know what's botherin' you. You can't give me the silent treatment without so much as a clue as to what I've done."

"It's not so much *what* you've done. It's just how things *are*." A moment later, she opened the door a crack.

"Sweetcakes, please let me in. We ought never to close the door on one another, you know?" Charlie dropped his head and sighed.

Claire opened the door the rest of the way and fell into his arms. "You're right, of course. You're always right."

He held her as she cried it out. Then he guided her to sit on the foot of their bed. He dabbed her eyes with his checkered handkerchief. "I'll be right back with a glass of water."

When he returned from the kitchen, he placed the glass into her still-shaking hands. "Take a sip and then see if you can help me understand why you're so upset, pumpkin." He sat down beside her, waiting while she not only drained the glass, but also blew her nose.

"It's Jake," she began, with a catch in her throat.

"Is it somethin' he said, or did, when you had your little talk back at Ruth's?"

"No, Charlie. It's that he's never going to be *ours*." She looked up at him with puffy eyes.

"So, that's it. Hon, listen, we talked about this before. Remember? We said if The Bureau for Children and Families would let us keep Jake a while longer, then with Ethan's permission, we would. But, that time is long past and—"

"I know," Claire interrupted. "But the time went by so quickly and now we're bonding, don't you think? And it would be a shame for Jake to have to go into foster care now."

"That's what I was afraid of. Here we go again, sweet pea. I told you it would be harder the longer we kept him. And here's the proof." He took her hands in his, astonished by their softness.

"Couldn't the news about him maybe bein' Sam's child be a *good* thing? Why, if it turns out he *is*, maybe Ruth will want to take him. See how this can be so much better than havin' him go to foster care where we might never get to see him again? I think we've formed a good enough relationship with Ruth that we'd be able to still be a part of the boy's life."

She looked deep into his eyes. "It could work out that way—if he's Sam's child."

Chapter 14

The morning after Ethan fled with Hound, he stood in front of the new "Dog Docs" veterinary office with the want ads from the local newspaper under his arm. He hated to lower himself to a vet tech position, but a job was a job. An elderly lady with bluish-gray hair held open the glass door for him. "Thank you. You're very kind."

He pushed the black metal glasses he'd purchased at the dollar store upward and onto the bridge of his nose with his forefinger. Not quite the right fit for his face, but the price was right. He slicked down his newly dyed black hair, dark residue remaining on his palms.

"Mr. Havens?" A petite young woman with a nose ring and long blonde hair smiled at him from behind the modern glass-topped desk. Her eyes dropped to stare in the direction of his missing appendage.

"That's me." Ethan scowled when she handed him a clipboard and a pen topped with a bright red flower made from pipe cleaners.

"Please fill out all four pages of the application and return it to me. You'll be given a brief interview when it's your turn."

"Thanks." He took the last chair available in the crowded waiting room. Open just two days and business is already booming. He looked down at the application. This was a total waste of his time. Half of the questions could be eliminated—or at least delayed—until a person was hired. He made up a fictitious list, including next of kin, last known address, and references. He supplied Sam's driver's license number. *Thanks, Sam, old boy. First, your knife and cabin. Now, your identity.*

Once the paperwork was turned in, he checked to make sure Hound remained in his "stay" position next to a large bush out front. His previous seat, stolen by an elderly gentleman with a cane, made it necessary for him to find a new place to sit. This time he found a vacant chair opposite an attractive woman in a blue suit and black patent heels.

No names had been called in the last fifteen minutes. It might be a long afternoon. He brushed stray hairs off of his stolen shirt, cleared his throat, and leaned toward the thirty-something female. "I notice from your name tag that you're a Realtor. Would you possibly know of anything for rent near here?"

"What is it you're interested in?" She stroked the head of a Maltese wearing a jeweled collar.

"I'd prefer a house. Something furnished, fenced and allows pets."

Her blue eyes sparkled as she turned her attention toward him. "I may have just the thing for you. It's an older home, though, and not exactly in the best condition. But, the rent is reasonable. Always glad to help out a fellow pet lover."

"Do you have a card?"

"A Realtor always has a card." After rummaging around in her over-sized purse, she produced one, smiling through ruby red lips framing perfect white teeth.

He grabbed it from her. A line drawing of a Victorian home was on the front along with her picture. "You're even more lovely in person."

"Ashley Farmington and Monique." A heavy-set young man wearing "Dog Docs" scrubs tapped his clipboard against the desktop.

Ashley picked up her dog and followed him toward the door marked "Exam 1."

She grinned goodbye, followed by an almost imperceptible wink.

"Sam Havens, you may go into the interview room, now. First door to your left."

Ethan reached for his crutches. *Hi, I'm Sam Havens...Hello, my name is Sam Havens...Hi, I'm Sam...Hey, Sam's the name. How' ya doin'?*

For the third day that week, Charlie drove to one of the towns on his list and spent the afternoon posting composite drawings of Ethan on tree trunks, light poles, and the sides of buildings. That guy didn't just drop off the end of the earth. Someone just had to recognize him from a flyer and give them a call.

He put the extra copies into his knapsack along a roll of masking tape and headed toward the Town Center parking lot. He reached onto the backseat of his SUV to retrieve the lunch Claire had packed and plopped down on a concrete bench next to the duck pond.

"Mind if I join you?" asked a short man with thick bifocals and a red handlebar mustache.

"Not at all. There's more than enough room."

"Robert Kenworthy." The man smiled as he held out his hand to shake Charlie's.

"Charles Claiborne. Folks call me Charlie."

"I haven't seen you around here before, Charlie." Robert raised a bushy eyebrow at Charlie as he surveyed his bright yellow SUV.

"I haven't been here before. Just puttin' up some flyers around town is all."

"Like that one at the entrance down there?"

"Yep. A guy we need to identify."

"Amnesia?"

Charlie wrinkled his nose. "Excuse me?"

"I mean, was the guy in an accident of some sort and can't remember who he is?"

"No. I think *he* knows who he is, all right."

"So you're a private detective? Trying to find him for a jealous wife, or such?"

"More along those lines." Charlie opened his lunch bag, retrieving a turkey and cheese sandwich on whole wheat. It would be too complicated to explain.

An overweight teenage girl approached the men just as he took his first bite. She gave Robert a playful peck on his cheek. "Gramps, we need to get going pretty soon. I have to leave for work at twelve-thirty and it's a good ways from here."

"Okay. Let me finish my lunch. Sure you don't want anything to eat?"

"Not really." The girl sat on the thick grass in front of the men and crossed her legs.

Robert turned toward Charlie, a proud smile on his face. "Charlie, this is my granddaughter, Trina."

Charlie swallowed. "Nice to meet you." He looked down at the girl, temporarily distracted by her bright purple hair and what looked to be a dog collar around her neck.

"What's that?" Trina nodded toward the flyer lying on the bench between the two men.

"A flyer with a guy's picture on it." Robert smiled at his grand-daughter.

"I can see that, Grandpa. I mean, what's it for?"

"Just a guy we're tryin' to find." Charlie held up the drawing. "Look familiar?"

Trina slapped her hands against her cheeks. "It's him!"

"You know him?" He let his sandwich fall onto his lap.

"He's the guy from the market—a customer from a couple of days ago."

"Trina, please tell me anything you can remember. It might be very helpful." Charlie wiped a large blob of mayo from his chin.

"I don't remember much, really, except he was very weird. He made the hair on my arms stand up."

From the looks of it, that wasn't the only hair standing up. "Did he have a dog with him?"

"Not that I saw. But, he had one leg and was on crutches."

Charlie let out a deep sigh of relief. "Yep. That's him. Can you think of anythin' else?"

"Um, not really." She pulled herself up to a standing position, brushing pieces of moist grass from her jeans.

"Well, if you do, please call me. My number is there at the bottom of the flyer." He gritted his teeth. *I'll find Ethan, yet. And he'll wish he was still stuck under that tree.*

❦

Ethan threw his prepaid cell phone across the room, shattering the dresser mirror and sending slivers of glass in all directions. He couldn't believe it. They hired an acne-faced teenager instead of someone that actually knew something about animals. He crumpled the want ads and threw the newspaper into the wastebasket. It was a good thing he had accepted the job at Pepperoni's as a backup. Just imagine. An educated vet making pizzas!

He lay down on the queen-sized bed in his second-floor room at the Cozy Pines Lodge. A breeze drifting through the open window brought appetizing smells of fried chicken from the take-out restaurant across the street. Three crumpled bills remained on the nightstand.

He looked at his bare foot and then at the glass covering the thin carpet. *Idiot!*

His heart double beat. The shards were tantalizing…promising. He reached over to pick one up and examine it in the sunlight. He raised his shirt, running its sharp edge across his abdomen. He laid his head back. Droplets of blood ran across his belly and onto the pale blue sheet.

The Hornet screeched around the corner and rolled to a stop in front of the library. Charlie hung his head out the open window "Goin' my way, doll?" That woman still made his heart go pitter-pat.

Claire smiled and rolled her eyes as she opened the door and slid into the comfortable leather seat. "I hope your afternoon was more productive than mine."

"Couldn't find anythin'?" Charlie gave her cheek a hurried peck.

"I searched through class lists and pictures from all of the veterinary schools in the eastern half of the United States. I'm afraid I'm going to have to look at schools farther away. I knew this wouldn't be easy."

"Well, I've got some good news!" He pulled into the cross-town traffic.

She brightened. "Really?"

"Well, I was startin' to eat my turkey sandwich—which, by the way, was really delicious. Thank you, pumpkin. Anyway, a guy asked to share my bench and, even though I wanted some time alone to think, I didn't want to be rude, so I said, 'sure.' He asked me about the flyer and I—"

"Charlie, please!" Her face reddened, her jaw set.

"I'm gettin' to it. I'm gettin' to it, honey bun. So, in the middle of our conversation, his granddaughter, Trina, no Tina, maybe Gina—oh well, it's not important—joined him. She took a look at the flyer—"

"Charlie, what does she have to do with anything?" She grabbed large clumps of her hair and faked pulled.

"She recognized Ethan. She saw him in the grocery store where she works just a few days ago. That means he's managed to put himself at least ten miles further down the road." Charlie's eyes danced in the waning sunlight.

"Did she have any information like a name or address or anything else to go on?"

"Nope. Afraid not."

She grabbed the map from the dashboard. "Still, it tells us he's headed northwest."

At one o'clock the day following his "Dog Docs" interview, Ethan leaned his crutches against the wall, sat down on the wobbly steps in back of Pepperoni's, and used his apron to wipe his face. He had already put in four hours—four of the longest hours of his life. And that included the hours he'd spent pinned under the apple tree. He removed his shoe and massaged his foot before raising his shirt to examine the painful chafing of his armpits. This was a job of minimum wage and maximum torture.

Pepper Johnson, the owner's son, stuck his head out the door. "Break time's over, Sam. We've got a lot of take-out orders piling up."

"I just sat down. Break is supposed to be fifteen minutes." His nostrils flared, hot anger just below the surface.

"I said break time's over, Sam."

"If I was a smoker, I wouldn't have even had time to light up!" He stared at the thunderclouds forming on the horizon, doubtful that he and Pepper were ever going to see eye-to-eye on this.

"Well, it's a good thing you're not a smoker then, isn't it?" Pepper stroked his long braided beard.

"Listen, I've been on the move for four hours. My whole body aches. I need my full break, man." He thrust his chest out, challenging the nineteen-year-old.

"This is the last time I'm telling ya. Get your tush off the steps. Put on a hair net and get back to work. If you're not back in the kitchen in two minutes, consider yourself fired." The boy spit into a leafy shrub and went back inside, letting the door slam behind him.

Ethan remained on the steps, rocking back and forth, his rage building. He clenched and unclenched his fists as he cursed under his breath. No punk kid was going to tell him what to do, owner's son or not. He would *give* orders—not take them—from anyone.

———

Ruth pulled off her scrubs and settled into a nice hot bath. She had worked a double shift, and was dead tired. On the drive home, she had thought of little else than the possibility of being a parent. It would be a hard job, but Jake really needed stability—

A loud knock at the door startled her. She grabbed a towel, and then her robe. Charlie and Claire were already standing inside the living room by the time she rounded the corner.

"Sorry to stop by unannounced, but we wanted to share the news in person."

Charlie helped himself to a glass of iced tea from the refrigerator. "We were just so excited."

"You shouldn't leave your door unlocked, you know," Claire chided.

"I'll remember that." Ruth finished tying her sash. "So, does this mean you have good news? Did someone call about the posters?"

Charlie scooped up a handful of jelly beans from the candy dish and jumped ahead with his story. "You see, I was about to bite into my sandwich, when this girl—"

Claire broke in. "A cashier at a supermarket about ten miles up the road from here saw Ethan a few days ago."

"That's great! We're getting closer." Ruth motioned Claire toward the sofa.

"She didn't know anything more, but she recognized him. Gave a good description. He's our guy, all right." Claire picked up Ethan's note from the coffee table, reading it for the first time while Charlie rummaged through the refrigerator for a snack.

"So, where would you like to eat?" He managed to say a few words between bites of a raw hot dog.

Silence.

He turned toward the sofa. "Dumplin'?"

Claire looked up from the paper with glazed eyes. Her hands trembled as she let it fall to the floor.

"Precious, what's wrong?" He crossed the room and offered her a sip of his iced tea. He squeezed her hand before bending over to pick up the note.

"What's upsetting you so?" Ruth sat down by Claire, placing an arm around her shoulders.

"Look at it closely, you two. He left a huge clue. I'm astonished you didn't see it before."

Charlie read aloud. "I know you…blah, blah…so I'm moving on… blah, blah, blah…There's no way I'm going *back* to—prison." His jaw fell open. "Well, I'll be. Now tell me, Ruth, how did the two of us ever miss that?"

Ruth's eyes widened. "*Back* to Prison. We just read right over it. That one word makes all the difference. Now that we know he's got a record, we'll have no problem finding out who he really is."

They were all bound together in a group hug when the door opened.

"What are you guys doing?" Jake chuckled as he headed for the refrigerator.

"It's called a group hug. Just a way of celebrating—" Charlie shut his mouth in response to a hard look from Claire.

Jake turned back toward them, a cluster of grapes in his hand. "What are you guys celebrating? Did you find Hound?"

"No, buddy, not yet." Charlie closed his eyes and shook his head.

Jake's smile faded. "So, then, what's that group hug all about?"

"Ah, well, um Claire and I met each other a year ago, today. Good reason to celebrate, don't you think?" Charlie grinned.

"I guess so. Sure." Jake shrugged, rubbing the back of his neck. "I already ate at Eric's. He wanted me to ask if I can go firefly catching when it gets dark."

Ruth tousled his hair, "Absolutely. Do you need a jar?"

Jake nodded. "This one okay?" He picked up an empty mayonnaise jar from the pantry shelf.

"That's fine. Make sure Eric's mom supervises when you make the holes in the lid. And remember to tell her 'thank you' for letting you spend the day over there, today."

Jake popped a grape in his mouth. "I'll spend next week with you guys, right?"

"We can't wait," the Claiborne's answered.

"Okay, then. Group hug!" Jake shouted.

—∞∞∞—

Ethan stormed into Pepperoni's and threw his apron at Pepper. "Give me my salary and I'm out of here."

"Whoa, 'salary'? What kind of vocabulary is that for a lowly pizza cook?" Pepper curled his lip.

"You have no idea who you're talking to, sonny." Ethan edged toward the open cash register, pushing the cashier out of the way. He raised the clip securing the twenties.

"Oh, really? I think I'm talkin' to a guy that just got himself fired." Pepper maneuvered around a stack of pizza boxes and shoved the drawer closed, smashing Ethan's fingers.

"Son of a—" he yelled as a searing pain traveled from his fingers up his arm.

The room went silent. The two other pizza cooks backed away, abandoning a Pepperoni's Special on the prep counter. Sheila, the cashier, left the phone dangling from the wall and scurried out the front door.

Pepper narrowed his eyes at Ethan, put up his fists, and squared his shoulders. "Go ahead. Bring it."

He wiggled his bleeding fingers. "Gladly." He'd seen Pepper's posters plastered all over the place. He might be planning on showing off his boxing skills, but Ethan would just use some old-fashioned ingenuity.

Pepper frowned at the cooks. "What are you standin' there for? Get the cops. I've got this under control."

As the pair scrambled out the front door, Pepper turned his attention back to Ethan just as he raised a crutch. It connected with Pepper's cheek with a loud *crack*.

Spitting out a single tooth, the teenager advanced toward him with everything he had, ramming into the end of the crutch with his stomach when Ethan raised it toward him. "Augh!" Pepper fell back onto the floor, pressed his elbows to his sides, and drew up his legs.

"What a wuss! Those posters are a joke." He gave Pepper's back one more jab with his crutch, snatched the twenties, and escaped out the backdoor. He hobbled down the alley to his motel room where he grabbed his knapsack and woke Hound from a sound sleep.

"Let's go, boy. We've got to get out of here. Now!"

Hound jumped up and followed him down the alley and into the field behind the motel. When Ethan heard the faint sound of sirens behind him, he dropped down, hiding in the tall weeds A string of patrol cars threw up dusty clouds as they rushed toward the pizza parlor.

Chapter 15

Charlie stretched as he got up from his recliner. Nothing but bad news on the tube. He clicked off the television. If Claire had managed to dig up some information about Ethan, now that would brighten the day for sure. He lumbered to the door to greet her. "Any news?"

Claire shook her head and planted a kiss on his lips en route to the refrigerator. "Not really. We need the inmate's last name or his department of corrections number in order to do a database search."

"And we don't have either of those." *Maybe we should contact America's Most Wanted.*

"We don't even know which state to search." Claire poured herself a glass of iced tea and took a seat at the kitchen table.

"How far back do those records go, do ya think?" Charlie closed the blinds, blocking out the late afternoon sun, and sat down across from Claire.

"They said fifteen years in some states. Twenty in others."

Charlie flinched as he noticed the time on the clock. "Oops! You need to hurry if you're gonna freshen up. I told Jake we'd get him from

Ruth's by six o'clock and go out for pizza. You don't mind havin' it again this week, do you?" Charlie turned a hopeful face toward his bride.

"I'm kind of getting tired of pizza, to tell you the truth. We just had it two days ago, if you count the one from that Take 'n Bake place you brought home." Claire rifled through the stack of restaurant coupons stacked on the Lazy Susan. She looked up in response to Charlie's silence and raised both of her hands in surrender. "But I know how kids—and men—are." Claire replaced the coupons and hurried toward the bedroom, a wry smile playing on her lips.

Charlie called after her as he finished off his tea at the kitchen table. "I thought we'd try some place different. I heard there's a good pizza parlor up near Clarksburg. Has a salad bar." That would clinch the deal. Claire was a sucker for salad bars.

The sun was ablaze on the horizon when a light drizzle of rain started to fall. Ethan pulled the collar of his Pepperoni's shirt up around his neck. His pulse quickened at the sound of a helicopter overhead. He might not have much of a chance against that kind of manpower. He ushered Hound between two narrow buildings, melting into the shadows.

A sudden clap of thunder sent Hound to look for safety next to him. Ethan allowed himself to enjoy a fleeting sensation of affection for his companion before he nudged him away. "You're still on my bad list, buddy."

The drizzle escalated into a shower, and soon the shower became a thunderous downpour. He cursed under his breath. As darkness dropped over the rooftops, he felt the tenseness in his shoulders begin to ease. He might be able to elude the authorities after all.

He pulled a flashlight from his knapsack. He clicked it on and used it to guide them to shelter inside an abandoned train tunnel.

Hound whimpered.

"No food, Hound. You haven't suffered enough for your transgressions. But you will, my friend. That you will." His lower lip curled up on one side. He tore open a packet of stolen jerky, moaning with delight as he ate each piece.

Hound tilted his head, his sad eyes looking up at him.

Ethan hesitated before sharing the last bite.

<hr />

The parking lot at Pepperoni's Pizza was lined with two Police cruisers, a fire truck, and an ambulance. The rain had stopped, but the darkness and the blinking caution lights provided mysterious overtones to an otherwise uneventful day.

"What's going on?" Jake rolled down the passenger window and hung his head outside. The tall gray house had a large wraparound porch and trellises laden with twisted vines. "Are you sure this is a pizza place? It looks like it belongs to the Adams Family."

Claire put her hands over her mouth, her shoulders heaving as she laughed. "Jake, you're definitely watching too much television. This isn't a haunted house. It's a lovely old Victorian home with a lot of character. Many older houses are being bought by businesses and renovated nowadays."

The large windows framed silhouettes of people hurrying back and forth. Thunder cracked overhead, signaling more rain for the coming hours.

"The sign on the door says 'Closed' but there are people in there." Big Charlie reached over the seat for his ball cap.

"What's happening?" Jake's nose made a print against the Hornet's window.

"Stay here and I'll find out." Big Charlie bolted from the car, making his way through the growing crowd.

"Once a newshound, always a newshound." Claire shook her head and chuckled.

Jake hung over the seat. "What do you mean? What's a newshound?"

"A newshound is an enthusiastic journalist or reporter—someone who digs up interesting stories for newspapers, magazines, or television. Charlie was a field reporter for six or seven years back in Texas. That was just one of the many jobs he's had over the years. I think it was his favorite, though. You might say he still has a 'nose for news.'"

Jake rolled onto the backseat, laughing. "Now I understand. He's kind of like Hound, then. Charlie digs up *stories* and Hound digs up *bones*."

Claire held her sides and bent over, giggling like a schoolgirl. "Oh, Jake. Only you could have said that."

"Well, I don't want to miss out on the fun. I'm going, too." Jake leaped out of the car, sprinted across the lawn, and skipped up the steps to the veranda, two at a time. He put his hands against the glass and peered inside. "It looks like we're gonna miss the pizza, but we're here in time for all of the hullabaloo, Charlie."

"What's goin' on, here?" Big Charlie asked a teenage boy to his left.

"Some guy assaulted the manager."

"That's terrible. Must be why the ambulance is here." Big Charlie motioned for Jake to follow him as he approached an officer just exiting the building. "You can stay, Jake, but don't get in the way."

"You folks aren't getting any pizza tonight. Break it up, now, and let these people clean up this place so they can be back in business to-morrow." Without answering any of the questions shouted to him, the officer went back inside and shut the door.

Big Charlie and Jake started down the steps, walking toward a large group of people assembled on the east side of the building. Jake jumped up and down, trying to look past the sea of bodies in front of him. Big Charlie grunted as he grabbed him under his arms, lifted him off the ground, and deposited him on top of the recycle bin.

"Don't be gettin' down from there, 'cause you're too heavy for this old man to lift again. And get that hood up over your head. You want to catch your death of cold?"

"Thanks, Charlie. Now I've got the best view in the house!" Jake pulled the hood over his shaggy hair.

"You stay put." Charlie sauntered over to a policeman talking to a guy on a stretcher underneath a parking awning.

"Please just describe his appearance. I don't need to hear the part about the assault again." The officer tapped his pencil against his note-pad, a hint of impatience in his voice.

The guy on the stretcher, face bruised and eyes swollen, remained silent. He seemed more intent on the constant flexing of his biceps than providing any useful information.

The officer leaned forward, nose-to-nose with the guy on the stretcher. "How much money did you say he took?"

"Sixt—" supplied a brown-haired girl standing at the foot of the stretcher.

"Hundred. Yeah. Six-hundred dollars." The victim smirked, giving her a hard look.

She cleared her throat. "Yeah, that's about right."

The officer rolled his eyes. "Could we try for that description just one more time?"

The teenager brought an ice pack up to his cheek. "About six feet tall. Black hair. Blue eyes. On crutches. Arrogant. Can't cook."

"Thanks. Finally some useful information." The police officer jotted down the facts on his notepad and then retreated back inside the restaurant.

Charlie steered a kid in a yellow slicker out of his path and moved closer to the stretcher. "Did you say somethin' about crutches?"

"Yeah. The guy beat me with them!" The victim narrowed his eyes at Charlie.

"Anythin' you can add to that description?" Charlie leaned in closer. He had to be talking about Ethan. "It's important. I may know him."

The victim raised up on one elbow. "You sure don't have very nice friends."

Charlie exploded at him. "I said I might know him. I didn't say we were friends."

Charlie and Pepper exchanged glances.

"One leg. The guy's only got one leg."

Charlie extended his hand in greeting. "I'm Charlie Claiborne. Sorry if I came on a little too strong there. It's just that I've been lookin' for this guy for a long time."

"No harm. No foul. My name's Pepper. My pop owns this place."

"You're lucky to be alive. We have reason to believe the guy's an escaped felon."

Feet crunched on the gravel driveway. "What's a f-felon?"

⸰⸰⸰

Ruth dragged herself into room #330 a few minutes before the stroke of midnight. She was unprepared for the battered face of her patient. Two black eyes indicated a broken nose. A jagged gash on his chin had already received stitches. "Wow. What happened to you?" She scanned the information the chart. "Pepper, is it?"

He nodded as he swallowed a spoonful of Jell-O. "Assaulted."

"There's nothing on your chart about bullet wounds." Ruth walked over to his bedside.

"I didn't get shot. The guy beat me." Pepper pounded his fist on his pillow.

"With a sledgehammer?" Ruth picked up his bruised wrist and found his pulse.

"No. Believe it or not, he did all of this with his crutches." Pepper jerked his arm away.

Ruth winced. "What did he look like?" She grasped his wrist again, and pulled it toward her.

"Ouch!" Pepper shook his head. "Why is everyone interested in what *he* looked like? I was the victim here."

Ruth scribbled on the chart. "It's just that I know a guy on crutches who has a terrible temper."

Pepper's eyes widened. "Early forties? One leg?"

"Yes. Where were you when this happened?"

"At Pepperoni's. It's a pizza place my dad owns. I'm the manager." He shot Ruth a smug smile.

"So, all this happened today?" Ruth removed the empty I.V. bag.

"This afternoon."

"Just where is this Pepperoni's?" Ruth hung a new I.V. bag and injected the pain medication.

"About five miles northwest of here, in Clarksburg."

Ruth headed for the door. "I'll be back in a few minutes with something for that high blood pressure." Of all the days to have to work a double shift and miss the evening news. Claire and Charlie always watched it, though. She'd give them a call.

———∞∞∞———

Charlie pulled Jake's bedroom door closed and crept into the living room to join Claire on the sofa. "He's finally asleep. It's plain to see the kid needs some counselin'." He ran his hand over his head. "I shouldn't have opened my big mouth. It was me that set the whole meltdown in motion."

Claire rubbed Charlie's back. "I'll make some phone calls in the morning and get a few recommendations for someone who specializes in children's abuse issues. We've buried our heads in the sand long enough."

He felt himself relax. "Thanks for the rub. I didn't realize I was so tense."

"You're welcome." She kissed his cheek, and then added, "You know, it might not hurt if you talked with someone yourself."

He jerked his head toward her. "Me? What for?"

"I know you've felt bad about not wanting Jake to stay with us much longer, and now you feel responsible for starting this whole incident. None of us can know which things will trigger memories and which won't. You need to extend the same grace you give to others and not be so hard on yourself. You're a good man. Anyone who says you're not will have to deal with me."

He kissed her tenderly on the lips. "I appreciate the confidence, even if it's not deserved."

She shook her head. "See, there you go again."

"All right, all right." His big hand folded around hers. Everyone needs a champion. She was his. No doubt about it.

"What really happened out there anyway? All I could see from the car was Jake running toward me. He was going on and on about his father trying to kill someone at the pizza parlor."

"Well, I suppose he might have tried to kill Pepper under other circumstances. But, it sounds like all he really wanted was to grab the money and get away as fast as he could. Let's pray he won't kill again. Bein' on the run, there's no tellin' what he might do—and to who."

"So, Ethan was at Pepperoni's tonight?"

"No, but it sounds like he'd been workin' there and got in a fight with his boss earlier in the afternoon. Beat him up pretty bad, too." Charlie's yawn was long and loud.

Claire grabbed both of his hands. "So, what sent Jake into a frenzy then? Ethan was gone by the time we arrived, right?"

"Right. I left Jake a hundred feet or so away while I closed in on a policeman that was interrogatin' the manager. I told him I'd be back for him and to stay where he was. I kept an eye on him from where I was standin'. From that distance, he wouldn't have been able to hear what was said."

"So, why did he get so upset then?" Claire's wary frown punctuated her question.

"I suppose he got tired of waitin', so he snuck up behind me. When he saw the guy's injuries and heard me talkin' about his father, he must've thought he was in the restaurant right then and there. Probably thought that one of us was next on Ethan's hit list."

Claire stood up and stretched. "It's hard to know, really, what's going on in someone else's head. He's probably seen—and even experienced—a lot of awful things in his short life. The conclusions he draws aren't always going to make sense to us, but a good counselor will be able to help him figure things out." She nodded toward the refrigerator. "Would a nice piece of apple pie and ice cream make you feel better? We didn't really get any supper, you know."

"No, thanks. Let's just get some shut-eye. It's almost one o'clock and this old man is tired." As Charlie rose from his chair, a flashing light on the recorder caught his attention. "We've got a message. I don't know why I didn't notice before." He pushed the *play* button.

"It's Ruth. If you don't know by now, Ethan's on the run from a fight with a restaurant manager in Clarksburg. He's actually one of my patients—the restaurant guy, not Ethan—and he filled me in on the whole thing. Call me if you want more details. Actually, I'd appreciate it if you'd give me a call anyway, and let me know you're all okay."

Charlie shook his head and looked up at Claire. "With all the excitement, I plum forgot about Ruth. I wish I'd thought to call her."

"Well, it's too late now. We'll have to get in touch with her first thing in the morning." She picked up her shoes from underneath the coffee table and headed for the bedroom.

Charlie spooned coffee into the old coffee pot, and set the timer on it to perk at six a.m. The whole town would be looking for Ethan by tomorrow. There would be nowhere for him to hide.

Chapter 16

*E*than waited across the street from the The End of the Road Motel as a hunched-over man with large spectacles placed an "open" sign in the office window. He roused Hound from his morning nap. "Let's go, boy."

He dropped three twenties on the counter, signed the register, and produced Sam's I.D. for photocopying. After leading Hound down the cracked and crumbling exterior walkway to room #20, he fanned the air in the dank space before pulling the string to turn on the single light bulb dangling overhead.

As his eyes adjusted to the dimness of the room, he surveyed the soiled wallpaper and worn carpet. The thin bedspread revealed a bow in the middle. He shook his head. Sixty bucks down the drain. He shouldn't complain, though. He'd lived for years in a lot worse conditions than these. And, anyway, the marquee said there was nothing else for the next forty miles...

Hound curled up on the floor next to the nightstand as Ethan shuffled toward the bathroom. The shower was small, but looked clean enough. He turned on the water and waited for it to get hot. The pipes whistled for the next few minutes, as he stood on the uneven tile and let the warmth of the water flow over his head and shoulders. Dark black water covered his foot and then ran down the slow-moving drain.

As he left the bathroom, he grabbed a white towel from the rack, using it to soak up the excess hair dye. Now the dang thing looked like a spotted leopard.

He sat on the edge of the bed and fiddled with the remote control for the television. It would be surprising if the TV even worked.

All of a sudden, the thing shot to life. An old episode of The Lone Ranger was on. It had been years since he'd seen a television show. He propped up his pillow, leaned back against the headboard, and massaged his leg.

Thirty minutes later, the local station interrupted the show with "Breaking News." The report focused on the "Pepperoni's Incident," complete with a hospital interview of the victim. It concluded by showing a sketch artist's amazing likeness of Ethan along with a reporter's description: "The suspect has blue eyes, black hair in a ponytail, and a full beard. He has one leg and uses crutches for mobility. He is approximately six feet tall and weighs one hundred sixty pounds. He goes by the name of Sam Havens and is traveling with a large brown dog answering to the name of 'Hound.' If you have any information on the whereabouts of this person, please call the sheriff's office."

He clicked off the television and rummaged in his bag for a razor. As he headed for the bathroom, he worked his stiff fingers back and forth. It was a miracle they weren't broken.

His stomach growled. He dressed, motioned for Hound to stay, and then left the room.

He caught a glimpse of a dark-haired woman as he passed by room #21. Her warm brown eyes met his as she walked toward the open door. "Hi."

"Hello." Ethan scrutinized her features in the dim morning light. Smooth white skin, slender waist, long legs in tight jeans.

"Kind of a dump, isn't it? I'm Lara, the housekeeper for these twenty-four exquisite rooms." She chuckled.

Ethan joined in with a good-humored laugh. "I'm Joshua. Just passing through." What was he thinking? He hadn't used his real name in years!

"Well, Joshua. It's nice to meet you." She flashed a big smile, revealing perfect white teeth.

His face felt hot. Was he actually blushing? "Um, could you recommend anywhere to eat around here?"

"There aren't any restaurants, but there's a small grocery over on the next corner."

"I guess that's where I'll head then. Maybe I'll see you later." He started off in the direction of the store.

Lara called after him. "Tell you what, if you'll buy a pound of bacon and some eggs, I have bread and orange juice. I could make us breakfast, if you'd like."

He squeezed his eyes shut. Had he heard her right? "You're offering to make me breakfast? That would be the first real meal I've had in who knows how long."

"I've got an hour before I have to start cleaning, so hurry right back." She winked as she shut the door.

He was glad he'd shaved off his beard and washed his hair. He used to be quite good looking—at least Ginnie had told him so. He whistled as he headed for the market.

Twenty minutes later, he was back at Lara's door with a plastic grocery bag dangling from his wrist.

She took the bag and turned to mute the T.V.

"Sorry that took so long. There were a lot of customers in there this morning. And, of course, I'm not the fastest these days." He hobbled inside and looked around. "No stove?"

"You'd be surprised at what a person can cook on a hot plate. Make yourself comfortable in my one and only chair over there. Looks like you picked up some extra items. Butter, jelly…" She set the bag down and picked up the coffeepot. "I started a pot of coffee. Would you like some?"

"Sure."

Her hands trembled as she poured the hot liquid into a cup with a small chip on the rim and handed it to him.

"Thanks. I can't tell you how long it's been since I had a fresh cup of coffee handed to me by a pretty lady first thing in the morning." *What's making this girl so nervous?* He flashed his most charming of smiles.

She opened the door to the outside, inhaled the early morning air, and returned to place slices of bacon in a small cast iron skillet.

"Expecting someone?" He wouldn't be surprised if a girl this attractive had guys dropping by all the time.

"No, why?"

"Well, you left the door open…"

"I just need some fresh air, especially when the skillet gets hot." She broke a half-dozen eggs into a small bowl, glanced at the television, then turned back toward him.

"You seem nervous." He explored the odd expression on her face. *She's acting like a lovesick teenager.*

"No—I mean, I guess I haven't entertained many men—any men— in my room before. Maybe I am just a little nervous. You understand."

"Of course." He'd give the girl a break, let her warm up to him— put her at ease before… He shook the thoughts from his head. "Have you worked here long?"

"Almost a year. This is part-time. I'm also a receptionist two days a week for a doctor in the high rise next to the hospital. You said you're just passing through. In a hurry somewhere?"

"You never know. I might find a reason to stay around awhile." He grinned, and then blew on his coffee before taking a sip.

Her face turned crimson. "I'm going to night school to finish my bachelor's degree. This is my last semester. I hope to get a teaching job after I graduate."

"Good for you. The kids will be lucky to have you." He just might get lucky, too...

"Scrambled okay?" She waited for his reply, a fork poised above the bowl.

"I'll like them any way you fix them." He raked his tongue along his lips.

She whisked the eggs and then poured them into the hot skillet vacated by the bacon. She buttered the toast, and poured orange juice into two Styrofoam cups. "Would you put these things on the picnic table outside?"

"Sure." He rose to take a cup. "One at a time, though." Her perfume smelled familiar. His pulse quickened. He made several trips in and out, over the threshold, across the sidewalk, onto the grass, and then back again. Each time he re-entered the room, he drank in her provocative fragrance. Lilac. Ginnie's favorite. His favorite.

Lara dished up two plates of steaming food. She placed them across from each other on the splintered wood of the old picnic table.

He went back outside, brushing the sweat from his forehead. He dropped onto a bench, admiring her graceful movements as she headed back inside. She was beautiful, but stupid. Couldn't she see he was handicapped?

"I'll get the pot and warm the coffee up. I'll be right back."

"Cold coffee doesn't bother me a bit. Let's eat before everything else gets cold." He closed his eyes, inhaling the lingering scent of... Ginnie.

"It's no trouble at all," she replied from inside the room.

He ate a piece of bacon while he waited. After a brief period of silence, he went over to the doorway and peered inside. *What's she up to?*

She was just emerging from the bathroom, a long telephone cord following her, when he hobbled through the door.

"What's taking so long with the coffee?" he snapped, his voice impatient.

Her face turned red, but she shot him a friendly smile. "Sorry. I took a minute to check on my mom. She's in the hospital."

"Yeah, yeah, but you said you only had an hour. Besides, I'm starving."

She placed the telephone receiver back in the cradle and breezed past him. "Me, too."

He dug in, scooping up the tantalizing breakfast. Coming up for air between bites, he observed her untouched plate. How long had she been just sitting there, staring at him? "What's the matter? I thought you said you were hungry."

She twisted her hands on the table. "I guess not. More coffee?"

"Not yet."

She grabbed his half-empty cup. "I'll warm it up for you."

When she turned her back to him, he grabbed the bacon from her plate and stuffed it into his mouth. Maybe he'd stay a day or two. He watched her as she glided back inside, her hips moving in graceful cadence with her steps.

"Ouch!" Lara's scream pierced through his thoughts.

He hobbled inside. "Here, sit down. What happened?"

"I got dizzy and spilled the coffee on my arm." She sank onto the foot of the bed.

"Probably from not eating." He grabbed a towel from the bed. "Okay if I use this?" *Still damp from her shower.*

She nodded, her face flushed.

He pushed the outside door closed. He couldn't have asked for a better opportunity to get near her. He blotted her arms with care. His eyes captured hers and held them for a long minute before a knock at the door brought him back to reality. He recoiled. "Expecting someone?"

"Probably my boss. He brings me a list of vacancies every morning about this time. Do you mind letting him in?"

He took a step toward the small window, pulled back the curtain, and looked out. He whirled back toward her. "Boss, huh? Does he masquerade as a sheriff, perhaps?"

Her face paled. She jumped up and retreated into the bathroom. He hobbled after her, wedging a crutch between the door and the facing before she could shut it. Once inside, he pushed her back against the shower door.

Chapter 17

*J*ake sat next to Big Charlie watching television as Claire cleaned up the breakfast dishes. "I can't believe we slept until almost nine o'clock. I bet we missed the morning news, for sure." *Had they caught Father, yet? Where was Hound?*

Sheriff Foley approached a waiting microphone. "Good morning. At eight o'clock this morning, the suspect in yesterday's robbery at Pepperoni's took Lara Middleton, a housekeeper at The End of the Road Motel, as a hostage. We are confident this man is the same one mentioned in posters up all around town. His dog was recovered from his motel room."

Big Charlie clapped his hands together, and then raised them overhead with a whoop. "I imagine he'll soon get apprehended. How far and fast can a man on crutches go?"

"What's a hostage?" Jake slid onto the floor and sat on his knees in front of him.

Big Charlie rubbed the bridge of his nose. "It's a person that someone takes with them when they're tryin' to run away. The criminal thinks if they take a hostage, the police will be more likely to negotiate a deal or that it'll help them escape. Let's pray he lets the poor girl go and she doesn't get hurt."

Jake jumped up from the floor. "Father's a murderer. He's the one that deserves to die." *Would he hurt that lady? Of course. Maybe kill her? He'd done it before.*

Claire stood by the recliner, drying silverware with a kitchen towel. "Let's not be worrying about that, right now. Let's focus on Hound. It looks like you're going to be getting your dog back, Jake!" She raised her eyebrows and gave Big Charlie a slight nod.

"Hound!" Jake grabbed Claire and twirled her around the room.

"Jake, I'm getting dizzy!" She grabbed onto a chair back and plopped down.

"Can we go get him now? Can we, Charlie?" He fell down on his knees in front of him and begged. "It's been so long. I don't think I can wait another minute!"

"Chores first. Hound second." Claire pushed herself up from the chair and steered his shoulders toward his room.

"Can I call Ruth?"

"After your chores are done." Claire called over her shoulder.

Jake stopped short of his room. "But, Claire, Hound's more important than chores—right?"

Claire remained silent. She picked up a hot cup of coffee and blew on it before taking a sip.

"Now, how did a man on crutches manage to get away from Sheriff Foley and his deputy and take a hostage, too?" Big Charlie shook his head in disbelief.

"I pray they're able to catch Ethan as soon as possible." Her eyes trained on Jake as he dawdled at the doorway.

They were ignoring him. Didn't they understand about him and Hound, after all? He smoothed the patterned quilt over the bed and yanked off his t-shirt and pajama bottoms. He pulled another t-shirt from the top dresser drawer and jumped back into the jeans he'd worn the day before. He rushed out of his room, dressed for the drive to town.

"Bed's made and clothes are in the hamper. Let's go!" He pressed his hands together, praying for Claire to give in.

She grinned and shook her head. "I think we've been overruled, Charlie. Do we have any travel cups?"

⤝❧⤞

The bright morning sun shined directly into Ethan's eyes. He pulled the visor down and looked over at Lara. Why was she driving so slow? "Let's pick it up a little. You cooperate and you won't get hurt." He watched out the passenger's window as the red Subaru Brat climbed the steep incline. The day had somehow veered off track. So much for his plans for a little romance.

"You hurt the pizza guy." She sobbed as she guided the car around a huge pothole.

"I had good reason. Turn, here." He'd need to keep her on the defensive…create the perfect balance of attraction and fear.

"I don't know where this road goes. It might be a dead end." Her eyes rimmed with tears as she steered the car on the single dirt lane.

"Pull over. Let me read this sign." He hung his head out the open window. "What's 'Brighton's Playhouse'?"

"A group of actors used to rent the building out to rehearse and stuff, but it hasn't been used in years."

"Abandoned. Perfect." He twisted his face into a grotesque smirk.

Her lips trembled. "If you're going to kill me, you might just as well do it, here."

"I'm not going to kill you. Pepper owed me money. He belittled me. He provoked me. As long as you don't do the same, I'll have no reason to hurt you."

She rummaged around in the glove box and produced a crumpled napkin. She dabbed at her eyes, a lone tear escaping down her cheek.

He reached over and brushed it away. His face grew hot. He withdrew his hand and looked out the window in the opposite direction. What was he doing? He reminded himself to show a little self-control.

They rode in silence for a few minutes before coming to a padlocked gate.

"Get out." He wouldn't let a little thing like a locked gate keep them apart.

"But—"

"I said get out!"

She opened the door. He hobbled around the car, placed a hand on her back, and pushed her forward. He yanked on the padlock and beat on the gate with his crutch.

"Let's see what you've got in the trunk."

"Just a jack and a tire iron. I don't think they'll be of any help."

"You never know. Now open up."

Charlie took up most of the space on the hard wooden bench across from the intake desk at the sheriff's office. He, Claire, and Jake had been waiting for almost an hour for a deputy to retrieve Hound from the animal shelter. Jake was having a hard time being patient, but he guessed he would, too, if he were a ten-year-old boy.

Jake jumped to his feet each time the door opened, only to slouch back down on the bench when Hound didn't materialize. "What's taking them so long? Let's just drive over there and get him ourselves." Jake scowled, crossing his arms.

"I'm sure it won't be much longer." Charlie stood and stretched his legs.

Claire smiled. "I'm certain they're trying to gather all the evidence they can in hopes it will help them get your father and the hostage back as soon as possible."

"Hound!" Jake shot to his feet when he heard the dog's familiar bark.

The door opened and Hound darted to Jake, jumping up and placing his paws on his shoulders. He whimpered as he licked the boy's face and neck.

The sheriff, tall and thin, followed behind his deputy. "No doubtin' whose dog this is!"

Charlie reached out to shake hands with Sheriff Foley. "I'm Charlie Claiborne; my wife, Claire. And this is Jake."

"Pleased to meet you all. If you'll follow me inside, we'll take your statement."

"Sure." Charlie grunted as he pushed himself up from the bench.

The sheriff bent down to look Jake in the eye. "Abby, please see to it that this fine boy gets a snack. Then, grab a pad and join us in my office." He gave Hound a pat on the head. "Fine dog you got there. We'll just be a few minutes, son."

Opening the first door to their left, the sheriff ushered the Claiborne's inside a cluttered, but otherwise spacious room. He placed his hat on top of the file cabinet, then fell into his leather chair and swiveled toward the desk. "Abby's good at answerin' the phone and makin' coffee, but I'll be darned if I can get her to go through any of this mail."

The couple struggled to find comfortable spots to sit on the loveseat facing the sheriff's large oak desk. Charlie hummed under his breath, and Claire pulled a stray thread from her sleeve as they waited for the secretary. The sheriff was stifling a yawn when Abby shuffled through the door.

Maybe they were married. She loved him, no doubt about it. Charlie could read these things. He gave his wife a smile when she looked in his direction. *She's probably wonderin' what I'm doin' starin' at the secretary for so long.*

"Land's sakes, Sheriff. Let me get you something to put on that." Abby's ample chin shook as she nodded toward the red welts on Ray Foley's left hand and neck. "How'd that happen, anyhow?"

"There was a little scuffle at the motel. The suspect was barricaded in the bathroom for a while, but then feigned surrender. He walked toward me with his hands up, but before I knew it, the crazy fool threw a skillet of hot bacon grease on me. I'll go over to Doc Brown's when we're done here. Let's get this over with and let these folks get back home. That okay with you?"

"All right, if you're sure." Abby tucked a stray gray hair back into place in the tight bun high above her neck.

"Okay, folks, explain what connection you have to this guy and why you've put up posters all over town."

Charlie didn't want to give him the impression that they had any connection to that son-of-a-gun. "He calls himself 'Ethan,' but we're pretty sure that's not his real name. He's the boy's father and—"

Charlie had barely begun before Claire interrupted him. "He's a dangerous man. He's already killed two people we know of." Claire twisted her fingers in her lap.

"He served time in prison at one time. We don't know how much time—or where—or for what," Charlie continued.

"We think he escaped. Why else would he have been holed up in the woods with very little communication with the outside world?" Claire raised her eyebrows at the sheriff.

"Accordin' to Jake, he hurt him on several occasions. He's not fit to be a father. We've been lookin' for him to get the boy's dog back and to convince him to have a blood test to prove for once and for all whose child Jake really is." Charlie rubbed his hands over the worn fabric on the arms of the loveseat.

"Well, from my experience, the courts will be lookin' to find relatives to take care of him." Sheriff Foley took off his reading glasses and placed them on the stack of mail.

Claire sat forward. "There's a lady we know that used to be a neighbor of his. It's sort of complicated, but she thinks her husband might be Jake's real father—not Ethan."

"Well, if paternity testin' verifies that, then her husband might be able to adopt."

"Not that easy, Sheriff. Ethan killed him." Charlie nodded in response to the sheriff's surprised gasp.

"My, this *is* confusing; and, while it's necessary to get it all sorted out, right now my focus needs to be on gettin' this guy apprehended and the hostage home safe. I appreciate your comin' in. Sounds like he's more dangerous than we first realized."

Charlie squeezed Claire's arm. "Wish we could've been of more help, Sheriff."

Ray Foley rose to his feet, a gleam in his eye. "I've caught people with much less to go on."

⸺ ∞ ⸺

Ethan and Lara stood facing the mangled chain link fence and gate. He pointed to the driveway ahead of them. "Too bad about your car, but ramming the gate was the only way to get through. You'd think this was Fort Knox."

She shook her head after surveying the bumper and hood of her vehicle. "Are you going to pay for all this damage?"

"What do you think?" Ethan sneered, as he hobbled past the twisted metal. "Help me shove this gate off to the side. There's no way a car this small can drive over it without the gas tank getting punctured."

Once the gate was no longer an impediment, he used a crutch to prod her in the direction of the car. "Get in." He dodged the open door, pivoted on one foot and slid into the passenger seat.

Lara started the motor and the battle-worn car moved forward. She guided it around a minefield of ruts and over grown weeds. "We're almost out of gas."

Ethan kept his eye on the needle. "Yeah. We'll soon be running on fumes. We should at least be able to make it past this clearing and into that stand of trees up ahead."

When at last they pulled up in front of Brighton's Playhouse, Lara placed her arms on the steering wheel and laid her head on top of them.

Ethan's shoulders relaxed. "Lots of nice trees. Ought to conceal the car quite nicely." He got out and motioned for her to do the same. As he hobbled up the creaky steps of the rustic building with his crutches, he stepped on a loose board at the top, causing him to lose his balance and stumble. Flailing, he grabbed onto a tall post. A large splinter dug deep into his hand. His outcry was punctuated with vulgarities.

He winced as he picked up his crutches and used his shoulder to push against the door. Lara stood a few feet away on one end of a small bridge over a dried-up pond. She looked beautiful, even in a setting like this with her arms draped over the rotting railing. But she was hatching up a plan. He could see it in her eyes.

A colony of ants scurried atop an unidentifiable animal's carcass. Cracked pavement in the parking lot was washed out in a number of places and windows were broken out in the main building. They were miles from the nearest gas station.

This just might work out for him—because he had a plan of his own.

Chapter 18

"The winner helps with the lunch dishes." Charlie bent Jake's arm behind him and forced him to the ground. "That'll teach ya to take on someone with years of experience on the mat." He couldn't do that again if his life depended on it. *I'd better end this little match now before the boy gets the upper hand.*

"High school was a long time ago for you, I bet." Jake chuckled as he squirmed free.

Claire looked up from her magazine. "Charlie, you're liable to hurt yourself, wrestling around with him like that."

Jake pinned Charlie down. "Okay Hound, you know what to do."

The dog romped over, licking Charlie's face and neck with his big, sloppy tongue until Jake called him off. After he retreated, they rolled onto their backs, gasping for breath and laughing on the thick carpet of grass.

"What's that?" Charlie pointed to the locket dangling out of Jake's shirt. *It couldn't be...*

"Ruth gave it to me. It belonged to Mama."

"Can I see it?" Charlie sat up, a somber expression on his face. *The locket had been custom made. There couldn't be another one like it.*

"Sure." Jake fumbled with the clasp.

"Here, I'll get it." Charlie's heart raced, a lump forming in his throat. When the necklace was free at last and dropped into his waiting hands, it released feelings in him he couldn't understand…couldn't describe…

"See how smooth it is, Charlie?" Jake's eyes connected with his.

"Yes. It is." Charlie brought the locket to his cheek and then clutched it to his chest in reverence. He choked up, unable to speak.

"What is it, dear?" Claire dropped to her knees, exploring his face.

Charlie tried to open the locket, but the clasp was sprung. He rose, plodding trance-like up the steps and into the cabin. He was sitting on the sofa when both Claire and Jake squeezed through the door at the same time.

"Charlie?" Claire knelt down beside him. "Is everything okay?"

Jake perched on the coffee table and crossed his legs. "Can you get it open?"

Charlie took out his pocketknife. "I'll let you know in a minute." His hands shook as he pried the locket open with great care, trying not to scratch the case. His breath hitched when he saw the two pictures inside. He ran his fingers over them, awed by the faces smiling back at him.

"Thirteen years ago, our daughter disappeared. We never knew if she'd run off or if she'd been abducted. But we never lost hope of findin' her." Charlie's shoulders shook. "Her mo—mo—ther went to her gr—rave a sad— and— broken woman— without knowin' what happened to her— only ch—child."

"Easy now, dear. You take all the time you want. We're here. No hurry." Claire planted soft kisses on Charlie's face and neck.

Charlie nodded and took a deep breath. He collected his thoughts before he continued. "This locket be—longed to her grandmo—ther.

It was passed down to—Anna and then to our daughter on her eighteenth birth—day. The picture on the left is of our little Virginia when she was just five years old. The one on the right is her grandmother at the same age." He pulled a handkerchief from his pocket and mopped the sweat from his brow.

"On the fifth anniversary of Virginia's disappearance, we packed up and moved to West Virginia to be near my wife's kinfolk. I thought it'd do Anna good. Cheer her up, you know. And I think it did for a while. But, then she got sick. I'm not gonna go through the details of all that, except to say that we never lost hope of findin' our daughter."

Jake scrunched his face. "I don't understand. If it belonged to *your* daughter, how did *my* mama get it?"

<hr />

Ethan hit his crutches against the wall. "The structure's still solid. Welcome home!"

"You can't be serious." Lara ran off the rickety bridge and up the steps.

"Sure am. It's as good a place as any to hide out for a while." He looked toward the horizon. Dark clouds were forming to the south, a strong breeze beginning to blow. Yes, this was a nice, secluded place.

"Listen. I'm sorry for whatever your problems are, but I've got a job and friends and—" Lara's voice trembled.

Ethan raised a crutch and pointed it toward her. "You don't want to know about my problems. Just be careful you don't become one of them."

"Look. You don't need me anymore. I gave you a ride. Let's just part ways." Her voice cracked as a single tear rolled down her cheek. She reached for his arm, but then pulled back.

"No, I don't think so. You see, you're a hostage. My ticket to freedom." His laughter filled the air. A second later, he gritted his teeth and pointed at the door. "Now, get inside."

She edged into the vacant building's spacious entry. Cobwebs stretched across doorways and were intricately latticed in corners.

Ethan brushed past her and into the outdated kitchen. He flicked a giant spider off the countertop and then rummaged through several drawers, coming up with a book of matches with Brighton's Playhouse embossed in fancy gold letters. "Should be raining pretty soon. Then we'll see if the roof leaks."

The view out the picture window over the double sink was beautiful. Pine trees overlooked a large common area. Strings of light bulbs rattled against the posts on the veranda as the winds picked up.

Lara shuddered, pulling her thin sweater around her. "It's cold in here."

"It won't get any warmer, either. There's no electricity." Ethan surveyed the kitchen. A folding chair leaned against the wall. A bucket of cleaning supplies, overrun with spiders, sat beside it.

He found an old razor blade in the bucket. He struck a match, ran the blade through the flame a few times and then, in one swift movement, slit his finger. He held it up to his mouth and used his teeth to grasp the splinter. He spit it out on the floor.

When Lara turned from the window, she cringed at the sight of Ethan's bloody grin. "I think I'll see if there's any food in the pantry." She hurried in the direction of the small room off the kitchen.

He wrapped a ragged-looking napkin around his finger, and followed.

The door creaked when Lara pulled it open. She stepped into the dark room.

Without notice, Ethan pushed the door closed, grabbed the chair, and wedged it underneath the knob. "You think I didn't know it was *you* that turned me in?"

Lara's screams echoed in the vacant room.

Jake fidgeted, impatient for the answer to his question. "You'd better not say Mama stole it. I know she'd never do anything like that."

"No. She didn't steal it. It belonged to her." Big Charlie ran his hand over his face. "I'll try to explain that. Just hang with me for a minute."

Claire laid her head on his shoulder. "They always say this is a small world, but I never knew just how small it was until I heard your story. I'm so glad for you, dear, that you finally have a clue as to what happened to her."

Jake shot to his feet and stammered. "Wait—do you mean that *my* mama is *your* Virginia?"

"I think so, Jake. As incredible as it sounds, I think my Virginia must've run off with your father all those years ago." Big Charlie continued to stare at the pictures in the locket.

Claire grabbed onto Big Charlie's arm. "You lived in Texas back then, didn't you? That means Ethan lived in Texas and was likely serving time there."

Serving time? That meant Father had done something bad before I was even born. He wedged himself between Claire and Big Charlie, listening with great interest to their conversation about Father's secrets.

"You're right. I think we're gettin' closer to findin' our answers!" Big Charlie sobered, turning to Jake. "I don't s'pose you have a recent picture of your mother, do you?"

"Sure." Jake headed for his bedroom, returning with his winter coat. He reached into the pocket and brought out his treasured picture. "I put it in here—to keep it safe." He stole a glance at her beautiful face before giving it to Big Charlie.

"Her hair is longer, a different color, and she's much thinner, but the smile is the same." He looked at Claire. "She's our Virginia."

Lara pounded against the pantry door. "Let me out of here, Joshua!"

Ethan finished off a candy bar from his knapsack. "Too bad it has to turn out like this. A few hours ago, I had different plans for you. But, you changed all that. If my dog could talk, he'd tell you what happens to traitors."

A crack of thunder sounded overhead, followed by the rain the weatherman had promised on the morning newscast. The drops intensified in sound as they fell on the metal roof, lightening zigzagging across the sky.

Ethan opened the outside door to watch the light show. He rubbed the back of his neck. He needed to accomplish some critical things in the next few days. Priority One: Take care of Lara. She knew his real name. Priority Two: Stay at least one step ahead of the law. They'd be checking this road sooner or later...setting up roadblocks...plastering that composite of him all over the place. Priority Three: Retrieve the package. Priority Four: Get Hound back—somehow. *Had he been returned to the boy?*

"Joshua! Where are you?" She continued to beat on the door.

He turned back around and lowered himself onto a cardboard box just outside it. He leaned his head against the wall. She reminded him of Ginnie. Good at small talk. Quick to blush. Cute way of tugging at her earring when she's nervous. "Yeah, what is it?"

"It's dark in here…I'm scared." Her voice trembled.

He closed his eyes. Should he change his mind? He drew in a deep breath, tempted by her perfume.

"Talk to me. You have a nice voice."

"Oh?" *Careful, Joshua, this is a dangerous game to play.*

"Let me out, Joshua, and we'll talk. I won't try to leave. I promise."

Ethan's hand grasped the doorknob. He hesitated. He knew what she was trying to pull. Just like Ginnie. Using her charms to get her way.

"About making that phone call…if you think about it, wouldn't any woman have done that?"

Sweat stood on his forehead. "You don't know me. I could be a killer. I might be a saint."

"Exactly my point. There was no way of knowing."

"But you judged me, Lara." He licked his lips, his eyes focused on the rusty doorknob. "So, now I'll judge *you*." He picked up his crutches and headed for the porch. "I sentence you to a *slooow* death." His heinous laugher echoed in the empty room.

"You can't just leave me here—"

"I've got a package to dig—I mean, pick—up. I can't have you getting in my way." He slammed the door behind him and headed for the glider. He lowered himself onto it, smirking at the faded hearts and blue birds painted on its back and arms. He put his foot on the deck and used it to push the glider back and forth. It wasn't long until his eyes grew heavy in response to the gentle rhythm.

Joshua's small fists beat on the smooth wood. "Mama, Mama! Get me out of here. Please. I'll be a good boy. I promise."

Gloria Harding whispered through the closed door.

"Shush, son. He's been drinking, again. You'll be safe enough if you stay quiet until he's gone up to bed. I'll be back before you know it."

He clapped his hands over his ears when he heard the sound of Father's slurred voice, the slap, the breaking of glass, and Mama's cries. "Christopher, stop!"

Mama, I can help you! Joshua fell to the floor and began to kick against the thick mahogany door.

Ethan woke with a start, his shirt and hair wet with sweat. He fought conflicting emotions as his erratic heartbeat returned to normal.

Christopher Harding's devilish laughter broke the silence.

Ethan drew his crutch up to his chest, swinging it in all directions. As he hurried to escape his father, he slipped on the top porch step, and fell headlong into the mud. Fighting for every breath, he crawled toward the gate, dragging his crutches with one hand, pulling himself forward with the other.

Later that afternoon, Ruth's car skidded to a stop in front of the summer house.

"Looks like she's got a bee in her bonnet." Charlie swung the door open wide.

Ruth ran up the steps, two at a time. She was breathless when she crossed the threshold. "Sorry—to interrupt—you all." She gave Jake a quick hug, placed her handbag on the table, and kicked off her flip-flops.

"Come on in and tell us what this flurry is all about." Claire motioned her toward the sofa.

Ruth sat down, crossing and uncrossing her legs. "Ethan's on the loose. I'm afraid he just might come back to the trailer. This is the first place I thought of. Would it be okay with you if I stay here until he's caught?"

Claire nodded. "Of course it is, dear. We were half-expecting you to show up this morning."

"So, you got my message?"

"Yes, we heard it late last night. We thought we'd remember to call you this morning, but we slept late and then Jake was clamorin' for us to leave and—" Charlie stopped short when Ruth shook her head.

"It's okay, Charlie. I guess you know all the details by now."

Charlie leaned forward. "We were at Pepperoni's not long after it happened, yesterday. Besides, it's been on the news for hours. Ethan's taken a woman hostage. I pray he does her no harm. She's young, with a life ahead of her." He closed his eyes and massaged his temples with his fingers.

"Don't you two think it's about time we go to the police and tell them everything we know?" Ruth ran her hand along Hound's smooth coat.

"Already have. In fact, we just got home from a long visit with the sheriff." Charlie sat back, relaxing the tenseness from his body. Ray Foley was nobody's fool. He'd bring Ethan in.

Ruth grabbed Claire's hand. "What about the hostage. Has there been any news about her?"

"Not that we know of." Claire gave Ruth's hand a squeeze.

Ruth's eyes opened wide with recognition and surprise. She sent Jake a questioning look. "Wait a minute. It didn't register until now that Hound is here. How did that happen?"

Jake plopped down on the floor and sat cross-legged beside Hound. "He got left behind in Father's motel room. But he's glad to be home now, aren't you, boy?"

Hound barked on cue.

Jake ran around in a circle, with Hound following behind, until dizziness caused them both to collapse onto the floor. "That was fun. Let's do it again."

"No, not in the house. If you want to play rough, you're going to have to take it outside," Claire chided.

"Okay, come on Hound!" Jake bounded out the door with Hound on his heels.

"Don't let the door—slam." Claire winced at the noise, and then smiled at Ruth. "Boys…"

"Well, now that you're here, Ruth, we have some news of our own to share with you. Don't we, Charlie?"

Ethan circumvented standing pools of water before arriving at a roadside rest area a quarter of a mile from Brighton's Playhouse. Outside the men's restroom, a lone light bulb cast a dim glow above the vending machines. He placed three quarters into the closest one, and reached for the soda as it slid down the chute.

Hobbling to a nearby snack machine, he took two more quarters from his pocket. He placed them in the coin slot, and pressed B1. He waited, salivating, but his favorite chips failed to drop into the chute. That had been the last of his money. He'd be darned if he was going to be robbed of it! He shook the machine back and forth, pressing the coin return button, over and over again. As a last resort, he lifted a crutch to strike the bandit.

"Whoa! Don't be doin' that," a voice yelled from behind. "Let's see if I can help."

"That's an amazing story, Charlie. You've learned a lot, but it looks like there could be more information for you back in Texas." Ruth handed the locket back to him.

"Yep. But that's gonna to have to wait." Charlie's eyes were red and his head ached. "I need to see where my baby spent her last days."

"Are you sure, dear? Maybe it's best not to see where it all happened." Claire put a gentle hand on his arm.

"She was murdered, Claire. I've gone through years of torment. Now I've got to see this through." Charlie blew his nose into his handkerchief and turned to Ruth. "I'm sorry, but I have to ask. Do you know what he did with their bodies?"

"Oh, Charlie, I wish I knew. But I wasn't thinking about anything other than getting out of there. I feared Ethan, for sure, but I also was feeling anger and sadness because Sam and my best friend had betrayed me. I was a jumble of emotions. I ran off, Charlie. I live everyday knowing that Ethan abused Jake. If I'd stayed, maybe I could have prevented it." Ruth broke down, sobbing.

Claire went to her side, put her arms around her, and let her cry on her shoulder.

"You couldn't have prevented the killing. It's likely you'd have been killed, too, trying to protect Jake. We know that."

Ruth turned to Charlie, her eyes red and swollen. "Can you forgive me, Charlie?"

Nothing would bring his Virginia back, but maybe he could stop Ruth from blaming herself. He squeezed between the women on the sofa, laying his hand on Ruth's back. "Ruth, you did what you could to protect yourself. None of us know the future or the exact ramifications of our actions. With God's help, we just do our best. Of course, I forgive you."

She smiled through wet lashes. "I would have never guessed that Ginnie would turn out to be your Virginia. It's amazing how things come together sometimes, isn't it?"

"God has a way of workin' things out—and teachin' us lessons along the way. He intervenes in the lives of those who love him so that he can bring about ultimate good for every situation."

Claire scanned the picture in Charlie's hand. "She was such a beautiful girl. I don't know why I didn't see the resemblance before."

Ruth blinked. " Do you two realize what this means?"

Chapter 19

"It's 9:00, dumplin'. Let's go inside. We need to get some sleep. This all doesn't have to be settled tonight." Charlie rose from his position next to Claire on the porch glider and walked toward the door of the cabin. He put his hand on the doorknob, but paused at the sound of Claire's trembling voice.

"Please, dear, you didn't want to talk about it last night. And I've had to wait all day until Jake went to bed so we could have this conversation in private."

He turned back around. How could he refuse with the moonlight shining on her face and all? Anyway, he knew she wouldn't let this conversation wait. He lowered himself into his favorite wicker chair. "Okay, but I'm wantin' to get an early start in the mornin'."

"It just seems like you don't want to look at this situation head on, Charlie." She dabbed a tissue at her misting eyes.

He shook his head. "No. I just wanted a chance to think it through before we talked about it. This news about Virginia has upset me all over, again. I thought this was all behind me, but now I know my daughter is dead. It's so final. And, then to top it off, there's all this mess about whose kid Jake really is." With elbows on his knees, he rested his head in his hands.

"I think it's also the fact that we now know he's your grandson, and it's forcing you to make some decisions." She laid a gentle hand on his arm.

"That's true, of course. And it seems like I just got you to agree with me about who the boy should live with and then all this has thrown a wrench in the works." Charlie rubbed the bridge of his nose.

Claire's face flushed. "Aren't you able to be happy about having a grandson at least?"

"Knowin' that he's a little bit of Virginia is an unexpected blessin'. That's for sure." He hesitated, focusing on the wooden planks he had helped his father nail into place more than thirty years ago. "This is gonna make me sound cold and callous and self-centered, I'm afraid." He raised his eyes to meet hers.

"No. Go ahead." She moved to the edge of her seat, her hands clasped in her lap.

Charlie ran his tongue along his lips. "I do love the kid, but we had plans for *us*— for our lives—and now it seems they aren't gonna work out. We'll have obligations—financial and otherwise. I guess it's just that we're gonna go off in a completely different direction from the travelin'-fishin'-relaxin' life I wanted for us. Instead, it'll be parent-teacher conferences, soccer games, and helpin' with homework at night." He pressed his lips together and rubbed the back of his neck with his fingertips.

Claire patted the place next to her on the glider.

He moved from his chair to sit beside her. She had that maternal look on her face. If anyone was meant to be a mother, it was Claire. He wished she had been able to experience motherhood when she was younger. If she had, perhaps Jake and his living arrangements wouldn't be such an issue between the two of them now.

She cleared her throat. "I understand, but let's try to put what we believe about God and His plans for our lives into the mix for a few minutes."

Charlie remained silent, hunched forward, looking down once again at the worn surface of the wooden porch.

Claire took his two pudgy hands in hers. "We know He can take the bad things in life and turn them into something good. Agreed?"

"You're right. Of course." Charlie raised his head to look into her crystal-blue eyes.

She gave his hands a gentle squeeze. "What happened with Virginia is something no parent should ever have to experience, but God gave you the strength to get through it. And how could Jake have ever endured the kind of treatment he's had from Ethan and still turn out to be kind and affectionate, except that God has been watching out for him? It seems to me that God has woven the tragedies of a mother and her son together and made a beautiful coat that you'll be able to wear proudly—one that will keep you warm with memories of both of them during the fall and winter of your life."

He nodded, overcome with emotion as he marveled at her eloquent words. He closed his eyes, regaining his composure. "It's just that we made all those plans."

Her eyes twinkled with understanding. "I know. But, in the sixteenth chapter of Proverbs it says that "A man's heart plans his way, but the Lord directs his steps.' So, what *we* might have planned isn't necessarily the way God is directing."

He put his arm around her shoulders, giving her a firm, but gentle hug. *Lord, help me say this in a nice way.* "It's easier for you to accept this because it seems like he's directin' us in a way more aligned with *your* thinkin'."

"I suppose so," she sighed, "but it hasn't always been that way. I've had my share of times that I needed to subject my wants to His sovereign authority." She turned to look into the starry night. "I look at it like this: we both had plans for our first marriages, didn't we? And even though they ended contrary to our expectations, God chose to bless us with each other."

He smiled, and then gave her a lingering kiss. "He sure did bless me. I know that."

He caressed her cheek with his fingertips. Each time he looked at her, he discovered something new. Like the tiny mole next to her lower eyelid. *When had that appeared?* He found it exciting to know that she was still changing, inside and out, settling into this new life of theirs in more ways than he'd ever imagined.

They were in their twilight years. It would be her inner beauty that would sparkle more and more as she reached the next plateau. Every line on her face would have a story to tell and he would be next to her as they experienced the rest of life's journey together.

"I realize this may be disappointing dear, but I'm sure there will be many blessings ahead, if only we'll follow His leading." Claire laid her head against his chest.

He brushed a lock of soft gray hair from her forehead. "Oh, I wasn't tryin' to argue with you, or with God—well, maybe I was, a little— Anyway, I guess I've been slow to admit it, but maybe God's hand has been in this all along. He knew we'd see Jake lyin' hurt in that clearin'. He knew I'd hear Ethan callin' for help. He knew Ruth would be there for Jake when he needed her. And, my darlin', he knew I'd need a strong woman like you to help me through this next phase of my life."

He closed his eyes and relaxed. How would he ever be able to find forgiveness in his heart for the man who'd killed his girl? That, too, would only be possible if the Lord changed his heart to accept what the Holy Spirit revealed to him as truth.

A strong hand shook Ethan by the shoulders. He awoke with a start. "Oh, what... day...um..." His thoughts were jumbled. Was it just yesterday that he left Lara at Brighton's?

"Hey, man. Wake up!" A dark-bearded logger in suspenders and a green flannel shirt gave his shoulders another push.

"What? Oh! I must have fallen asleep. Your logs are so comfortable, and all." He sneered at his own humor. He should be more gracious. After all, a ride was a ride. He pulled himself up to a sitting position on the dilapidated flatbed truck.

"Let me help you down from there. You'll have to walk a little ways. I can't get this rig on up there any further without the chance of getting stuck." The logger nodded toward the single-lane dirt road ahead, then turned back to Ethan. "Hey, man, what kind of operation left scars on your stomach like that? I never saw any like those before."

Ethan grabbed at his T-shirt and pulled it down over his belly. "None of your business." Ethan put his crutches under his arms and leaned forward as the logger steadied him. "Drop by anytime. The door's always open." He chuckled as the rig pulled away. "Yeah. Right."

Ethan stopped several times to rest, wiping the sweat from his forehead as he plodded toward the blackened landscape that had been his home for thirteen years. He sat down on a charred, but otherwise sturdy tree trunk and shook his head at the scorched boards and misshapen metal objects protruding from the ashes. A shiver ran down his spine. With the moonlight shining on them, the scene looked like a graveyard.

That was the kitchen there. Yes, across from the fireplace. The old stove had practically melted in the fire. He kicked at what may have been a soup pot and looked toward the back of the property. The shed was still standing, totally unscathed.

He took a bite of a granola bar and a sip from his canteen. He focused on the lock, still securing the door. He balanced himself on one crutch, picked up the other, and made his way toward the tree stump where the boy sometimes played with his rocks. From the grouping, he picked up a large one and hobbled to the shed, balancing himself on one crutch. He repeatedly hit against the bracket until it broke loose on one end and fell to the side. He dropped the rock onto the ground and pushed the door back.

Ruth searched the telephone directory for Happy Moon. She'd order Chinese for everyone and take hers with her to eat in the break room later in her shift. As she picked up the phone, a drawing of Ethan filled the television screen. She dropped the receiver into the cradle and turned up the volume. "…hostage, Lara Middleton, has been taken to Davis Memorial Hospital in Elkins. She spent two days without food or water. The suspect is still at large."

Ruth drew in deep breaths. She dressed in a hurry, putting a frozen burrito and a can of soda into her lunch bag. Her hands shook as she reached for the doorknob and stepped onto the porch.

Claire looked up from her *Cook's Illustrated* magazine. "Going so soon?"

"I wasn't planning on it, but I just heard on the news that the hostage was found and taken to the hospital. If I go in early, I may be able to get some useful information from her." Ruth winked as she gave Claire a quick hug.

"Oh, I hope she wasn't hurt."

"I don't think so. I'm sure they'll just keep her overnight as a precaution."

"Are you taking anything for supper?"

Ruth held up her lunch bag. "A burrito. I'll be fine with that. I intended to buy Chinese for all of us tonight, so I left money on the table.

I hope you'll go to that little place you like. Sorry not to be going with you, but this trumps a meal—at least I think it does."

Claire shook her head. "Now, there's no need for that. You're our guest."

"I want to do it and I'm going to ask Jake if he had Chinese, so please don't disappoint me. I appreciate your letting me stay here. So let me do this one little thing." She waved goodbye and sprinted down the steps to the Camaro.

Ethan reclined against the wall of the shed. The floor had been hard and uncomfortable, but at least it provided shelter for a few hours. If things went well today, he might go back for Lara. He'd remind her how nice things had started out for them, how they could be again—if only she'd cooperate.

His eyes fell on the ladder, standing next to the cracked window. "I could've used you not so long ago." He picked up the shovel from the corner and went outside.

As the early morning sun pushed its way through the remaining clouds, he scanned the area for landmarks. *Now, this is where everything gets tricky. Four steps from the corner of the cabin; turn right. Four more steps; turn left. Or was it left and then right? And where's the corner? Uncle Ethan had been a fool to build a structure on a wooden foundation.*

He struggled to keep his balance as he dug down a few inches. Nothing. Okay, he'd go four to the left and then four to the right. He counted off the paces, dragging the shovel behind him. Again, he dug down several inches—still no luck.

"Dang it!" He flung the shovel through the air. It landed against the wall of the shed with a resounding *bang* that echoed through the trees.

If he didn't find it, someone else would stumble upon it someday. He couldn't take a chance on that happening.

Sometime later, after several more failed attempts, his shovel *pinged* against the metal of the old cash box. He crumpled onto the ground, wiped his face on his sleeve, and pulled the reclaimed container from the ashes. His lips curved into a sly smile as he brushed it off and placed it in his knapsack.

He staggered to his feet and shaded his eyes with his hands, assessing the impact of his digging on the land. He wiped his forehead again and took a long drink of water before he stumbled back into the shed. Sunlight danced through its roof and onto his uncle's crudely made workbench. There wasn't much here of any value. A rusted rake, Uncle Ethan's old dental tools and a bucket with a hole in the bottom.

"What happened here, Joshua?"

Ethan scrambled into the corner, hiding his head in the crook of his folded arms. That was Cleo's voice. What was she doing here? He raised his head. "What went on here is none of your concern." He panted, fighting hard for each breath.

Cleo's eyes bore into his. Her silent stare chilled his blood. "You need to face what you did, Joshua. Face your wretchedness."

He hung his head. He'd only wanted to talk with his uncle…plead for his help, if necessary. He had envisioned having a pleasant visit with him while Ginnie shopped in town for clothing and other necessities. He had never meant for it to be a confrontation.

He had leaned against the wall of the shed as Uncle Ethan sat at the workbench.

> "Ginnie and I need a place to lay low for a while.
> I thought of your cabin and how isolated it is. This
> would be the perfect place for us to hole up."

He swallowed hard, closed his eyes, and forced himself to relive the horror of that day.

"Joshua, you must take me for a fool if you think I'd ever let you live under my roof!" Uncle Ethan rose to his feet, his nostrils flaring and fire in his eyes. "You're a murderer of the worst kind—a coward!"

Joshua towered over him. "So, you think I should spend years of my life in prison because of an out-and-out accident?"

Uncle Ethan leaned against the workbench opposite the open door. "The jurors must not have seen it the same way, or they'd have never convicted you! My brother's partly to blame in this. You were born with a silver spoon in your mouth. He never made you accountable for anything in your life. He's been bailing you out of trouble since you broke that boy's nose in the first grade. No wonder you turned out just like him."

Joshua felt his defenses rising. "You're my favorite uncle. I've always wanted to be like you. And now to hear you say such horrible things... Doesn't family mean anything to you?"

Ethan walked toward the back of the shed and leaned his crutches against the ladder. He wedged his hand into the small crevice between the workbench and the back wall, working his fingers back and forth and writhing as splinters from the brittle wood dug deep into his fingers. He froze as he once again felt the cold handle of the carving knife and the last of the horrid memories burst into his consciousness.

His pulse raced as he shoved his uncle down onto
the floor and grabbed the carving knife.

I hadn't even realized I'd grabbed it from him. He placed the weapon on the
workbench, a grim reminder of what he'd done. He buried his head in
his hands.

"It's not over, Joshua." Cleo leaned closer, her eyes piercing his very
soul. "You dragged the body down by the creek, didn't you? You dug a
shallow grave that the wolves found even before you'd brought Ginnie
back from town the next day. You told her that you'd found him dead
at his workbench…that he must have been there, for who knows how
long. You said you'd buried him in a private, but tender ceremony. You
couldn't talk about it anymore…you were so overcome with grief."

—⚬⚬⚬—

The nurses' station was deserted. Ruth picked up the duty schedule,
ran her finger down the list, and paused at Lara Middleton's name –
Room #417. Her heart beat erratically as she pulled the chart and then
stole a patient tray from an unsupervised food cart. She was taking a
chance, but she needed to hear what happened—firsthand.

She breezed into the room and set the tray on the table in front of
Lara. "Good evening. How are you doing?"

"I'm all right. A little restless, I guess." Lara gave Ruth a feeble
smile. "Do you always serve supper so late?"

"Not really, but I thought you'd be hungry. So, I snagged you a tray."

"You were right. I'm literally starving." Lara unrolled her napkin, took out a knife, and buttered a crescent roll.

Ruth's stomach growled, yearning for her burrito. "If you can spare me a couple of minutes, I'll take your blood pressure and then leave you to eat in peace and quiet." She placed the cuff around Lara's arm. She couldn't believe she was doing this. She didn't even work on this floor. "You don't look hurt and there's nothing on your chart about any wounds…"

"No. I had the scare of my life, but really all it amounted to was a few missed meals and a damaged car." She took a bite of bread and rolled her eyes. "It's kind of stale but, still, it's food."

"So, the—um—suspect didn't lay a hand on you?" Ruth's heart raced. The nurse assigned to Lara would come on duty any moment.

"He locked me inside the pantry, but other than that, it was only his threats and language that were abusive. I told the deputy I felt fine, but he insisted I stay here one night. Something about department rules."

"I guess they just want to be on the safe side."

Lara nodded. "I guess so."

Ruth looked up from the chart. "Kidnappings don't always turn out so well, you know."

"Somewhere along the way, some bad stuff must have happened in that guy's life. My mother says there's got to be some goodness—even if it's just a little—inside of everyone. I believe that, too."

"Maybe." There was no reason to tell Lara that she'd just escaped the clutches of a man who was capable of almost anything. Indeed, she was fortunate to be alive and unharmed.

Lara took a bite of pot roast. "This is really good—for hospital food. I wonder if you could heat it up for me in your break room, though. It's a little cold."

"It might have been sitting out there a little while. I'll see what I can do." Ruth ran the thermometer over Lara's forehead. "98.6. Perfect. I'll take your tray with me and get it heated up. After you eat, you should try to get a little sleep. The sheriff will probably be here early in the morning to question you."

Ruth headed for the door with the tray, then paused. "By the way, did the kidnapper say anything that might give you a hint as to where he might be headed?"

"Not really." Lara laid her head back and closed her eyes. "No, wait!" She sat up, wide-eyed. "He might be going to the post office."

Ruth cocked her head and walked back in her direction. "Really? Why would you think that?"

"He said he had a package to pick up. No...dig up. He said *dig* up."

"Are you sure?"

Lara raised up on one elbow. "Definitely. 'Dig up' is what he said, but you wouldn't do that at a post office, now would you?"

Full from a breakfast of bacon and eggs, Jake sprawled on the sofa watching cartoons while he waited for Big Charlie. When a composite drawing of his father filled the television screen, he rolled onto the floor and crawled over a sleeping Hound to Big Charlie's recliner. He grabbed the remote off the seat cushion, turning up the volume. "Claire! Charlie! I think they've found him."

"My goodness. What's all the ruckus about?" Charlie ran in from the bedroom, wiping shaving cream from his face with a towel. "Are you okay?"

"Yes, but look!" Jake pointed to the television and perched on the arm of the sofa, giving Charlie his usual seat in the recliner. "I hope he gets locked up forever."

A reporter stood in front of the courthouse, holding a microphone in front of the sheriff. Ray Foley cleared his throat before talking. "Late last night, a team of FBI officers located and freed the hostage in a local kidnapping case. I'm pleased to report that Lara Middleton was found approximately twelve miles east of town at the deserted Brighton's Playhouse. She was unharmed, and is now hospitalized as a precautionary measure. The suspect in this case is still at large."

Claire stood in the doorway, thick white cream covering her face and neck.

"Actually, Ruth heard about it on the news report last night. She hurried off to the hospital to see if she could get some information from the hostage. I meant to tell you this morning, but I guess the television beat me to it." Claire hugged Jake, leaving smudges of cold cream on both of his cheeks.

"Claire, you got that stuff on me!" Jake grimaced, rubbing it off with his hands and wiping it on his jeans. Then he bolted off the sofa in Hound's direction, calling over his shoulder to Charlie. "Father will be headed this way. You know what kind of guy he is. He'll come for Hound. I just know it." Jake put his arms around Hound's neck. "You've got to help me hide him, Charlie! How about you fly us out of here on your airplane?"

"Whoa. Not so fast. We're not gonna be runnin' away. Ethan has no way of knowin' where we live. I'm gonna call Ruth, though. I want to find out if she got any useful information from the hostage." Big Charlie shuffled toward the phone.

Jake pulled his knees up to his chest and buried his face between his arms. Father would do anything to get Hound back. He'd make Ruth tell where they lived. He'd end up killing all of them.

Chapter 20

Half an hour later, Charlie and Jake set out for Ethan's old cabin site, as planned. Charlie rolled down the Hornet's windows. The crisp morning air felt good and the smell of pine trees was invigorating. Jake rode in the passenger seat, playing his hand held FROGGER game. He was a fine young man. Resilient. Clever. Virginia would be proud.

Charlie wished Ruth hadn't given him that game for his birthday, though. It was nothing but a distraction. But, then again, a distraction might be just what he needed. He'd been skittish ever since he'd heard about the kidnapped woman being found—thinking his father would be coming for Hound. Truth was, maybe he would... Charlie slowed the car down. "We should be close now. Look for the turn off."

Jake moaned, laid his game aside, and sat forward. "There it is. Turn right at the fork in the road, then left up there by that big tree. We're almost there." His voice wavered and trailed off.

Charlie brought the car to a stop. He shook his head at the blackened earth where the cabin once stood. The chain-link fence, stone fireplace, and shed were all that remained. When they had been out here before, there hadn't seemed to be any point in even getting out of the car, so he had just driven on over to Sam's. *Horrible sight...such a horrible sight...*

"Why didn't Claire come with us?" Jake melded back into his seat.

"Because she and Hound had a hard night chasin' gophers. I told her it's just part of livin' in the woods, but she was havin' none of it." The real reason, though, was that she thought this trip would traumatize Jake. She said she'd be no part of that, so he had to use his trump card: he was the grandfather. He hoped she'd still be speaking to him when they got back home.

"Charlie?"

"Yes, Jake?"

"My stomach hurts. Can I stay in the car with Hound?" He scrunched his face and nodded toward his dog, stretched out on the backseat.

Charlie gave his head a reassuring pat. "I think you're just a bit nervous. But, as you can see, there's nothin' here that can hurt you anymore."

Jake's hand froze midair above the door handle. "But, Charlie—"

"I'm just wantin' to visit the place my Virginia lived, Jake. I saw the orchard when I found your father pinned under that tree, but I didn't see the cabin, of course."

"It's burned down, though, Charlie."

"I know, but there still might be somethin' here worth seein'."

Jake hesitated, but finally opened the Hornet's door, slid out of his seat, and walked toward the fence. He gave the chain link a hard kick, his eyes darting beyond it to the tree line. "Father could be hiding around here, Charlie."

"I suppose it's possible, Jake. So, I brought a little protection—just in case." Charlie put his hand behind him and pulled a revolver from his waistband.

Jake's eyes opened wide. "Whoa! I didn't know you had a gun."

"I keep it put away for safety's sake. But, well, I thought it might make you feel safer comin' here today—not that I think there's really any reason for concern. Like I told you, it's the first place the law would look for him—and I'm sure Ethan knows that." Charlie put the gun back in his waistband, scanning the land from one stand of trees to the other. "Naw, he's a long ways from here."

"Claire should see this, huh?" Jake stretched his hand out, indicating the dozens of holes on the property.

Charlie pushed back his ball cap and frowned "Well, I'll be. It looks like a passel of gophers have been here, too. But let's get on with our business and leave the gophers be." He bent down and put his hands on Jake's shoulders. "This visit really means a lot to me, so can you stick with me—for just an hour or so?"

⚬⚬⚬

Jake stood motionless, eyes darting back and forth from Big Charlie, to the car, and back to Big Charlie again. His eyes rested, at last, on the handle of the gun. *I can do this. I can do this.* His heart double-thumped.

Big Charlie put his arm around his shoulders and guided him onto the property. "The shed's still standin'." He pointed his finger at the small building at the back of the property, nestled between two large pine trees.

Jake's eyes shifted toward the creek. "Let's go to the orchard, if you want. Then we can be back home by lunch time."

"That's a good idea. I'm gonna see if there's a basket of some kind in there. Maybe pick some apples for Claire. You know how she loves to make apple pies." Big Charlie lumbered toward the shed.

"About as much as we do eating them!" Jake rubbed his stomach.

"All the more reason to see if we can find a somethin' to put 'em in."

Jake shrugged his shoulders. "Father always kept the shed locked."

"Well, let's take a look anyway, seein' as we're here and all."

Jake hung behind, pushing the toe of his shoe around in the ashes. "You go first." The last time he'd been in the shed was when he was punished for raiding the scrap bucket—a memory he didn't want to relive.

Big Charlie reached for the door handle.

A lump formed in Jake's throat. *Father's around here. I know it.* "I'll just wait here. I don't want to see it all again."

Big Charlie reached back and grabbed his arm. "See all what?"

Jake wriggled from his grasp, cowering behind him, as the door pushed open from the inside. The edge of it smacked Big Charlie in the forehead.

"Aaugh!" He cradled his head in his hands.

Father emerged from behind the door, his face twisting into an evil smile. "What in the world are you two doing here?"

Jake's body stiffened. "What did I tell you, Charlie? Now we're both going to get killed!"

The muscles in Big Charlie's face twitched. He pulled a handkerchief from his pocket and dabbed at the trickle of blood. "I wanted to see where my daughter lived out her last days, as hard as it is for me to believe she preferred the likes of you to bein' at home with her family." He took a step backward, shielding Jake.

"What are you talking about? What do you mean, *your* daughter?" Father glared at him, his eyes cold as ice.

"Virginia Claiborne, that's who!" Big Charlie's fingertips examined the raised knot on his forehead.

"Virginia...Virginia," Ethan repeated. "Ginnie was *your* daughter?" The knife Father held by his side glistened in the morning sun.

"Yes. It was *my* beautiful daughter you murdered."

"That's not true. Whoever told you that?" Red-faced, he lunged forward with outstretched hands.

Big Charlie jumped back, pulling Jake out of Father's reach. He held his chin high. "More than one person will be willin' to testify."

"Without evidence? There's not a jury in the country that would convict me." Father spat.

Jake leaned out from the safety of his position behind Big Charlie. "You did kill Mama—and Sam, too! You told me so yourself." His heart skipped a beat. "And I'm not the only one who knows."

"Hearsay from a toddler?" Another devilish laugh escaped Father's lips.

"And Ruth, of course," Jake exclaimed.

"Yes. Ruth's husband cheated on her, too. You know how it is, old boy, 'a woman scorned'." Father chuckled, licking his lips as he transferred the knife back and forth between his hands.

"Are you tryin' to suggest that *she* was the one that did the killin'?" Big Charlie demanded.

"Maybe... Yeah... Sure." Father started toward them.

"You don't sound very convincin'." Big Charlie dodged the knife.

Father's face contorted in a monster-like snarl. "It's not *you* I have to convince."

"You're right about that. Does this state have the death penalty?" Big Charlie raised his eyebrows, and then squinted his eyes.

"What makes you think I'd stay around for a trial anyway? And if you believe what you've been told, then why shouldn't I just add two more notches to my belt?" Father pointed the knife toward Big Charlie's chest.

"I'm not afraid of you, Ethan." Big Charlie's nose flared as he sneered at Father, his fingers edging behind his back toward the handle of the gun.

"Maybe you should ask the boy if I keep good on my threats. He knows what I'm capable of." Pure evil flashed in Father's eyes.

Jake recalled the evening Papa sat on the porch steps, crying for
Mama. *That was when he stopped loving me. He turned into someone else...
someone I didn't know... Father.* "You can't hurt me anymore. And you're
not going to hurt Charlie either!" He lowered his head and charged at
Father, swiping at the knife with his bare hands.

"That's where you're wrong." Father snatched Jake's wrist, pulled
him to his chest, and brought the knife up to his throat.

Jake's body shook in uncontrollable spasms. "Father, please—"

"Ethan!"

"Come on. Answer!" Ruth bit her fingernails as she waited for Claire to
pick up. She'd hoped they hadn't already left for the cabin.

"Hello," answered a sleepy voice.

"Claire? It's Ruth."

"Oh. Hi, dear."

Ruth exhaled. "I'm glad I caught you before you headed out."

"Oh, Charlie and Jake did leave, but I stayed home to rest." Claire
yawned.

"They're not with you?" Ruth chewed yet another fingernail.

"No. Charlie let me sleep. You see, all night long, I—"

"Claire, listen. I talked with Lara Middleton—the girl Ethan
kidnapped—and what she said gives me reason to believe he might
be going out to the cabin to dig up something. He may be there right
now!"

Claire's voice trembled. "Call— the sh-sheriff. I'll stay—by—
the—phone."

———∞∞∞———

Jake wrestled to free himself. *Please…Charlie…the gun…*

Father snarled at Big Charlie through gritted teeth. "Back off! Get in your vehicle and drive away. Or, I'll show you no mercy!"

"I'm not leavin' without Jake. Now, let go of him." Big Charlie edged toward Father, his eyes fastened on the blade. "Hurtin' the boy will only make it worse for you."

Father chuckled and tightened his grip. "You might think you did a good thing by taking him in, but you're an old goat that's gotten in over his head. What's the boy to you, anyway?"

"He's my grandson!"

Jake's eyes widened. When they were fishing at the lake, Big Charlie had explained about grandfathers. So, why hadn't he realized before that the secret in the necklace—the picture being Mama—Big Charlie's daughter—meant that Big Charlie was *his* grandfather?

He tried to speak, but Father's arm pressed hard against his throat. *God, Claire says when we're weak, you're strong…*

Father's grip tightened. "Your Ginnie was a cheatin'—"

"Watch your mouth!" Big Charlie growled as he inched closer.

"Listen, man, I loved Ginnie. But she and Sam were together behind my back—behind Ruth's back. This boy is Sam's. I don't doubt it for a minute." He wiped at the corner of his eyes. "I loved him once, too. But then I found out he wasn't even *mine*. How do you think that makes a man feel?"

"Pl—" Jake moved his foot back, hooking it around Father's crutch. With all his might, he kicked it away, causing Father to lose his balance and fall to the ground.

Jake landed on the dirt nearby, free from Father's clutches. Hound growled in the distance, jumping from the Hornet's open window and racing toward them. He growled incessantly at Father, covering the distance from the car to the shed in mere seconds. He stood over his adversary and clamped his mouth around his wrist.

Father kicked at Hound with his foot, but the dog's teeth only sank in deeper. "Auugh! Get him off me, or I'll use the knife. I swear I will!" Father raised his hand, the knife pointed at the dog's underbelly.

A gunshot echoed through the trees.

Father's arm flew back under the impact, the knife soaring overhead and then plunging into the ashes.

Chapter 21

*J*ake shared a tree stump with Big Charlie as they waited for the sheriff's deputy to finish questioning Father. He clutched onto Big Charlie's arm, wiping his eyes against the soft flannel of his shirt.

Big Charlie's hands trembled as he blew his nose into his handkerchief. "You're okay, aren't you, Jake? Not hurt anywhere?" Big Charlie looked Jake over from head to toe.

"I'm fine. But, I sure was scared—for Hound." The rhythmic breathing of the dog's broad chest, as he lay sleeping in the shade of the old shed brought him a sense of reassurance… thankfulness. Then he stole a glance at Big Charlie. "I don't know what I'd do without either of you, Charlie."

An EMT closed the door to the ambulance and took off down the driveway, the tires spraying a mixture of mud and water onto everything in its path. The deputy strode toward Charlie and Jake, a notepad and pen in his hand. "It looks like you two had quite an adventure this morning."

Charlie gave Jake's shoulders a firm squeeze. "We sure did."

Jake furrowed his eyebrows. "Is Father going to die?"

"Not at all, son. Bullet only grazed his arm. Just sent him to the hospital per department guidelines." The deputy smiled at him and winked.

Jake frowned. The deputy might believe he was worried about Father, but he wasn't. He was glad Big Charlie shot him.

"My partner and I are going to collect what evidence we can, so you two go on home. The sheriff had an ornery tooth pulled earlier, today. If he feels like coming in tomorrow morning, he'll have his secretary schedule an appointment with you. For now, I think I have enough information from your statements to write my report."

Charlie grunted as he stood. "Jake, get Hound into the car and let's head home. Claire's probably worryin' about us."

Jake whistled. "Come on, Hound. Time to go home." Hound jumped up, wagging his tail. He took a long drink from a puddle of yesterday's rainwater and then followed Jake down the sloping driveway.

Before he reached the car, Jake looked back at the remains of his home one last time. He hoped one day he'd be able to forget all that happened here.

He raised his hands to the sky, twirling around and around, as the sun warmed his face.

"We're free, Hound."

"Ruth!" Jake ran to give his friend a big hug as she entered the Claiborne's cabin.

"Are you all right, Jake? I heard a little of what happened today." Ruth placed her hands on either side of his face.

"I wasn't scared. Grandpa was with me."

"Grandpa?"

"Yep. See, he was my mama's father, so that makes him my grandpa."

She raised her eyebrows at Big Charlie. "Yeah, I know how that works, but—"

Big Charlie shrugged his shoulders. "You were right. Jake hadn't put two and two together, yet. He didn't realize exactly what Virginia bein' his mother meant as far as *our* relationship was concerned."

Ruth laughed good-naturedly. "So much for our big surprise."

"Father's in the hospital." Jake balanced himself on the arm of Big Charlie's recliner. "Hound bit him—and then Grandpa shot him when he tried to hurt Hound."

Claire placed a bowl of steaming corn-on-the-cob in the middle of the table. "As a rule, I'm against guns, but in this case I'm glad Charlie didn't listen to me about taking it along."

"Jake, I'm sure Ethan will be fine, but you may have to testify at his trial."

He looked over at Ruth, clutching his arms to his chest. "What does 'testify' mean?"

"The court will ask you questions about how he treated you, what kind of father he was, and about what he did to your mother and Sam. Just tell the truth. You'll be fine." Ruth let out a deep sigh. "The worst of it's over. From here on out, you're going to have a nice life. We're all going to see to that."

"Right." Big Charlie beamed. "You're part of our family. I'm your grandfather and Claire, because she's married to me, is your grandmother."

"What about Ruth?" Jake turned and gave her a big smile.

"I'm still your friend. That will never change. We have a special bond, don't we?"

"Yep." Jake answered. "Just like me and Hound."

Ruth blotted her running mascara with a tissue. Then her voice took on a serious tone. "The thing is, Jake, we need to determine who your real father is—Ethan or Sam."

Jake sat up straight. "Father said Sam is my real father."

Ruth bit her lip. "Maybe, maybe not. It's very complicated. Your mother isn't here to ask, so we need to do the next best thing. There's a medical test that can be done to determine the truth, once and for all."

Jake scrunched his face. He hoped it had nothing to do with needles. "Maybe I'd rather not know. Neither one of them was very nice— oops. Sorry, Ruth."

"That's okay." Ruth tousled Jake's hair. "But knowing who your real father is will make the decision of who you will live with an easier one."

Jake pulled on Big Charlie's sleeve. "Can't I just go back and forth like I've been doing?"

"For a while, I suppose," Big Charlie interjected. "But, when it comes to things like registerin' for school and gettin' treatment at hospitals—you know, important stuff— there needs to be one person responsible for makin' decisions. Just remember, we all love you and want the best for you."

"We're ready to eat, Jake, so go wash up, please." Claire slid the garlic bread out of the oven.

Jake left the bathroom door open while he plunged his hands under the faucet. He grabbed the towel and headed back into the kitchen, pausing at the sound of Claire's hushed voice.

"I couldn't bear it if Jake went into a foster home. Can we all agree that one of us should adopt him?"

"What's 'adopt' mean?" Jake stood in the doorway, head cocked to the side.

"Jake!" Big Charlie raised his eyebrows. "You sure have a way of comin' around in the middle of conversations. Sit down here for a minute, son." Big Charlie relocated to the sofa, making room for Jake between him and Ruth. "The law allows people to adopt, or take a child into their home...let him or her live there...take care of them…love them… raise them just like their own. Legally, the child is no longer connected to the parent of their past. They can look forward to a bright future with a new and loving family. Do you understand?"

He nodded. "A kid sure would be lucky to get adopted. But I suppose that only happens to really good kids—not ones that get in trouble or think bad thoughts."

Ruth took Jake's hands in hers. "Hey, slow down! People don't adopt children because they're perfect—or ever could be. It's because the adult *chooses* to love the child. No conditions."

———

"Come on in, folks. Good to see you." Sheriff Foley extended a hand to Charlie as he arrived at the sheriff's office with Claire and Ruth. Charlie pulled a straight-backed chair next to the loveseat, giving the ladies the more comfortable seats facing the sheriff's cluttered desk. "Sheriff, this is Ruth Havens."

The sheriff closed the blinds to block out the late afternoon sun and then reached over the desk to shake hands with Ruth. "Nice to meet you. Thanks for comin'."

Claire was the first to speak. "It was Ruth that talked to the hostage in the hospital. And, because of her good detective work, she played a hunch that Ethan was headed to the cabin to retrieve something important. It was her phone call to your office that sent your deputies out there just in the nick of time."

The sheriff nodded. "So they said. Thanks for all you did, Ms. Havens."

Ruth blushed, looking down at her clasped hands.

Charlie cleared his throat, anxious to get on with the meeting. "I guess your deputies already filled you in on what took place out there yesterday."

"That they did. However, when firearms are used, we need to be careful to get in-depth witness statements. Get our ducks in a row, so to speak." He leaned back and crossed his feet atop the edge of the desk. "Basically, I need each of you to write in your own words, when you met this man, any and all interactions you've had with him, chronologically, all the way up until the shootin'."

Charlie nodded. "I've never been one that was good at letter writin', but I'll make this an exception."

"I know what you mean." The sheriff shook his head and sighed, his eyes focusing on a tall stack of paperwork. "An attorney will be contactin' each of you, too. This may be a nasty case that'll tie up the courts for some time. Joshua Harding has a prior sentence to serve in Texas and we've got accusations of child abuse, assault, kidnappin', identity theft, and two murders here in Virginia."

Ruth's mouth fell open. "*Two* murders?"

The sheriff referred to his handwritten notes. "Yep. Sam Havens, and Joshua's uncle, Ethan Harding."

"We didn't know anything about Ethan Harding." Claire looked at Ruth and Charlie with raised eyebrows.

"That's right," Charlie nodded.

"This is being confirmed, as we speak, but we have every reason to believe that Joshua...er, Ethan to you, killed his uncle and then stole his identity. The cabin he'd been livin' in for the last thirteen or so years actually belonged to him. When we searched Joshua's knapsack, we found a small metal box. Inside it was some cash, the driver's license of the deceased uncle, as well as his own. Looks like he'd been masqueradin' as Sam Havens. Found Sam's license in Joshua's pocket."

"The social security office told us they hadn't received a death certificate for Mr. Harding. They figured he was still alive. So, we can probably add social security fraud to the growin' list of things he'll have to account for. Those monthly benefits probably added up to quite a bit over the years. His post office box here in town had several checks in it when my deputy got it opened this mornin'. Up until a few months ago, Joshua had probably been pickin' those up on a regular basis."

Claire shook her head. "Are you saying Ethan's real name is Joshua Harding?"

"Bingo." The sheriff pulled another paper out of his folder. "According to Miss Middleton, he told her his real first name. The license we found in that box, yesterday, provided his last name. We put all of that information into the computer this mornin' and he was easy to identify. He's a wanted man in Texas. Looks like he'll probably stand trial here for the murders. Once they're over, he'll have his prior sentence added to whatever he gets here. Nothin's been decided yet, of course."

Charlie pushed his ball cap back on his head and sat forward. "Did you find out what he was in prison for back in Texas, Sheriff?"

"He was convicted of killin' two children in a hit-'n-run. Left those sweet little girls for dead. Just hours before he was to be moved from jail to prison, he got the slip on one of the guards."

Claire grabbed Charlie's hand and squeezed. "Tell the sheriff the rest of what we found out, dear."

Charlie hesitated. He hoped to say this without losing control and sounding like a blubbering old fool. He knew a grown man wasn't supposed to cry and get emotional, but she was his daughter. He cleared his throat and took a deep, calming breath.

"Since we talked to you before, Sheriff, we've discovered that we have a more personal connection to Joshua. Back in Texas, he somehow got mixed up with my daughter, Virginia, and talked her into runnin' away with him. He ended up killin' her, along with Sam Havens. Guess you can add a third murder to your list. I'll never know how he managed to talk her into runnin' off with him, but it sure hurts, I can tell you. It sure hurts." Charlie blinked away his escaping tears.

"My, my. Small world." Sheriff Foley stuffed the papers back into the folder.

"My condolesences. At least I hope it's of some comfort to you to have him locked up. And, at least you have more answers than you did before."

Ruth stood. "Sheriff, are you going to need to get a statement from Jake?"

"Counsel will need one from him in order to make his case. If he's got any idea where Joshua's rifle might be, that'd be a big help. We've already taken prints from the knife he was holdin' yesterday, and started that new-fangled DNA testin'. Pretty sure that's gonna be Uncle Ethan's murder weapon. Found traces of blood on it."

Claire put her arm around Ruth. "Speaking of DNA, Sheriff, we'd like to ask you to get a sample from Ethan—sorry, Joshua—so we can confirm paternity for Jake. This may be the best chance we're ever going to have of finding out, once and for all, who his father really is."

"I understand. I'll talk to his public defender and get the ball rollin'. It may take a while, so we all need to practice a little patience. It'll all come out in the wash."

Chapter 22

*C*harlie stared at the envelope on the kitchen table, noting the return address label and embossed seal. He picked it up and turned it over, again and again. It had been the longest thirty days of his life. Whatever it says, their lives would be changed forever. He knew Ruth wanted the boy to be Sam's. She'd be a good mother for him. He was certain of that. But if he turned out to be Ethan's son, she would have no legal claim on him at all.

Claire padded into the kitchen and leaned down to kiss his cheek. "Is that what I think it is?"

"Letter from the president? Nope."

"Charlie Claiborne, you're such a jokester."

"Yeah, it's the results. But I don't want to open it without Jake and Ruth bein' here."

"It's almost seven o'clock. They should be back from the movie, soon. I think I'll bake an apple pie and we can celebrate." Claire walked toward the pantry.

"Celebrate? I don't think so." Charlie craned his neck in her direction. "Jake'll be disappointed to be either man's son. And who'd blame him? He never says who he wants to live with. Afraid to hurt someone's feelin's, I s'pect."

"Yes." Claire placed a sack of apples on the counter, grabbed her paring knife, and started peeling. "We have a lot to be thankful for, and no matter who his father is, we have a wonderful grandson. Period. The rest, we'll just deal with as God gives us the wisdom and strength to do so."

"You really mean that, don't you?" Charlie's mouth watered as Claire doused the cut apples with a mixture of cinnamon and sugar and placed them in the bottom crust. She topped the concoction with several large pats of butter.

"Yes, I do. I've been watching the way Ruth is with Jake these past couple of weeks. I hate to admit it, but I think I've been slow to acknowledge what has been under my nose all along." Her voice was calm and her face serene.

"You seem to be at peace, whatever the outcome." Charlie walked over and put his arms around Claire's shoulders from behind, giving her a playful hug, followed by a slobbery kiss on her cheek.

"Ruth has all the qualities we could ever hope for in a mother for Jake. Most of all, she loves him and wants him." A single tear rolled down her cheek. She brushed it away with the corner of her pink apron.

He nodded. *Thank you, Lord, for hearin' my prayer and changin' my sugar's heart.* "So, does that mean what I think it means?"

"It means I'm going to try to be content with being Jake's grandmother."

"So when do you think we should talk to Ruth?" Charlie raised one eyebrow.

"Whenever you think the time is right, you have a talk with her— alone. I know I'd just cry if I was there and I don't want her to misunderstand and think I don't agree with this decision." She put her forehead against his. "This is the right decision—for all of us."

"I'll talk with her in private, if that's what you want." Charlie poured two cups of coffee, placing one in front of Claire. "That cinnamon sure smells good."

"I'm glad I had these extra crusts in the refrigerator. Makes the job go that much faster. This pie is almost ready for the oven." Claire covered the mixture with a second crust. She was just pinching the two layers together when Ruth and Jake returned.

"Hi, you two," Claire greeted as she carried the pie toward the oven. "How was the movie?"

Ruth sat down at the kitchen table. "Lots of action. We were on the edge of our seats the whole time. Weren't we, Jake?"

"Yep." Jake grabbed a tennis ball from Hound's toy basket. "Come on, boy. Let's go outside and play." He ran toward the door, Hound trotting at his heels.

Charlie stood and faced them, the thin envelope in his hand. "Hey, not so fast. Let's have you join us in the living room for a little family pow-wow."

"Ahhh," Jake protested.

"This will only take a few minutes. Besides, it's important." Charlie gave Jake a stern look and pointed his index finger toward the sofa.

———— ꙮ ————

With the light of the full moon shining through the window behind him, Jake fidgeted as Big Charlie slid his finger under the flap of the envelope. He was sure this was the letter they'd been waiting for. To him, cheating was better than murder, so he hoped it would say he was Sam's son.

He'd like to live with Ruth. His friend Eric was right when he said it was best to just visit with grandparents and let them spoil you. A kid should live with someone younger who has more energy. Eric should know. He'd lived with his aunt ever since his parents died in a car crash six years ago.

Big Charlie opened the folded paper with a flourish. After a careful read of its contents, he put it back inside the envelope. He closed his eyes and exhaled before he spoke. "You know, Jake, these results are only for legal purposes. We all love you and want you in our lives. Whoever your father is has no bearin' on our futures together. It's only a confirmation of what happened more than ten years ago. We've been through all that. Right?"

"Right." Jake nodded, wiggling in his seat.

"And Ruth, same goes for you. Except maybe this letter will help you forgive Sam."

Ruth twisted several strands of her hair around her finger. "So he's not Jake's father?"

"No. Ethan is the confirmed father—ninety percent reliability on the testin'."

Jake tugged on Claire's arm. "What does 'reliability' mean?"

"Well, it means they are certain that Ethan—Joshua— is your father, just like he's always been." She patted his knee with her soft hand.

Jake jumped up, yelling at the top of his lungs. "I don't want a father! And I especially don't want *him* for a father!"

"Now, calm down. We understand, Jake, but things are how they are. We knew you had to be somebody's son. Right?" Big Charlie laid a hand on Jake's head and drew him to his chest for a big bear hug.

Jake pulled back and looked into his eyes. "I guess. But I wanted Sam to be my father." *Big Charlie didn't know how it felt. His father never killed anybody. Anyway, Ruth wouldn't want the son of a killer to live with her.*

"I know, but things aren't always how we'd like them to be. And now that we know this, we have some talkin' to do with Ruth—some things to decide. Don't be concerned. Nothin' needs to change right away. Let's just take our time until we get used to this news."

"I'm never going to get used to it."

Ruth slid her chair back from the table. "I'll be back in a little while. I need a minute or two— alone." She hurried out the screen door and onto the porch.

Charlie placed the envelope on top of the refrigerator with the rest of the day's mail. He turned toward Claire. "I s'pect this news is a mixture of both relief and disappointment for Ruth."

"I'm going to my room. Come on, Hound." Jake stalked down the hall with his dog by his side.

Big Charlie called from behind him. "Hey, aren't you forgettin' about that apple pie?"

Claire jumped up from the sofa. "Oh, the pie! What else can go wrong?" She grabbed her potholders and ran for the oven.

"I don't smell anythin' burnin', so you're probably savin' it just in the nick of time." Big Charlie inspected the pie as Claire brought it out of the oven. "Just a little crispy around the edges. We don't mind that. Do we, Jake?"

"Nope."

Big Charlie put his arm around Jake's shoulders. "Let's you and I go outside and talk with Ruth a bit while the pie's coolin'." He guided him out the door and into the cool night air.

Jake stood under the kitchen window, lost in the shadows. He knew what Ruth was going to say. She'd decided to move away and start a new life in a big city. There, she could meet a nice guy and settle down and have a bunch of her own kids. She'd say it would be better for everyone. But he knew it wouldn't be better for him.

Ruth stood by the railing, moonlight bathing her in a soft glow. Big Charlie put a burly arm around her thin shoulders and gave her a squeeze. "Hey, how you doin'?"

"I'll be okay." She dabbed at her swollen eyes with the edge of her sleeve. "I guess I didn't realize just how much I wanted to be a mom— Jake's mom. I just have to adjust to this news on my own."

Big Charlie took a seat in the chair facing the empty glider and reached across to pat the cushion. "I know you're disappointed, but if you think about it, nothing has really changed."

Ruth left the rail to sit across from him. "That's easy for you to say, Charlie. He's your grandson, no matter what."

"True. But Ruth, love knows no boundaries…hereditary, or otherwise. You and Jake have a special bond. What you do *now* will determine just how strong that bond really is."

Ruth sniffled. "What do you mean?"

"Well, you can use this news to defeat you, or you can show Jake unconditional love—no matter who his father is." Big Charlie hoisted himself out of the chair and turned to face the small pond. He watched a fat toad hop from one lily pad to another. "You're right. I'm still gonna be the boy's grandpa, but you have the choice of walkin' away or remainin' his friend. Why, you might even want to adopt him." The corners of Charlie's mouth curled into a slow smile.

Ruth blinked. "Really? You and Claire aren't going to try to get custody or adopt him, yourselves?"

"Ruth, we love Jake. But, he needs to be livin' with someone younger—someone who can relate to him better, who has the energy for raisin' a growin' boy. Of course, we'll do that if you decide you don't want the responsibility, but we're happy just to be his grandparents. We've seen you interact with him these past months. There's no doubt in our minds that you'd be a good mother for him—and we'd be glad to have you as part of our family."

"Thank you, Charlie. I can't think of a nicer family to be a part of." Ruth's smile was as bright as her silver earrings. "You have no idea what your words mean to me."

"You can still be his mother, you know—in every way that really matters." He nodded in Jake's direction. "You have anythin' to add to what I've already said, Jake?"

Ruth gasped. "Jake, I didn't know you were out here."

He ran to her side, giving her a giant hug. "Yeah. I've been here the whole time. I heard the part where you said you wanted to be my mother. Is that really true?"

"Nothing could be more true, Jake. How would you feel about that?"

Her closed eyes reminded him of Sam's picture as he made his wish before blowing out his candles. "I was hoping that's what you'd say." Jake took her hands in his and twirled her around, her long skirt a kaleidoscope of happy colors reflected in the moonlight.

She grinned at Big Charlie. "It looks like we have some celebrating to do. I'm ready for some pie!"

"Me, too!" Jake held the door open for Big Charlie and his new "mom."

It wasn't even nine o'clock, yet everyone else in this antiquated jail was already asleep. Ethan examined the official-looking envelope in his hands. It was probably notification of his hearing date. If he was so sure of that, why was he so nervous? And why hadn't he opened it hours ago?

He tore open the end of the envelope and slid out a single folded sheet of paper. He unfolded it and held it up to the window, reading it in the glow of the full moon. He squinted. "Dear Mr. Harding, blah, blah... results are conclusive...you are—." As the letter fluttered onto the floor, he sank onto the hard bunk, his crutches clattering onto the concrete. He lowered his head to rest in his hands. So, the boy was his son, after all. He would have bet good money he was Sam's.

Blind fury propelled him to the cell door. He clutched the bars, shaking them back and forth. His guttural scream horrified even him.

A burly guard careened around the corner, rapping his flashlight on the bars. "Hey, keep it down in there. People are tryin' to sleep."

"You really think I care about them?" Joshua screamed.

"We have a solitary cell for guys like you. Keep hollerin' and we'll move you over there for the next few days." The guard gritted his teeth.

"Suits me just fine. I've never been one to socialize anyhow." Joshua spat in his face.

The flashlight was shattered, and its light extinguished, when the guard smacked it against the bars for the second time. "Now, look what's happened. All because you couldn't keep your big trap shut!" He grunted as he crouched down to retrieve the broken glass. He raked his hands back and forth over the rough floor, gathering fragments and placing them into his empty Styrofoam coffee cup. Then he strode back down the hall and closed the door separating the cells from the rest of the station.

Joshua dropped onto the small cot. He rolled over and closed his eyes.

Ginnie smiled as she held the baby in her arms. "Joshua Harding, you have a son. A beautiful baby boy."

He ran his finger over the baby's soft cheek. "I'm your father, little Jake. I love you and I'll always be here for you and your mama."

A crack of thunder overhead jolted him awake. He sat on the side of the bed, running his fingers through his hair. Lightning illuminated a small piece of glass next to his cot. He picked it up, lowered himself onto the floor, and wedged himself into the darkened corner between the toilet and the bed frame. He raised the sharp edge of the glass to his wrist as fresh tears traveled down his cheeks and onto his neck, finally coming together at the place on his chest that had once housed a heart.

This time, he'd go deeper. This time, he'd cut along the vein and then the artery underneath. He'd soon know the peace that had eluded him for so many years.

His movements were swift and sure. He'd need only to wait for the sweet release...

His breathing slowed. It would soon be over—the years of abuse at the hands of his father and the subsequent abuse of his own son. The cycle would now be broken. His last act here on earth would bring about Jake's safety and his own self-retribution. Justice for them both.

Minutes later, he felt his body being pulled, and then lifted. Sounds of muffled voices, then a gush of air as doors opened. *Where are they taking me? The hospital? The morgue?*

Ginnie, is that you?

She had never looked more radiant. Her skin glowed. Iridescent. The beautiful rainbow behind her was alive with pulsating colors. He held out his hand to touch her, but she faded away, leaving behind a vast emptiness.

His body felt heavy. It started to fall through an intense cold fog—faster and faster—colder and colder. Then silence, followed by darkness—utter and complete darkness.

———

Charlie inhaled the heavenly aroma as he lowered himself into the chair across from Jake. His mouth watered for pie.

The phone rang just as he tucked his napkin inside his shirt collar. "What now? Can't a man eat without interruption? Is that too much to ask?"

Claire answered it, gesturing to Charlie that it was for him. She mouthed the word "Sheriff" and held out the receiver.

"I hope my ice cream doesn't melt." He grabbed the phone in a huff. "Charlie Claiborne here."

"Charlie, I thought I should keep you in the loop. Joshua Harding tried to take his life down at the jail tonight."

Dear God! And all I had on my mind was apple pie. "Do you have any details?"

"Only that he's at Davis Memorial Hospital, here in Elkins. Doin' alright, as far as I know."

"I appreciate the call, Sheriff. Keep me posted, will you?"

"Sure will. Bye, now."

Charlie turned to look in Jake's direction. There was no reason to break the news to his grandson until he knew more.

"So, what did the sheriff have to say?" Claire poured coffee for Ruth and Charlie, placing the cups next to their desserts.

"Ah—um." He cleared his throat. "Joshua's in the hospital. No details yet. The sheriff said he'd call again when he has more information."

Claire sank into her chair. "Odd. I wonder what happened?"

"He probably has a stomach ache from eating jail food. Otis had the same problem on The Andy Griffith Show." Jake shoved another large bite of pie into his mouth.

Ruth raised her eyebrows toward Charlie.

He read the silent question in her eyes and nodded in her direction.

Ruth rose from her chair, pasted a smile on her face, and planted a kiss on top of Jake's head. "I didn't realize it had gotten so late. I have just enough time to drive home and get changed before my shift. See you this weekend."

Jake looked up from his half-eaten dessert. "Okay. If you see Eric, will you tell him I can play Saturday?"

"Sure will." She turned to Charlie. "I'll call you about...you know."

Charlie wiped vanilla ice cream off his chin. "I'd appreciate it. See you Saturday morning. 'Bout ten."

Jake's brow furrowed. "What's going on, Charlie?"

Charlie shook his head. "Why do kids always have to be so inquisitive? How's the pie?"

"Deeeeeeeelicious!" Jake replied between bites.

Ruth squeezed Claire's shoulder. "Sorry to waste the pie."

Jake slid her plate over in front of him. "It's not wasted!"

Chapter 23

*C*harlie stopped at the nurses' station later that evening and waited for Ruth to finish on the computer before he interrupted her. *Lord, what am I doin' here, anyway?* Maybe he'd just turn around and go back home. The hospital surely had a pastor or a counselor on call... He coughed.

Ruth jumped. "Charlie!"

"Didn't mean to spook ya. Just thought I'd come down and offer some moral support. Claire sent you another piece of pie, too." Charlie reached over the counter and thrust a small foil-covered plate into her hands.

"Thank her for me, will you?" Ruth peeked under the foil, inhaling the aroma.

"Sure will." Charlie cocked his head in the direction of the guard at the end of the hallway and lowered his voice. "That his room down there?"

"Yes." Ruth's eyes opened wide. "Surely you don't want to see him, do you?"

Charlie shrugged. "I s'pect he won't have any other visitors."

Ruth shook her head. "After all he's done?"

How could he explain to Ruth that he didn't really want to see Joshua? It was just that the Holy Spirit was prompting him, as He'd done when he saw Claire sitting all alone at that group meeting last year. "True, but still—everyone needs a friend."

Charlie waited for Ruth to walk around the counter and join him. They took a dozen cautious steps down the hall, approaching the lanky guard at the door of room #340.

When Charlie produced his driver's license, the guard stepped in front of him. "Gotta frisk ya, too. No offense. Just the rules."

Charlie raised his arms overhead as Deputy Watkins patted him down. "I understand."

"I'll call you about Friday night, Ruth." The guard flashed his toothy grin in her direction as she and Charlie neared the door.

Ruth's face reddened and she lowered her eyelids. "Okay, Earl."

Charlie smiled. *Seems like Ruth has a buddin' romance. I wonder if Claire knows anythin' about it...*

Charlie stood still for a minute, letting his eyes adjust to the darkness. What little light there was came from the bathroom, the door being left slightly ajar. He froze in the shadows as Ruth checked Joshua's pulse. *Give me, strength, Lord. I need you, now.*

Joshua's eyes fluttered open. "Who is it?"

"It's Ruth." She turned on the small bedside lamp. "How are you feeling?"

"Sleepy."

"Charlie's here, too, but don't be alarmed. He's only here out of concern for you. I'll let you two visit for a few minutes." Ruth gave Charlie's arm a squeeze, then disappeared through the door.

Charlie stepped toward Joshua. His leg was shackled to the bed-rail. One wrist was also handcuffed to it, the other bandaged up to his elbow. They weren't taking any chances. He was a killer, after all. His throat tightened. What could he say to the man who'd killed his daughter? Why had the Lord even brought him here?

Joshua tried to rise up from the bed, but sagged against the pillow. His eyes closed, twitched, and then opened wide. "If you're here…to kill me, Charlie, get…on with it. I…know we both want…me dead. You should…have finished me…off at the shed."

"I didn't want to shoot you. I did it to protect Jake and Hound." Charlie's body shook as he lowered himself into the soft leather chair at the far side of the bed.

Joshua cleared his throat. "But, you…hate me."

Charlie couldn't find the words. He gulped, forcing himself to talk. "Let's just say that you've done things I could never forgive on my own. It's only outta obedience to God—with the help of the Holy Spirit— that someday I'll be able to." Beads of sweat formed on his forehead.

Joshua's wrist turned red as he pulled against the handcuff. "But, Ginnie—"

"Don't try to talk. They've probably given you somethin' to help with the pain."

"Ah…the pain." Tears filled Joshua's eyes as his face contorted. "What…about the…pain…I've…caused…all of you? Got anything… for…that?"

Charlie rose from the chair and stood over the bed. "As a matter-of-fact, Joshua, there is somethin' for healin'—"

"No, I want…to die!" Joshua spat the words at Charlie.

He shook his head and wiped the saliva from his face. *He deserves to die. But Lord, you don't always give us what we deserve. You extend mercy— to even the likes of him.* "You will die, someday. We all will. But, I'm talkin' about the healin' of your eternal soul." Charlie ran his hand along his chin. *The words, Lord. I need your words…*

Joshua's blue eyes twitched. "Eternal soul?"

"Yes. I believe we were all created by God as eternal bein's."
Charlie grabbed a handkerchief from his back pocket and mopped his
forehead.

"Well, I prefer...to believe life...is just one...long...movie that
will...eventually... end. And, when...it does...well..." Joshua's voice
drifted off.

"So, that's what you were hopin' for? The end of your movie? The
end of your pain?" *He deserves to suffer, Lord. Why are you willin' to let him
off so easy?* Charlie clenched and unclenched his fists.

"Something like that."

"The Bible says—"

"Listen old man, I don't... need ... a sermon."

Charlie rested his arms on the bed rail and bent over. "What you *do*
need is forgiveness."

"You said you can't forgive me." Joshua snarled.

"I'm not talkin' about me. I'm talkin' about God."

Joshua continued to pull against his shackle, straining to rise and
meet Charlie face-to-face. "God's not going to forgive me. I tortured
my own kid. I killed Ginnie."

*Lord, he's every bit a murderer and abuser, but if you see somethin' in him
worth savin', then I'm not the one to argue that point.* "God knows what
you've done. But, as incredible as it may seem, He's willin' to forgive
you—to forgive anyone—who truly repents."

Joshua's voice was sarcastic. "Now why would he want to forgive *me?*"

Jake's stomach flip-flopped again. Too much pie. Too much ice cream.

"Here. Drink this." Claire shoved a glass with fizzing bubbles into his hands. "It'll help. I promise."

He recoiled at her strange brew. He wasn't so sure about that. When the next wave of cramping hit, he held his breath, pinched his nose, and drank the concoction down as fast as possible.

"Let's get ready for bed now. It's late. No use waiting up for Charlie." She turned off the light over the kitchen table.

Jake started down the short hall toward his room. He stifled a yawn when he reached the door. He wished they'd tell him what's going on. He wasn't a little kid anymore. "I know he went to see Father."

"You do?" Claire's voice squeaked in surprise.

"Yeah. That story about needing to get some milk for breakfast didn't make sense. I'm the only one who drinks it and there's still plenty enough in the fridge." He flashed her an impish smile. "Anyway, stores aren't open this late and the drive is too far."

When she returned his smile with one of her own, her blue eyes lit with a familiar twinkle. "Okay. Yes. He did go to the hospital. He was concerned."

"How can he be concerned about Father? He's been nothing but bad to him."

Claire leaned against the hallway wall. "Your grandpa is a good man, Jake. He feels things deeply—one of which is his commitment to God. I'm certain he went to see Joshua because God laid it on his heart to do so."

"If God is all about goodness, why would he care anything about Father? He's bad—all the way through!" Jake stomped into his room, dove beneath his favorite quilt, and drew it up over his shoulders. He had killed Mama and hurt him more times than he could count. He didn't know why Big Charlie thought God could ever forgive Father.

Claire followed him into his room and sat down on the side of his bed, massaging her right foot before placing it back into the soft fluffiness of its white slipper. "Charlie's definitely better at explaining these things, but all I know is that because God is 'all about goodness' as you put it, he loves every person he ever created. That includes your father. He often doesn't love what people *do*, but he loves their eternal soul. He gives them chance after chance to come to him and let him change their lives for the good."

Jake sat up. He had thought about Father as being bad for so long that the possibility he might someday be different had never entered his mind. "You really believe God can change Father's heart? Change him into a good person?"

"I definitely do, Jake—but only if Joshua will allow him to. The Bible says that God stands at the door of our hearts and knocks. He doesn't force himself in. We have to be the ones to open the door. When we do, he says he'll come in." She gave his head a pat and headed for the door. "Let's get some sleep. We can talk more in the morning if you want." She turned out the light and started to close the door.

"Claire?"

"Yes, Jake?"

"What will it be like to be adopted?"

"It's just like we discussed before. You'll live with Ruth most of the time so that you can get established in school, but you can spend weekends with us whenever you want."

"Will I be her son then, really and truly?"

"Yes. You'll be her son and a part of her family. And, in the future, we're hoping that you will accept Jesus as your savior and get adopted again."

"What do you mean?"

"The Bible tells us that when you accept Jesus as your savior, you will be adopted into God's family, too."

I wonder what it would be like to have God for a father... Jake yawned and stretched once more, but he sensed that the tingling warmth spreading throughout his body wasn't because of the quilt.

As soon as Claire left the room, Jake slid from the warmth of his bed down to the rug where Hound slept. He snuggled close. "Hound, you don't mind having company down here, do you?"

Hound licked his face and settled back to sleep, his big droopy eyes closing as he drifted off. It wasn't long until he was snoring.

Jake reached up for his pillow, scrunched it, and lay his head down. Pillows were a great invention. Come to think of it, so were beds. He guessed Father had a bed in jail. Claire said this is a civilized world—not barbaric. He wasn't so sure what that meant, though.

He clutched a tuft of fur on Hound's back. "Grandpa Charlie said that my insides could get ruined if I keep so much hate inside me. He said if I would ask God to help me, someday I'd be able to forgive Father for all the things he's done. But, I'll tell you a secret, Hound. I don't want to."

He raised up on his elbows. "Things are changing for us, Hound. They're just getting better and better." His eyes fell on the framed photograph of his new family on his dresser—Grandpa Charlie, Grandma Claire, and his special friend, Ruth. "I'm going to have a mama, but I think I'll still call her Ruth." His eyes were soon too heavy to hold open any longer.

Mama kissed his forehead. She smelled like cinnamon and spring flowers.

It was still dark when he was roused from a dream in which he and Hound romped and played in the remote woods. They had cornered a toad between two smooth rocks, wet with morning dew. As Jake's hand inched forward to grasp the creature from the deep, a voice startled him and the toad made his getaway.

"Jake. Jake."

"Wh—what?" Jake opened his eyes and blinked.

An angelic figure with pale blue wings etched in silver sat down on the side of his bed and stroked his damp hair. "Your Papa needs your help, Jake."

"What do you mean?" Jake blinked twice and rubbed the sleep from his eyes.

"You know he's in the hospital."

"Yes."

"He's tried to hurt himself again." Tears rimmed the angel's perfect blue eyes.

"Don't cry. He's not worth it." Jake clenched his teeth.

"He can't live with what he did. How he's treated you all these years. He doesn't know how to apologize or make it up to you—but he wants to, Jake, he really wants to. To him, ending his life seemed to be the only option." Her fingers caressed his cheeks. "He was a boy like you, once, Jake. He had hopes and dreams like all boys do, but his father abused him, too. He did what he had to do to survive."

"Did his father kill Father's mother, too?"

"No. But he abused her. She wanted to help him, but she didn't see any way out. She took her own life when your Papa was just nine years old."

"Why are you telling me this?"

"Because although it doesn't make the things he has done *right,* it helps explain how he came to be the way he is. And it should show you what may lie ahead for you, too, if you aren't able to put your own hurt aside and help him."

"You're wanting me to forgive him? I just can't—not now. Not ever!" He squeezed his eyes shut, but hot tears still managed to escape.

"You've come so far, Jake, from that frightened little boy in the cabin. You thought you were running *away*, but you were really running *to* this very day, this place in time, where you will make one of the most important decisions of your life."

The angel's reassuring smile lingered as he contemplated her words. Had God sent her here to guide *him* the same way Claire said Big Charlie is guided by the Holy Spirit?

Chapter 24

"Well?" Joshua raised his chin in defiance. Charlie had been staring at him for at least a full minute. Maybe this was one question he didn't have an answer for.

Charlie's lips trembled. "Love. Plain, simple, unconditional love. God's very essence is love and, by his very nature, he acts accordingly. From that love flows mercy and forgiveness."

"I'm not stupid. What's the catch?" Joshua growled. There's always a catch...

"All you have to do is repent. And, like the Bible says, 'turn from your wicked ways'."

"That's it? I simply promise to be a good little boy from now on?"

Charlie paused, shut his eyes and took a deep breath. "You've gotta face what you've done—who you've become." He balled his fists at his side. "When Jesus died on the cross, he paid the ultimate price for the sins of all of mankind. That includes yours. By comin' to the end of yourself and placin' your confidence in him, you can be forgiven and start a brand new life—in Christ."

"So, I get off scot-free?" *New life? I don't think so. Why am I even listening to this old coot?*

"Not at all. Each one of us is subject to the consequences of our actions. You'll have to pay the price on this earth for what you've done."

So, it was just as he thought. "Then nothing will have changed, will it?"

"Of course it will. You'll become a child of God." Charlie laid his trembling hand on Joshua's shoulder. "You'll know his eternal forgiveness of sin. You'll be with him in heaven one day when you *do* die."

"I'd—I'd like to believe you, but—" His head was spinning. Maybe it was the drugs. *Was Ginnie's father really here in his room, telling him that God actually could care about someone like him? That he could forgive the things he'd done?*

Charlie leaned closer. "Let God begin to work in your life. Let him heal your heart of stone—restore it to what it was when he first created you. Let him teach you to love yourself —and your son."

Something flickered in Joshua's heart. He recognized the same emotion as kindled in Charlie's pleading eyes. Could it be *hope*? He bit his lip, then nodded. "I don't know how to talk to God."

"I'll help you." Charlie let out an audible sigh. His shaking hands took Joshua's in his own.

How can Charlie stand to touch me? These hands killed Ginnie. These hands hurt Jake. He closed his eyes.

Charlie cleared his throat. "Just repeat after me. God, I believe that you sent your Son, Jesus, to the cross to die for my sins. I accept your forgiveness for the wrongs I have done. Give me the strength to turn from a life of sin to a new life in Christ. Amen."

Joshua's soft, whispered voice joined Charlie's. "Amen."

As they finished praying, Joshua gave Charlie's hands a squeeze. His eyes filled with tears. "I feel different, Charlie—like a massive weight has been lifted."

Charlie nodded. "That load of sin was pretty heavy, wasn't it?"

Claire was sleeping soundly, snoring like a freight train, as Jake tiptoed past. He pulled Big Charlie's holster off the bedpost, and slung it across his body. The buckled end of the belt rested on his shoulder, the holster itself against his opposite hip. He retrieved the step stool from the corner of the kitchen and placed it in front of the hall closet.

Jake stood on the top step, stretching his arm as far as it could reach. Charlie had stored his gun on the top shelf following the shooting incident at the shed. With any luck, it would still be there. He moved his hand from side to side. When he felt the cool metal, he slid it from its resting place.

The weapon was so heavy that even using both hands, it slipped from his grip. He let out a sigh of relief when it landed in the clothesbasket on the closet floor. Whew!

He jumped down the steps and hurried to look into Claire's bedroom. He peeked around the corner, his heart still pounding in his chest. Her position on the overstuffed pillow had not changed. *That was a close call.*

Back at the closet, he licked his lips, bent over, and recovered the revolver. He heaved it into the holster. He knew the rules about the gun. He wasn't supposed to touch it—in fact, he had promised not to—but this was different. Big Charlie couldn't possibly fault him for following an angel's request.

He snuck out the kitchen door and trekked the short distance to the highway. He drew the hood of his sweatshirt over his head and sprinted the quarter mile to the roadside rest area. He waited behind the men's restroom until a truck pulling a horse trailer parked nearby. When the driver headed into the building, Jake jumped into the bed of the truck, landing on soft, warm hay.

Just before sunup, the truck stopped at the familiar rodeo grounds where Jake had experienced his first circus. He held his breath as the driver strode around the truck and toward the back of the trailer. Then he hopped out and ran down the pavement toward the hospital.

He had worried about gaining entry to Father's room, but it had been easy to walk past Ruth and the officer who was laughing with her at the desk. It had been trial and error, though, to find the right room. Behind one door he opened was a man with a cast on his leg raised high in the air. Another door led to a room with two beds, but no people.

Father was in the third room.

He crept forward, trancelike. He fumbled a moment as he un-zipped his sweatshirt and withdrew the gun. It gleamed in the light of the bedside lamp.

There are three reasons to kill, boy:

> <u>One</u>, *for food;* <u>two</u>, *for sport;* <u>three</u>, *to put an animal out of its misery.*

Jake's nod was almost imperceptible. His heartbeat and his breathing raced against each other. His hands shook as Father's words replayed in his head. He swallowed hard, raised the gun, and took aim. Tears streamed down his face.

Why didn't the doctors just let him die? Nobody in the world would care, especially him.

But, the angel had asked him to help Father. So, he'd do it Father's way—like he'd said should be done for any animal.

He pulled the stiff hammer back on the second try.

At the sound of the click, Grandpa Charlie woke with a start. He rose from the chair where he had been sleeping to turn in Jake's direction. His eyes fell first on the wall where Jake's shadow loomed over Father's bed, then widened when he saw the gun. His face, ghostly white, was frozen on one side and twitched on the other.

Grandpa Charlie edged around the opposite side of the bed toward Jake. "Give… give…m-me the gun. You-you d-don't really w-w-ant to do…this," he stuttered. He inched closer, one arm stretched toward Jake, ready to take the weapon.

Jake waved the gun at him. "Stay back! I'm here to put Father out of his misery." His heart felt like it would beat out of his chest. His face grew hot and he struggled to breathe. Fear, hate, and pity swirled in his head. He squeezed his eyes shut.

He had a new life ahead of him. He was going to be part of a real family. Once Father was gone, he could start his new life without the fear of ever being hurt again. He hated Father. He had every reason to.

Father's voice broke through the twisting emotions. "Jake. Son—"

Jake looked up, squinting his eyes at the intensity of the bright light that was somehow slicing through a lifetime of memories, going backward in rapid succession and stopping, finally, at a long-forgotten day—the last, happy, carefree day of his life with Papa.

Mama had packed a wicker basket and set a red-and-white checkered cloth on the ground by the creek.

She and Papa laughed while he and Hound played by the water's edge.

When Papa picked him up and slid him over his head to ride on his broad shoulders, he squealed with delight. Papa trotted him around a few minutes before depositing him near Mama. "I may not tell you every day, Jakie boy, but always remember that I love you—and I always will."

Papa's voice grew fainter.

Jake glared at Father. "You told me you'd always—"

"Love you." Father's voice was low, unaccustomed to speaking the words.

"That's what you said, but you *lied*." The gun wobbled, heavy in his outstretched hands.

Tears ran down Father's cheeks. "I was hurt. I believed a lie. I turned the hate I felt inward and it destroyed me. I wasn't capable of loving you. I'm so...very...sorry."

Jake crept forward. Father's eyes told a lifetime of stories—tales of abuse, struggles, disappointment, betrayal—even murder. But tonight he saw something different. A mingling of sorrow and—could it be—*love?*

Was it possible that his father could really change? That the words he had said to him as a young child could possibly be believed? That they could give Jake hope and a reason to trust the one who had been there all along—the one who had clothed and fed him in the wilderness—the one who had protected him and his best friend—the one who stood at his heart's door and knocked?

His hands quivered. His ears pounded with each heartbeat. He wavered, unsure of what he should do.

It was then that he felt the angel's presence. She laid her hand on his shoulder. He cocked his head and returned her smile.

He knew at once if he would empty his mind of the past, he could look forward to a future filled with endless possibilities.

When he released the gun to Grandpa Charlie's waiting hands, for the first time he felt capable of forgiving the man who had hurt him so many times—the man that had taken Mama's life.

He turned back toward the stranger in the bed.

"Papa?"

About the Author

Brenda Poulos is a former teacher and elementary school guidance counselor. She is a member of American Christian Fiction Writers and is current president of Christian Writers of the West. She lives in Gilbert, Arizona with her husband, John. They have four adult children, seven amazing grandchildren, a wayward rescue cat and an energetic fifteen-year-old dog that needs constant reminders to act his age.

Brenda blogs on spiritualsnippets.com, focusing on "Seeing Life's Events in the Light of God's Word"; she offers new writers encouragement on brendapoulos.org and at 5scribesandtheirstories.com, a website she shares with other writers.

Printed in Great Britain
by Amazon